The Nightgown
a rural love story

Bob Bancks

Paradise Creek Books

Paradise Creek Books
Elgin, Iowa
Seattle, Washington
www.ParadiseCreekBooks.com

Paradise Creek Books
Elgin, Iowa
Seattle, Washington

www.ParadiseCreekBooks.com

Editor: Gary Anderson
Cover design: Stephanie Fox
Interior design: Stephanie Fox

Printed in the United States of America
First Publication: September 2011

ISBN # 978-0-9836652-1-2

The Nightgown
a rural love story

Bob Bancks

"A farmer loves his land.
If you fall in love with a farmer,
you learn to love the land, too.
They both will love you in return and
be a part of your very soul."

–Sara Maas

Table of Contents

1. The Gift   1

2. Jenny Grows Up   15

3. The Boarder   21

4. Little Paul   35

5. Girl Meets Boy   41

6. The Big Itch   57

7. Hot Turkey, Cool Christmas   65

8. Cool Waters   75

9. We've Only Just Begun   93

10. Hi-Lo-Hi   107

11. A Bump in the Road   121

12. Old Blue Wins One   135

13. The Family Begins   145

14. It's a Girl!   161

15. Sara's Chickens   167

16. Dry as Desert   173

17. Sweet Corn Party   189

18. Paul's Close Call   197

19. Good Neighbors   209

20. Triumph and Tragedy   217

21. Moving On   227

22. Goodbye at the Dune—The Nightgown Moves On   241

Chapter One
The Gift

Sara reached into the top drawer of the old dresser. Her hands, tanned and wrinkled from more than a quarter of a century of farm work, pulled out a tattered and yellowed Petersen's Department Store box. She opened the lid gently and unfolded the paper surrounding a white cotton nightgown with lace around the top and buttons down to the waist. It had held up well, she thought, considering it was more than sixty years old. She carried it lovingly over to the bedroom window and sat down in an old rocker.

As she sat down, a card sifted to the floor. Sara picked it up and read: *Mr. & Mrs. John McWilliams invite you to attend the wedding of their daughter, Sara Jane, to Paul William Maas, the son of Mr. & Mrs. George Maas, on July 26, 1975 at First Church of Christ in Muscatine, Iowa.*

On the back of the card, in her own handwriting, was: *Nightgown from Mr. and Mrs. B.*

Sara gently rocked back and forth, her mind drifting back to many sweet nights of rocking her babies to sleep. The creaks and groans of the chair sounded like the strains of a familiar old song. She loved that old house. It was built by Paul's grandparents after they picked it out of a Sears & Roebuck catalog, which listed the model as the Prairie Queen.

The front porch stretched across the entire north side of the house and featured an oversized swing that hung from the ceiling. There were four bedrooms and a bathroom upstairs. The large kitchen, which Sara had always loved, was on the main floor and was the heart of the home. Everyone used the back door to enter the house, which opened into the kitchen.

The house sat well back from the road, connected by a long driveway. The yard contained several old oak trees and the large lawn on the east side of the house ended in a vegetable garden. The south side of the house, where the backdoor was located, had a narrow sidewalk that led to the farmyard. The outbuildings included a two-and-a-half car garage, a combination machine shed and shop, a gambrel-roofed barn that sat between two large cattle sheds, an old corncrib that was no longer used, and several grain bins.

When the corn was high, the house and lot were completely isolated, which suited Sara's free spirited lifestyle well, since a certain amount of nudity was accepted as normal in her household. It made Sara smile to remember how many times members of the family would come upstairs from the basement shower wearing only a towel without anyone giving a second look.

"Oh, Paul," Sara thought as she shook her head sadly, "who could have imagined that you wouldn't be here for our daughter's wedding?"

Paul had been strong and active—the last person anyone would have expected to suffer a stroke—but one day they were eating lunch and the next day Paul was in the intensive care unit. Sara had spent all that night praying that Paul would recover, but as a late spring thunderstorm swept across the Heartland, Paul passed away.

Sara missed how Paul could always make her laugh. She had planned to grow old with her man, sitting on the porch, watching the amazing Iowa sun go down on silky summer nights. Why had God taken away the only thing she had ever really cared about? It made no sense—and now Jenny, their darling daughter, was about to leave her, too. The very thought of living all alone in that big old farmhouse sometimes threatened to overwhelm her.

Farming was a difficult life, but Sara wouldn't have traded her life for anything else on Earth. She and Paul were blessed with three wonderful children. The first was Ed, who had returned to the farm after college to continue their farm operation. He and his wife, Carol, and their three children lived a half mile away. Tim, who never really wanted to farm, was good at math and mechanics, so he became an engineer at

John Deere. He and Angie lived in Dubuque with their three girls. Jenny, Sara's baby, was a typical farm girl, tall and slim like her mother—and a 100 percent tomboy. Jenny was a teacher like her mom, except she taught vocational agriculture, something girls weren't allowed to take, let alone teach in Sara's day.

While Jenny was attending Iowa State, just as her brothers and dad had done, she met Jason Wulf, who was studying to be a veterinarian. After graduation, Jenny began teaching at Durant. Jason accepted a position at a clinic in Eldridge. They were a perfect match. Jenny had always loved animals and now she'd be able to help her husband-to-be treat them. The wedding was to be in August.

Paul farmed with his dad, George, until his parents decided to retire. Even after they moved to Wilton, George still came out to help during the busy part of the spring and fall. Sara had always loved George. He helped her in the garden, since she was a city girl and knew little about growing vegetables.

Sara grew up in a middle-class section of Muscatine, and she knew everyone in the neighborhood, but she was especially fond of a couple who lived across a ravine behind their house. They were the Baumgardners, whom she'd always called Mr. and Mrs. B.

As Sara sat and rocked, lost in her thoughts, the bedroom door suddenly burst open and Jenny walked in, saying cheerfully, "Hi, Mom. What's up?" A moment later, sensing Sara's melancholy mood, her voice softened as she asked, "Mom, what's the matter? Are you okay?"

"I'm fine, sweetheart," Sara said, trying to compose herself. "I'm just missing your dad. I miss him so much." She paused a moment, then asked, "How was your day?"

"Oh, the usual—hectic—but we've got everything under control now, I think," Jenny said, her excitement rising. "The caterer called and wanted to know if he should plan on more people. He said he could bring more food but not put it out unless it was necessary. The florist will be at the church about 11:00. Heather, Sue, and Beth will come about ten. That should give them plenty of time to get dressed before the ceremony. Jason called to tell me that he'd forgotten to ask for the day off—it took me a second to realize he was kidding me. Thankfully, this is a slow time at the clinic, so they're giving him three weeks off."

As Sara smiled at Jason's joke, Jenny asked, "You said you wanted to see me, Mom? If it's to have a heart-to-heart talk about married life, you had that years ago, remember?"

Sara smiled again and replied, "It's nothing like that, sweetheart. Are you in a hurry? I want to tell you something I've never told anyone, not even your dad."

"No, Mom, I've got all night. Jason's having his last night out with the boys, if you know what I mean," Jenny said, rolling her eyes.

"Good," said Sara. "Sit here on the bed, please. I want to show you something. Do you remember me telling you about Mr. and Mrs. B, the older couple who lived across the ravine when I was a girl?"

"Yeah," replied Jenny tentatively. "I remember Mr. B. He seemed like a gentle and kind man. He'd come out to the farm with Grandpa and Grandma McWilliams. He could do card tricks. I never met Mrs. B because she died before I was born."

"Well, I was going to wrap this nightgown and give it to you, but since you got here before I could wrap it, I'll give it to you now," said Sara, handing the nightgown to her daughter. "This was Mrs. B's wedding nightgown. Mr. B gave it to me just before my own wedding."

Seeing the puzzled look on Jenny's face, Sara continued, "He told me that Julia would have loved for me to wear it. You see, she only wore it on the night of their anniversaries. Of course, I was pleased, because I loved Mrs. B like my own grandmother. I used to sleep at their house when Mom and Daddy were gone or just out late."

"I see," Jenny said, although her puzzled expression failed to match her words.

"By the time I was born, their boys, Jim and Bill, were teenagers and treated me like a kid sister," Sara continued, "but they were the same age as your Uncle Tom, so they spent a lot of time at our house. Jim was good with cars, and he and Tom spent hours working on engines and transmissions."

Seeing that Jenny was still struggling to follow the story, Sara smiled and said, "Okay, here's where the nightgown comes in."

"Good," said Jenny. "I was starting to wonder."

"Grandpa and Mr. B used to keep the ravine mowed between our houses. It was often the quick way over. One night when I was about eight, I was looking out my bedroom window and saw Mrs. B standing on their sleeping porch in her nightgown, looking toward the ravine. Then Mr. B came out, put his arms around her. He kissed and began undoing her nightgown and sliding it off her shoulders."

"Oh, my!" said Jenny, her eyes widening.

"Well, Mrs. B stood nude in the moonlight, her long black hair flowing over her back. They stood on the porch for a long time, holding each other, kissing, and caressing. Then they disappeared below the railing."

"That must have been something to see," Jenny said with a smile.

"It was something I wouldn't soon forget, that's for sure," Sara agreed. "A year later, Mr. and Mrs. B threw a party at their house for their thirtieth anniversary, and that night, I saw them do the same thing on the porch again."

"So it was sort of a ritual," Jenny said, nodding her head.

"Right," said Sarah. "Over the years, Mrs. B's long black hair turned silver and she cut it shorter, but the same thing happened on every anniversary. I thought it was the sweetest thing I'd ever seen. Then, when I was fifteen, I learned that Mrs. B had pancreatic cancer and only had six months to live."

"Oh, that's terrible," Jenny said softly.

"Yes, but on their thirty-seventh anniversary, I saw them reenact that scene one last time. She was in her nightgown, but all she could do was reach up and give Mr. B a kiss. Then they held each other longer than I'd ever seen them do. The next day she went to the hospital and she died a week later."

"That's the saddest thing I've ever heard," said Jenny, wiping away a tear.

"I learned something very special from watching those two old people over the years," Sara said. "I saw two human beings who shared a complete love, always giving and never taking. I worried about Mr. B, all alone in that house after Mrs. B died."

"What happened to him after that?" Jenny asked.

"He kept to himself. He'd only come over when someone was celebrating a birthday. Then one night in July, when I was eighteen, I was home alone because I had a job at Penney's. My parents were visiting Uncle Bob in Kansas City. I was in my room looking out the window, and I saw Mr. B, standing on the back porch. I could see he was holding his wife's nightgown."

"Don't tell me," Jenny said. "It was their anniversary, right?"

"That's right," Sara replied. "He stood there for a long time, then sat on their porch swing, holding the nightgown up to his face. It broke my heart, so I ran downstairs and headed across the ravine. I was almost to the porch when he finally noticed me. I felt bad that I had startled him, but when he realized it was me, he smiled and invited me onto the porch."

When Jenny said nothing, Sara continued, "He just smiled and asked me to come sit on the swing with him. When I sat down, we sat in silence for awhile, then he asked me if I knew what night it was."

"Did you tell him you knew about their ritual?" Jenny asked. "I bet it was kind of awkward."

"A little," Sara agreed. "I told him I knew it was their anniversary and he said it would have been their fortieth if Julia had still been alive. Then he held up the nightgown and said, 'This was a special nightgown for Julia and me. She only wore it on our anniversary. I don't know what to do with it, because neither of the boys wants it.'"

"Without thinking, I just blurted out, 'I'd like to have it someday.'"

"What did he say about that?" Jenny asked with a smile.

"He was surprised, for sure," Sara replied, "but I told him that Mrs. B had always been like a grandma to me and having the nightgown would give me something special to remember her by."

"And how!" Jenny said with chuckle. "He had no idea they'd had an audience on all those anniversaries over the years."

"And I definitely didn't tell him!" Sara said, joining Jenny in her laughter. "I just told him about how special it was to have Mrs. B babysit me and let me help her make cookies."

"And to let you be a Peeping Tom for about ten years," Jenny added.

"Well, I left that part out," said Sara, "but when I had finished telling him how much I loved Mrs. B, he held up the nightgown and said, 'Then you're the one who should have it. On the day you get married, I'll give it to you as a wedding gift.' I was surprised, but happy."

"So he didn't give it to you on the spot?" Jenny asked.

"No," Sara replied, "but I knew it would be that much more special when he finally did give to me."

"Hmmm," Jenny said, nodding slightly.

"Mr. B got up and asked if I wanted something to drink and then went into the house to get us some ice tea, but before he left, he set the nightgown down on the swing."

"Really? What happened next?"

"Well, after he went into the house, I reached over and picked up the nightgown. It was soft and still like new, but I knew why, since she only wore it on one special night every year."

Jenny held the nightgown up to her cheek and said, "It *is* soft."

Sara smiled and said, "As soon as he disappeared into the house, I took off my blouse and I slipped the nightgown over my head." Seeing Jenny's shocked expression, Sara added, "Don't worry, sweetheart, I was wearing a bra, and Mr. B had seen me in a bikini many times while I was sunbathing in our backyard anyway."

"But why did you do it?" Jenny asked.

"I'm not quite sure," said Sara. "Maybe I just wanted to feel closer to Mrs. B at that moment. I'd watched her slip out of that nightgown so many times over the years, and it just felt right somehow. It's hard to explain."

"I think I know what you mean," Jenny said softly, "but did you get it back off before Mr. B came back out?"

"No," replied Sara. "I was still wearing it when he returned, carrying two glasses."

"What did he say when he saw you? Was he angry?"

"Not at all," said Sara. "In fact, his eyes filled with tears and I was afraid that I had made him feel worse than he already did. Collecting himself, he put the glasses on the railing, and walked over to me. He put his arms around me and hugged me."

"Oh, now you're starting to scare me, Mom," Jenny said, looking at Sara intently.

"Hold on," Sara said, shaking her head. "He held me in his arms for a short time, then pulled back and kissed me—"

"He *kissed* you?" Jenny said, her voice rising.

"Yes, he did," Sara said slyly, "right on the forehead."

"Oh, you had me worried there," Jenny said, breathing a sigh of relief.

"He looked at me, smiled, and said, 'You've been like a granddaughter to me for a long time, Sara, and I want to thank you for this moment. It was a kind thing for you to do. You've helped me more than you can ever know. Until you came over, this was the saddest night of my life, but now I know I'll live through it—and try to move on with my life.

You became Julia for a moment. I heard her tell me to love life and she was waiting for me.'"

"Wow!" Jenny said, whistling in awe. "That's some story, Mom."

"But that's not the end of it," Sara said. "He also told me that the nightgown was magical."

"Magical?" Jenny repeated.

"Yes, and I can tell you that he was right, but that's a story for another time," said Sara. "That night, he discreetly turned around while I slipped out of the nightgown and put my blouse back on. We talked for awhile as we sat on the swing and drank our ice tea, and then I went back home. Neither one of us ever mentioned the incident again, and Mr. B continued to be like a grandfather to me. He came to my graduations— both from high school and college—and he was eighty-one when he died."

"I've gotta say, Mom, you definitely surprised me today!" Jenny said, looking down at the nightgown in her lap.

"I figured you wouldn't be expecting a story like that when you got here," Sara said with a laugh.

"And you were right," Jenny said, smiling broadly. "And you never told Dad?"

"Or anybody else. There was nothing to tell, really. It was a private moment between Mr. B and me, and I didn't see any reason to tell anybody else."

Jenny leaned forward. "Look, Mom, you can't stop there. I'm not going to wait around for you to tell the rest. I've got all afternoon, so start talking!"

Sara smiled. "Well, true to his word, Mr. B handed me the nightgown in the box you see next to you on the bed on my wedding day."

"Did you wear it on your honeymoon night?" Jenny asked eagerly.

"I did, and your dad was okay with it, because it wasn't really on for very long, if you know what I mean."

"I have a pretty good idea," Jenny said knowingly.

"From then on, I wore it on our anniversary night, but just like when Mrs. B wore it, it never got a whole lot of wear. It was usually on the floor pretty fast."

"Funny!" Jenny said, laughing heartily.

"The year I was pregnant with your brother Tim, I waddled into the bedroom wearing the nightgown on our anniversary night, and it barely covered my stomach. Your dad burst out laughing, but I was eight months pregnant, cranky, and in no mood for jokes."

"Did you tell him off?" Jenny asked.

"No," replied Sara. "I caught sight of myself in the mirror and saw how silly I looked and started to laugh with him, so it all turned out alright. We spent that anniversary night just talking. I was so miserable that I didn't want anything to do with hanky-panky that night."

"I guess I can't blame you," Jenny agreed.

"Another anniversary, we were all down in the basement because of a tornado warning. Ed was only about eight at the time and he asked why I was wearing a white dress instead of my pj's. I told him it was our anniversary and I always wore this white dress to bed."

"Good thinking, Mom," said Jenny.

"Ed asked, 'What's an anniversary?' and I told him it was like a birthday, but it was to celebrate when two people got married.

"He said, 'Okay, Mom, but I think you look prettier in your pj's.'

"I thanked him for the compliment," and he said, 'Sure, Mom, but I'm a guy, and we notice those things.' That comment has stuck with me all these years."

"How come I don't remember anything about this nightgown?" Jenny asked, holding it up to look at it more closely.

"Well, we didn't tell you kids about it, really, and I usually didn't put it on until you were all asleep," Sara replied thoughtfully. "One anniversary we were baling hay in the afternoon. You were about seven and you and I took lunch out to Dad and some of the neighbors who were helping. You asked if you could ride on the hay wagon on the way home, and a teenage neighbor, Jake, lifted you up to the top of the load.

"Your dad started the baler while I went back to the house. When the load was about full, Jake climbed to the top of the bales on the wagon, but you weren't there!" Sara said.

"You know, I remember that!" said Jenny. "I fell off the wagon and got knocked out."

"That's right," said Sara. "They rushed you back to the house, and though you were shaken up, you weren't hurt bad. That night, I put on the nightgown, but I spent most of the night rocking you in my arms to make sure you didn't have a concussion."

"I remember that," Jenny said, nodding her head. "But I was fine the next day."

"Yes, but by the time I tucked you into bed and went into our bedroom, your poor dad was sound asleep from working so hard all day, so I just gave him a quick peck on the cheek and let him sleep."

"That wasn't a very romantic anniversary," said Jenny with a smile.

"No, but it was memorable," said Sara. "Another anniversary, your dad decided we should hike to the dune, just like we had on our first night as a married couple. There was a full moon that night, and after all you kids were asleep, we headed for the dune. When we got there, I sat on the bench and instantly felt something squish underneath me. It was a big bug of some sort, and it left a stain that I've never been able to get out, no matter how hard I try."

Jenny held up the nightgown and Sara pointed out the stain, though it was hardly noticeable, probably because it had been treated with so many stain removing remedies over the years.

"One more story before I quit," said Sara. "If you look, you'll see a seam up the back, because I tore it one wild anniversary night. I can't remember why you kids weren't home, but it was just your dad and me. It was hot and the weatherman had predicted some severe weather, and the wind was already starting to pick up. Thunder and lightning flashed about. Your dad and I were in the kitchen. I was wearing the nightgown and he was wearing boxer shorts. Suddenly, we looked out the window and saw the cattle gate had blown open and the steers were heading for the opening!"

"That would be a mood killer, for sure!" Jenny said with a laugh.

"No doubt about it!" said Sara. "We grabbed some tennis shoes and ran outside, where your dad headed for the lane while I ran toward the barn so we could head them back. As I ran through the yard gate, I caught the nightgown on the latch and ripped it, top to bottom. I felt a definite draft on my backside, but I couldn't worry about it at the time.

"This is where the magic of the gown really showed itself. As I was running toward the cattle yard, I could see the first steers about to make a break. I waved my arms and hollered at them, but the wind was drowning out my voice. Just as the cattle reached the gate, the wind caught my nightgown, making it flutter like a big white flag. Then a huge flash of lightning lit up the farmyard, and all the steers slid to a halt—just long enough for your dad to slam the gate shut. As I ran over and started latching the bottom, a gust of wind caught the nightgown and blew it up over my head. There I was in the middle of the barnyard—with my butt in the air and my boobs hanging down."

As Jenny laughed, Sara continued, "Your dad was laughing even louder than you are now, and he said, "Having a little problem with your nightgown? Here, let me help."

"Then he reached out and pulled the gown all the way off! Now I was standing in the middle of the farmyard, wearing only my tennis shoes!"

"Oh, my gosh, Mom!" Jenny said, shaking her head in disbelief.

"Well, your dad gave me a big hug and a kiss, then said, 'I love you—especially when you're naked.' The wind was really starting to pick up, so I gave him a playful slap on the cheek and said, 'Get your mind out of the gutter, Big Boy—especially since we may die out here when the tornado hits!'

"We made sure the gate was secured and made a mad dash across the barnyard, but the rain had started to fall and we got drenched before we got back to the house. We hurried upstairs and took a shower together—"

"Okay, that's enough, Mom! I get the picture," Jenny interrupted. "I guess I'm lucky that the gown survived long enough for you to hand it down to me."

"I suppose," agreed Sara. "The next morning I sewed up the tear, but even though it will never be the same as it was, I hope you'll take this nightgown and wear it with love. It hope it will bring you the sort of happiness it brought Mrs. B and me. Mr. B told me it was magical, and I can tell you that he was right. It's been magical for me."

"Thank you, Mom," Jenny said, standing and giving her mom a warm hug. "I will wear it, I promise, and I can also promise that I'll never forget this afternoon!"

Jenny stayed for supper that night and they had a wonderful time reminiscing. Sara even asked if Jenny and Jason might want to live in the old farmhouse someday. Jenny smiled and said she'd talk to Jason about it.

Jenny decided to stay the night, and before she went to bed, she asked, "Would you mind if I try the nightgown on?"

"No, sweetheart," Sara replied. "I figured you'd want to."

Jenny slipped it over her head and it fit her perfectly. She twirled around letting the gown flow outward. Before she went to bed, she changed to her own pajamas and carefully refolded the gown, putting it carefully back in the box. As she drifted off to sleep that night, she wondered if a nightgown could really be magical. At that moment, it seemed entirely possible.

Chapter Two
—Jenny Grows Up

The next day, Sara and Jenny talked more about the nightgown over their morning coffee.

Jenny asked somewhat sheepishly, "Mom, you mentioned being naked in the farmyard. Did that happen often?"

"No, Jenny, you know better than that," Sara replied with a laugh. "You lived here and you know we didn't run a nudist camp. It's just that many of the experiences involving the nightgown happened to include some nudity, with your dad and me, and with Mr. and Mrs. B before that. It seems on an isolated farmstead you are able to be freer with what you wear outdoors. Sometimes in emergencies you didn't think about dressing properly and it wasn't necessary before leaving the house. "

"I guess that's true," Jenny said, nodding in agreement.

"Here's a story about being naked that you've never heard," Sara said, her smile widening, "and it didn't involve the nightgown."

"Do I really want to hear this, Mom?" Jenny asked.

"Well, this one involves you—" Sara began.

"What?" Jenny said, cutting her mom off.

"It involves you, Tammi, and Amy. Amy's mom, Annie; Tammi's mom, Barb; and I were going to meet to plan the church's Young Adults Picnic for August that year, but since the weather was beautiful, we decided to meet here instead of at the church. The three of you were playing outside and you found hickory nut shells that you thought would make great little canoes."

"I remember that!" Jenny said, smiling.

"You came in the house and asked if you could float them in the creek, but Barb was worried about letting you girls play down there without adult supervision. Annie and I convinced her you'd be fine, so we let you go. You were dressed in shorts, t-shirts, and sandals, but Tammi had on a new pair of shorts and Barb warned her not to get them dirty."

Jenny looked at her mom warily as the story unfolded, making Sara smile even more broadly.

"Before you girls left, you promised you wouldn't get dirty, then you ran off to play in the creek while we went back to planning the picnic. After awhile, Barb started to worry, so we decided to go down to the creek and check on you. I gave Barb an old pair of sneakers to wear so she wouldn't step in a cow pie and ruin her fancy sandals. As we got closer to the creek, we could hear laughter coming from the creek, so we crept up so you girls wouldn't see us."

"Oh, no," said Jenny. "I think I know what's coming next."

"Yup," said Sarah. "When we looked over the bank, we saw the three of you playing in the creek—without a stitch of clothes on!"

"Oh, my gosh!" gasped Jenny. "You *saw* us down there?"

"We sure did," said Sara, "and Barb started to head down there, but I grabbed her arm and pulled her back before she could say anything. I pointed to your clothes, which were all hanging neatly on branches of a nearby tree, and I told Barb, 'You told Tammi not to get dirty, and she's obeying what you told her."

"We never knew you were there," said Jenny, shaking her head.

"No, but we sat there and watched you girls play for quite awhile. Even Barb thought it was funny. I even suggested we join you, but Annie threw cold water on that idea.

She said, "Our naked old bodies would probably stampede the cattle and we'd end up having to chase them out of the cornfield."

"That is amazing," Jenny said.

"A little while later, you girls climbed out of the water and sat on the bank and began drying in the sun, so we tiptoed away. When you finally got back to the house, we were waiting for you on the porch.

"Barb asked Tammie if you girls had fun, and she just said, 'Yes, Mom, we had a great time, and I didn't get dirty at all.'"

"Well, it wasn't a lie," said Jenny.

"Right, but we moms had a terrible time not laughing. Finally, Barb said that next time they'd bring a swimsuit for Tammie so she could play in the water. We all laughed, but you girls never knew why."

"Until now," Jenny said, joining her mother in laughter. "I remember Tammie and I got our underpants mixed up down at the creek and she and I had to take our panties to Sunday School to exchange them. If anyone would have caught us, we would have been mortified."

Now it was Jenny's turn to smile mischievously as she said, "You know, Mom, that wasn't the only time I went skinny-dipping in the creek. Most of the time, I was either alone or with Amy, but there were boys involved once or twice!" Sara looked surprised as Jenny added, "So you see, I didn't tell you everything, either."

"Well, I'm not surprised. Skinny-dipping just seems to be a ritual young farm kids go through," said Sara. "I hope they were little boys."

"I'm not telling," Jenny shot back with a sly smile.

Jenny thought a moment, then said, "You know, Mom, why don't you write down all those stories? You've got a computer."

"I've thought about it," Sara replied.

"Well, why don't you think about it after the wedding? You and Grandma Madge probably have hundreds of great stories between the two of you, and I'm sure Grandma Emma could tell a few, too. It would keep you busy—and out of trouble," Jenny said with a wink.

"It's something to think about," Sara replied, "but now you've got a wedding in two days, so let's get that out of the way first, okay?"

* * *

The wedding went off without a hitch. Jenny wore Sara's wedding dress, and it fit perfectly. Tim and Ed gave Jenny away. It was an honor that would have been reserved for Paul, but his sons did a great job.

After the wedding, everyone headed for the reception. The wedding party drove all around Wilton in a long white limousine. There was a funny moment when Jason's partner, Ken, answered a call on his cell phone during the reception. He asked Jason if he wanted to go out on a call to Greater Iowa Hog Farms. Jason just smiled mischievously, gave Jenny a big hug, and said he was going to be busy the rest of the evening!

Everyone got a good laugh from that exchange, but Jenny knew it was going to take a little time to get used to being a veterinarian's wife. There would be many times when she'd have to go to a function alone or be late because of some animal emergency. It was a good thing she'd been raised on a farm and understood such things.

When Jenny and Jason returned from their honeymoon, their lives had to snap back to reality quickly. Jenny had to get ready to start teaching again and Jason had to catch up on calls and clients. One afternoon, Jenny visited Sara to show her some honeymoon photographs.

"I wore the nightgown our first night in Jamaica," she told her mother. "I went out onto the veranda and stood in the moonlight, trying to imagine all the other moonlit nights it had witnessed. Then magic must have kicked in, because when Jason came out of the shower, he let out a low whistle and told me that the moon shining through the gown didn't leave much to the imagination. We did manage to make it back inside before he ripped it off."

"Good for you!" said Sara with a laugh. "I told you it was magic."

"I know!" Jenny agreed. "I never wore anything to bed the rest of the honeymoon, and when Jason asked why I was wearing a nightgown with a stain on the butt and a repaired seam up the back, I told him the whole story."

"What did he have to say about that?" asked Sara.

"He just laughed and said he hoped we'd be able to contribute our own stories over the years."

"It sounds like you're off to a good start," Sara said with a smile.

Chapter Three
The Boarder

In mid-August, during one of Ed's morning check-ins, he announced to Sara that he wasn't buying any feeder calves that fall. The market was in the dumps, and since Paul's death, he no longer had time for feeder calves. Instead, he would try to maintain the stock cow herd and just sell their calves in the fall.

Sara knew how hard it was for Ed to tell her the news, but she comforted him by saying, "Son, you're the farm manager now, and you have to do what you think is best. I'll miss the calves, but I know we have to change and I'm sure your dad would approve."

Then Ed took a deep breath and told Sara the rest of the story. "Carl Samuelson dropped in last night and offered me a chance to farm his ground. He wants to retire and Jim Baker at the bank suggested me. Grain prices are improving and I think it's a good time to farm more ground instead of raising more livestock. It would mean an extra 275 acres of crop ground and 45 acres of pasture, and I'm excited about the possibilities."

Sara was silent for only a moment, then surprised her son by saying, "You know, son, I think your dad would be proud of you for wanting to take on a new challenge. I think you should take it."

As Labor Day approached, Sara considered subbing again as the new school year drew closer, but after talking to Principal Mary Gordon, she decided that too many years had passed. As they talked, however, Mary asked if Sara would be interested in boarding Susie Collins, the new high school English teacher, who needed a place to stay until she could find her own. Sara agreed when Mary assured her it would only be for a few weeks. Sara decided Susie could stay in the Ed's old bedroom. Since

Susie would go home on the holidays, she could still have family stay overnight.

The next day, she met Susie Collins from Ottumwa, Iowa. Susie was a tiny person, standing about 5'2" and weighing less than 100 pounds. With coal black hair and almond-shaped eyes that indicated an oriental background, she was far different from Sara, who stood 5'11" in her stocking feet.

As they sat at the kitchen table drinking coffee, Susie offered a brief version of her life story. "I'm the product of an American soldier and a Vietnamese mother. My mom was a boat person who escaped from Saigon with her family, and they were adopted by our church in Ottumwa. My dad is an agronomist with a seed corn company in Hendricks, Iowa. Mom and Dad met at church. I have a younger brother and sister, I graduated from UNI last June, and this is my first teaching position."

It felt like a good match, so they agreed that Susie would move in over the Labor Day weekend. Sara was actually excited at the prospect of having a young person in the house again. They worked together all day Sunday setting up the room, and on Labor Day they went shopping for new curtains and a bedspread. Late that afternoon, they took their ice tea out onto the front porch and sat in the swing. Susie had a knack of making people feel comfortable, and almost before she knew what was happening, Sara had told her several stories about Mrs. B's magical nightgown.

As they laughed, Susie asked, "Are any of these stories on paper?"

Sara said, "No, but you're the second person who has encouraged me to do it, so maybe I should start thinking about it seriously."

"If you do, I will help with the writing," Susie volunteered.

Fall went well for Ed. For several years the Maas's had been renting a farm from Lila Becker, a long-time friend and neighbor. The Becker place was more than a mile away and it was slow going with a tractor, so two people were required to haul the grain home to the bins, and Sara became one of the drivers. She enjoyed being part of the work force again. Ed also hired, Keith, a retired worker from Alcoa, to help drive the other tractor. Sarah helped Keith when he couldn't keep up with the combine and when she wasn't busy. Carol considered quitting her job, but the health benefits from her employer, Burt, were too good to leave, and Burt had promised her, she could start her own business next year, because he was retiring. She would have the choice clients.

Although they had only planned for her to stay a month or two, Susie stayed on throughout the fall and into the winter. She liked the quiet of the farm as she graded papers. Sometimes she showed Sara examples of good papers—and of pathetic ones—which helped Sara learn more about what it took to write well.

One cold Saturday in January, a snowstorm was in the forecast, and when Susie and Sara woke up, they saw ten inches of blowing snow in the front yard and it was still snowing. By noon the roads were impassable and the lane to the house had drifted full.

At four o'clock, Ed called. "Mom, I'm going to be late getting there with the snow blower," he said.

"That's all right, son," Sara assured him. "Don't worry about us. Susie and I will check the cows. We've got heat and power, so we'll be fine."

As Sara hung up the phone, Susie said, "Did you say *we* were going to check the cows?"

"You betcha," Sara replied with a smile. "I don't want to go out there alone. What if I fall and can't get back to the house?"

Susie was so petite that she easily fit into some of the clothes Ed had worn in seventh grade—with room to spare. She rolled up the pant legs and sleeves as they bundled up and headed for the barns, where they found the cows huddled together, unwilling to venture outside to the bale feeders.

As Sara was getting ready to toss several bales of hay down from the hay mow, her cell phone rang. It was Ed. "Be careful out there, Mom," he said. "Don't let any of the cows knock you down. Is Susie there with you?"

"Yes, I'll toss the bales down to her. How many should we give them?"

"Twenty or so should hold them until I can clear a path to the bale feeders."

As Sara tossed bales from the haymow, Susie dragged them down the alley and hefted them into the feed bunk that ran the length of the barn, the cows went crazy. They were hungry and this was prime hay, normally used only at calving time. When Sara came down from the mow, she noticed that several smaller cows were being pushed away from the bunk. The only way to remedy the situation was to carry some bales out to a little free-standing hay bunk some twenty-five feet from the barn.

She opened the small gate at the end of the barn and started to carry the bales out. Susie followed and soon found herself surrounded by hungry cows. It was only a matter of time until one of the jostling cows knocked her to the ground. Sara dropped her bale and hurried to help her. Luckily, none of the cows stepped on Susie, which was probably due to the screaming she was doing at the time.

"Here, take my hand," Sara said, reaching down to pull Susie from the muck.

Susie reached up, but Sara lost her footing and ended up landing right next to Susie. As the cows huddled around, intent on getting their share of hay, Sara and Susie looked at each other for a moment, then burst out laughing.

"Can you get up?" Sara asked.

"I think so," Susie replied, putting her hands down in the manure and pushing herself up. Then she reached down and said, "Here, let me pull you up."

A moment later, they were both standing, brown soup dripping from their work clothes and surrounded by hungry cows who looked at them as if to say, Well, now you know how it feels to be one of us. We lay in this stuff all the time."

"Well, let's see about getting back to the house so we can get out of these clothes," said Sara, turning back toward the gate.

After they had shuffled the length of the barn and reached the outside door, they had to struggle to get it open. The wind had piled snow against it and they had to push with all their might to move it open even slightly. Susie squeezed through first and promptly fell into the snow.

Sara was intent in holding the door and didn't see Susie fall.

"Susie, where are you?" she called, her voice almost disappearing in the screaming wind.

"I'm right here below you," Susie yelled. "You're about to step on me."

Sara reached down again and helped Susie struggle to her feet. "Walk behind me," she shouted against the wind. "I'll break us a path."

As they trudged through the snow and wind, they could see the back porch light glowing faintly across the farmyard. They braced themselves against gusts that threatened to send them sprawling. Their wet clothes turned as hard as boards as they pushed forward. At the yard gate, the drift was too deep to push the gate open.

"Help me raise the gate off its hinges," Sara shouted into the howling wind.

They grabbed the gate and gave a mighty heave. It hesitated briefly, then popped off. Then they plowed through and dropped the gate into a snowdrift. Leaning forward, they waded through the ever-deepening snow until they finally reached the back door.

Sara grabbed the handle of the storm door and pulled it open, then leaned against it to hold it open against the wind.

"Susie, you'll have to turn the doorknob."

"Okay," Susie said, shaking off a glove.

As she turned the knob, both women almost fell into the kitchen as a huge gust of wind blasted them from behind. They stumbled downstairs, their fingers so cold that they had to use pliers to grip the pull tabs on their zippers.

"You sit on the chair and I'll pull your boots off," Sara said. "Then you can help me with mine."

Susie sat as Sara tugged at her boots. When the first one came off, brown wet ooze poured out. Her socks were soaked. Then Sara helped her take off her coveralls. Then it was Sara's turn. Susie struggled with the boots and coveralls, but finally got them off.

Their fingers were stiff, but they finally managed to strip down to just their undergarments, because their jeans and sweatshirts were wet and stained with manure. Then they headed upstairs, clad only in their underwear, their legs and feet so numb that they had to hold on to the rail to keep from falling on the slippery steps.

"You take your shower first," said Sara. "I'll grab a comforter and sit in the rocker till you're done, but don't take too long. I can't stand smelling like this much longer."

Susie dashed into the bathroom and emerged after about five minutes. Covered only in a towel, she said, "Okay, I'm out. Are you okay?"

"I...think so," Sara said through chattering teeth. "I'm just a little cold."

As she tried to get to her feet, Sara stumbled, but stopped herself from falling by grabbing onto a nearby dresser. Susie rushed to her side and helped her into the bathroom, where Sara managed to get her panties off, but her fingers were too numb to work the clasp on her bra. Susie unhooked it for her and then turned on the water and helped Sara into the shower. Sara sat on the corner seat of the oversized shower stall. She was shivering too much to stand without hanging on to something.

"I'd better help you," said Susie, slipping out of her towel and joining Sara in the huge shower. She began rubbing Sara's legs, and then started rubbing her back. "Bend over," she said. "I'll run some warm water on your head and back. Mom always said you lose heat from your head, so it stands to reason you'll get warm that way, too. You just sit here while I go get some towels."

Susie stepped out of the shower, dried herself, then rewrapped the towel around her body as she looked in the closet for more. Then she helped Sara out of the shower and helped dry her off. Finally, she draped Sara's robe over her shoulders and led her back to her bedroom and threw a blanket over her.

As Sara sat on the edge of the bed, Susie said, "You sit tight. I'll be right back. I've got to get some clothes on."

When she returned, she helped Sara into her pj's.

"Let's go down to the den," Sara suggested. "It's the warmest room in the house."

"Okay," said Susie, "but take it slow. I don't think your legs are working right yet."

As Sara sat on a recliner in the den, Susie went into the kitchen to make hot chocolate and soup. While she was working, the phone rang and Susie answered.

"Yes, we're alright," Sara heard her say. She guessed it was Ed on the phone, checking up on them. "We both fell in the cow yard and your mom got a little chilled, but I think she'll be alright. We had quite a time getting back to the house. Oh, the cows are fine. I'll have your mom call you back in a half hour or so, okay?"

Susie finished the drinks and returned to the den, but just as she was handing Sara her mug, the phone rang again. Sara picked up the phone.

This time it was Jenny, asking, "Mom, are you all right? How deep is the snow?"

"Yes, we're fine, sweetheart. A little cold, but Susie got me all cleaned up and we're working on getting warm again. She's been an angel. I'll tell you all about it later—oh, and the snow is about a foot deep— maybe more."

"Okay, but you call me if you need anything," said Jenny. "Jason's stuck at the Warner's. He just called to say he was going to stay there for the night. I bet that's a first for a vet."

Susie flipped on the TV while Sara called Ed to reassure him that she was alright. The news was dominated by cancellations and postponements.

"They could have saved time by telling people what wasn't canceled," Sara joked. "It would have been a shorter list."

The weather forecast was for more snow in a band stretching from Ottumwa to Clinton—possibly dumping another 6" to 8" on top of what they already had. The total could reach 18", a record. The wind was supposed to die down the next day, but it was still going to be very cold.

"Well, I think I'm ready for bed," Sara announced. "That will warm me up quite a bit—but I may need some help up the stairs."

Susie helped Sara up the stairs and waited while she used the bathroom. Then she tucked her into bed and said goodnight. However, a short time later, Susie returned and stood sheepishly in the doorway.

"Sara," she said, "would you mind if I slept with you tonight? We could keep each other warm, and it's lonely in my room with the wind howling like it is."

"Sure," Sara replied, "crawl in. I could use a little extra warmth tonight myself."

Susie climbed into the bed and was asleep within minutes.

As she listened to Susie's rhythmic breathing, Sara prayed, "Thank you, Jesus, for sending Susie to me. She saved my life today." Then she fell asleep herself, enjoying the feeling of having another warm body next to her. It was something she hadn't experienced since Paul's death, and it felt good.

It was still dark the next morning when Sara slipped out of bed. Susie rolled over sleepily, but Sara said, "You go ahead and sleep a little longer. I'll make some coffee and rolls."

As Sara slowly descended the stairs, every bone in her body ached. She got the coffee going and popped some cinnamon rolls into the oven, then went to the basement and started the washer. It would take some serious washing to get all the stains out of their clothes from the night before. When she returned to the kitchen, she found Susie was sitting at the table.

"How was your night?" Susie asked, obviously still sleepy.

"Fine," replied Sara, "and warm, thanks to you."

The phone rang, and when Sara picked it up, Ed asked, "How are you, Mom? How's Susie? I'll be over about eight with the blower. Carol and the kids will be coming, too. Carol says she'll bring the toppings if you'll make some pizza dough."

"It's a deal," said Sara. "We'll see you at eight."

As Sara hung up the phone, Susie asked, "Have you ever braided pigtails?"

"Heavens, yes," Sara said with a laugh. "I used to do it all the time when Jenny was little. Why?"

"Could you braid my hair?" Susie replied. "I'd like to keep it out of my eyes when I go outside."

"You don't have to go outside. Ed will blow some paths when he gets here."

"But I want to. Who knows when I'll get a chance like this again?"

"Okay," Sara said. "You sit on that stool while I go get some rubber bands."

When she returned, Sara braided Susie's long black hair into two pigtails, and when she had finished, Susie twirled her head, causing the pigtails to wrap clear around her neck. Then Susie chirped, "Now I'll go find some more clothes and start shoveling the walk."

After Susie had put on every warm article of clothing she had, she went back downstairs, where Sara told her to wear mittens so her fingers wouldn't get so cold. Then she grabbed a snow shovel and began working her way down the sidewalk toward the driveway. She was almost done when she heard Ed coming up the lane, snow shooting high into the air and Carol and kids slowly following the snow blower in the pickup.

Once everyone was in the house, Ed started giving orders like a drill sergeant. "Isaac and Izzy, you stay in the house and help Grams. Aaron, you're big enough to watch the gates so the cows don't get out. Carol and Susie, you dig out the door to the skid loader so Carol can start clearing the cow lot. I'll blow a path for the cows to get to the hay and cornstalks."

Like a well-oiled machine, everyone threw themselves into their assigned tasks while Izzy, Isaac, and Grams started making the pizza dough. As Sara looked out the kitchen window, she could tell that things were going smoothly outside, because the crew had begun playing in the snow. A short time later, they all came into the house, stomping and shaking the snow from their boots and clothes. After taking off their snowy coats and boots in the basement, everyone sat at the dining room table and quickly devoured two large pizzas.

Smiling broadly, Ed looked at Susie and said, "You're pretty good at helping around here. Would you consider hiring on as farm help?"

Before Susie could reply, Sara said, "Well, I'll tell you one thing. Susie saved my life last night, so she's a keeper in my book."

Susie laughed. "I'd say we're even. You got me up off that awful floor. My clothes will never be the same."

"Well, I think you both deserve new outfits, courtesy of Maas Farm," Ed announced.

"Hey! What about me? I could use some new duds, too, you know, "Carol quickly added.

"Okay, okay," Ed said with a mock sigh. "The three of you go to the mall and get whatever you need."

Ed and Carol and the kids stayed a while longer so Ed could make one last check of the cattle barns. When he returned, he said, "We'd better head for home. There will be school tomorrow and Carol will have to go back to work. Thanks for the pizza, Mom. See you, Susie. Thanks for taking care of Mom."

"No problem," Susie replied.

Susie and Sara had leftover pizza for supper that night, then Susie said, "I'd better go up and get my study material ready for tomorrow. It's been quite the couple days. It'll make another great story."

Susie ended up staying with Sara the entire school year, always encouraging Sara to keep writing down her stories. A week after school ended, Susie went back to Ottumwa, where she volunteered to teach English to new immigrants through her church.

Sara's summer passed quickly. She helped with bible school and babysat Aaron, Isaac, and Izzy for two weeks while Carol's regular babysitter was on vacation. They had a great time splashing in the creek on some days and going to the pool on others. Her gardening and flowers took up the rest of her time.

At least once a week, Jenny stopped by on her way home from checking on her students' projects. In July, she stopped by after supervising a detasseling crew for NK Seeds. She drove a detasseling machine aided by ten teenagers, most were Durant students. In August, she was helping students get ready for the state fair. Durant FFA had entered a demonstration team and several members were showing livestock.

Susie returned on August 10th and brought Jon along. He was a medical student in Iowa City. Susie had met him while she was teaching at the language help center and Jon was volunteering at a health clinic across the street from her church. Jon was a pleasant young man, and when Sara asked where he planned to go after graduation, he replied, "I hope to stay at the university and do research in cerebral-vascular accidents—you know, strokes. My dad died from a stroke and there was little they could do for him at that time. My dream is to find out if they can be prevented or forecasted."

"That's what my husband, Paul, died from," Sara said, nodding her head.

"Interesting," said Jon. "If you wouldn't mind, could you write down what happened that day and what your husband did that day, right up to the time of his attack? It might help a lot."

"I sure will," Sara said eagerly.

"I'll help you, if you want," Susie chimed in.

As the school year went by, Susie and Jon got together almost every weekend. He often stayed at the farm, but they respected Sara's rule about separate bedrooms.

In the evenings, Sara pretended to be tired and went to bed early so they could be alone, but she could hear them talking and laughing in the den. It made her recall her own happy times with Paul, and she loved every moment of it.

One warm October afternoon, Sara walked them to the dune. When they arrived, she explained, "The dune was on the edge of a prehistoric lake that dried up. There are several other dunes in the area, but this one was special. Paul and I had some great times on this pile of sand. It's a quiet, out of the way place and I've always loved it here. The kids used to come here often, too. This dune could tell lots of stories if it could talk, including some the kids would prefer I didn't hear, I'm sure."

Susie stayed the whole school year again, but there were no blizzards. If fact, there was very little snow that year. In late May, Jon appeared at Sara's door before Susie got home from school.

He was silent for a long time, then asked, "Sara, can I ask some advice from you as a woman?"

"I'd be honored," Sara replied.

"Well, I was wondering," Jon said, searching for the right words. "Do you think it would be alright if I proposed to Susie on the dune?"

Sara broke into a wide smile. "I can't think of a better place!" she exclaimed. "Paul proposed to me on the dune. I won't go into the details, but it's been a special place to me ever since."

"I'd like it to be a surprise," said Jon happily. "I talked to her parents about it yesterday."

"I love it!" said Sara. "Why don't you put your car in the machine shed before she gets home and then hide in the den? I'll act like no one is here, then you can suddenly appear and offer to take her for drive in the UTV. I'll put in a blanket and some bug spray. There are always bugs this time of year."

"That would be perfect!" Jon said, already heading for the door.

Susie arrived a short time later, her arms loaded with papers to grade. As she sat at the kitchen table, Sara asked, "How was your day?"

"It was fine, but I have all these papers to grade before Tuesday. They're the senior's final papers and the grades have to be in early. I'll have to work overtime to get them done on time."

Just as Susie finished her sentence, Jon stepped out of the den, sneaked up behind her, and put his hands over her eyes. "Guess who?" he said, and as she turned around to give him a hug, he added, "How about taking a ride on the UTV? I think you could use a break."

"You are so right!" she said, standing up and giving him a kiss.

"Well, let's go then!" Jon said excitedly. He gave Sara a wink before turning to lead Susie out the door.

In about an hour, they returned, which was a shorter time than Sara had expected, but Susie was aglow with excitement. "Congratulate me, Sara," she announced. "I'm getting married! I guess the dune has worked its magic again."

"Congratulations, kids," Sara said, giving each of them a warm hug. "The dune always promises long and happy marriages."

Although she didn't say anything about it, Sara had to smile when she noticed that the buttons on Susie's blouse didn't match up and her skirt was twisted around backward. She also noticed that Jon had lipstick on his face.

Susie and Jon continued to meet at the farm, and they often told Sara how much they loved it there. The end of the school year was a bittersweet time, because as she hugged Susie goodbye, she knew that

Susie would no longer be returning to live with her. Susie promised to visit often, but they both knew that things would never be the same.

 Chapter Four
—Little Paul—

As summer rolled by, Jenny arrived one August afternoon with wonderful news. "Mom, guess what? I'm pregnant! The baby's due in January!"

Sara hugged her daughter and said, "Congratulations. I figured you'd be starting a family before too much longer. Let's hope the weather is good for you in January. I wouldn't want you to have to head for the hospital on a snowmobile."

Jenny laughed, and said, "I've got more news. Jason and his partner just bought out the Muscatine Clinic. Jason will run the clinic and teach two days a week at the community college. They're starting a vet tech course and he'll be one of the professors." Sara braced herself for what was coming next. "Of course, that means we'll have to move. We've been looking at places in Muscatine."

Sara said nothing because Jenny was so happy.

"I just can't believe this is all happening at once. Do you think I'll have to quit teaching? Will you help me decorate our new place?" Jenny babbled.

"Whoa!" Sara finally said. "You've got time." Then she added, "Do you remember when you got married, I asked if you and Jason might want to live here? I've talked to some women at church who moved to the new condos in Wilton and they really like them. No lawn to mow, no snow to shovel, and plenty of company. Maybe it's time I get out of this old house and let a family live here again. What do you think?"

"I don't know what to say, Mom," replied Jenny. "I know I'd love to raise children on a farm, but what about Ed? Do you think he'd mind?"

"Heavens, no!" Sara said. "We've already talked it over and he and Carol love their new house. He's going to build a shop at his place so he won't have to run back and forth so much, and he even talked about asking Jason if he might want to manage the cow herd with him. What could be better than having a veterinarian on site"

"Wow!" exclaimed Jenny. "That's great, but do you think you can stand living in town? You've lived here for so many years, and you'll have neighbors in town, you know."

"I think I can get used to wearing clothes all the time, I suppose," Sara said with a chuckle. "I'll just pull the shades when I get the urge to run around in my underwear."

"I'll ask Jason about it tonight," Jenny said, giving Sara a hug, "but I know he'll say yes. It's all like a dream! Maybe I should wait and ask him on the dune. What do you think?"

"Why not?" Sara replied. "That old dune has made history many times over the years."

"I'll bring him out as soon as he gets home. I know he's not on call tonight," Jenny said happily. "Well, I'd better get going." As she turned to leave, she added, "Oh, and Mom, could you put a blanket and some bug spray in the back of the go-getter? We might need it. "

"Consider it done," Sara said as Jenny rushed toward the door.

* * *

In late October, Sara moved to Wilton and Jenny and Jason began moving their meager amount of furniture to the big farmhouse. Sara left some of her furniture because it wouldn't fit into the condo, and together she and Jenny began painting and redecorating.

Several days after Thanksgiving, Susie called to say, "I need a wedding coordinator, if you've got time. I just can't seem to get everything done by myself."

"I'd love to!" Sara said, "but I've never done something like that before."

"I think you'll do fine," said Susie. "I'll stop by next weekend and we'll talk about it."

The next few weeks were busy as Sara spent her weekends in Ottumwa, helping Susie pull together all the loose ends. As Christmas approached, Sara wondered what to get Susie—and came up with a great idea. She'd give her a special nightgown of her own.

She looked for the right cotton fabric, but she quickly discovered that everything seemed to have some polyester mixed with it. Finally, she found what she was looking for at a Mennonite store—100 percent cotton. She bought a little-girl size pattern and sewed a nightgown identical to the one she'd been given by Mr. and Mrs. B.

The day after Christmas, Sara went to Ottumwa to stay until the wedding on the twenty-eighth. The wedding went off perfectly and Susie was thrilled with her nightgown, saying it would always remind her of the two wonderful years she'd spent on the farm.

When Sara returned home, she turned her attention to Jenny, who was looking very pregnant and hoping to have the baby during semester break. The school agreed to give her a two-month leave of absence after the baby was born. Cliff Twill, one of Jenny's former teachers, agreed to come out of retirement to sub for her. He missed the kids and was looking forward to coming back for a while to be with the students.

The last couple of weeks were torture for Jenny, and she had her students do most of her leg work while she sat in a chair during class. Sara stayed at the farm on the nights Jason was on call, and he was out the night the baby decided to arrive. The sky was clear at 8:00 that night and the thermometer was hovering around zero when Jenny started having contractions.

"I think we'd better call Jason," she told Sara, but as another contraction began, she added, "Maybe we'd better head toward the hospital now."

"I'll start the car and get it warmed up," Sara said. "Then we'll call

Dr. Julie, Dr. Julia's daughter, to let her know we're on the way. We can call the vet clinic on the way to have them get hold of Jason."

"Okay, Mom," Jenny said, her face distorted as another contraction began to wash over her, "but I think we'd better hurry!"

After Sara had helped Jenny into the car, she called 911 and said, "Hello, Jill. This is Sara Maas. Jenny needs to get to the hospital right now and we're going to need an escort. Could you have one of the deputies meet us at Y48 and 170th?"

"You bet," Jill said. "I'll have Tom there in three minutes."

As they started down the driveway, Sara said, "Don't have the baby in the car. I don't want to have to clean up the mess."

"Okay, sarge," Jenny said, smiling weakly. "I'll do my best."

Just as they reached the blacktop, the deputy pulled up beside them. He turned on his lights and siren and Sara followed in his wake until they finally reached the hospital. The emergency crew rushed out, sat Jenny in a wheelchair, and disappeared into the hospital.

Sara was about to put the car into drive when Deputy Tom stepped up to the window, opened the door, and said, "I'll park your car, Sara. You'd better go inside. I'll bring you the keys in a few minutes."

"Thank you very much," Sara said, jumping out of the car and hustling toward the building.

Just as she walked through the door, Sara slipped on a wet spot and fell to the floor. She was immediately helped into a wheelchair by a young attendant who began pushing her toward the maternity ward. They were met by Dr. Julie, who was just arriving herself.

"Do you want to be in the delivery room with Jenny?" the doctor asked.

"If it's alright, I would," Sara replied.

"I think it will be okay," the doctor said. "I'm told that Jason's on his way, but it would be better for Jenny if someone was with her during the delivery and if he can't make it, who better than her mother?"

They quickly got Sara into a gown and wheeled her into the delivery room, where Jenny said, "Hi, Mom. Are you okay? They said you took a pretty nasty fall."

"I'm fine," Sara replied. "I just got going too fast. How are you doing?"

"I wish Jason was here," said Jenny. "He's probably delivering pigs somewhere. We could have saved some money by having him do the delivery."

"Well, at least you're not lying on a cold barn floor while you're having your baby," Sara said with a smile.

Just as Dr. Julie announced, "The head is coming," Jason burst through the door.

"Did I make it in time?" he asked.

"Just barely," Dr. Julie replied. "Okay now, Jenny, one more push!"

A moment later, the doctor looked over at Jason and asked, "Well, Dad, would you like to cut the cord of your new son?"

"Yes, ma'am, I sure would," Jason said with tears in his eyes.

Jason cut the cord and held his son for a moment, then handed him to Jenny. "Paul James Wulf, meet your mommy," he said softly.

"I'm glad you made it," Jenny said, smiling at her husband and squeezing his hand.

"This is the first time I've been in the delivery room as an observer," said Sara. "All the other times, I was the main attraction."

"I know, Mom. In fact, the last time you were here, you were having me," said Jenny, smiling through her own tears. "I'm glad you were here."

Two days later, Jenny and little Paul went home. Sara stayed for a few days to help, then went back to her condo, where she faced her own dilemma: It was time to start writing, but where should she start?

Chapter Five
Girl Meets Boy

Sara was born May 10, 1951, the only daughter of John and Emma McWilliams. Her dad was a tall slim man. He always wore his hair in either a butch or flattop. If he'd had a beard, he could have passed for Abe Lincoln. John loved to fish and would spend hours in his leaky old johnboat. He and Emma owned a cabin on the Cedar River where they spent most summer weekends.

Emma was considered tall for her time. She was five-eight and fine-boned, with fine black hair and long, slender hands. Emma was a tireless worker, and when she had time, she loved to sew, knit, or do needlepoint. Never going beyond eighth grade, she worked as a cook, cleaning lady, and nanny for many prominent Muscatine families over the years.

Sara had two older brothers, Tom and Bill. Growing up in a small city of 20,000, she took part in all the activities little girls did in the fifties, but having older brothers also made Sara a total tomboy. She could play basketball, baseball, and tennis better than most boys her age, but there were no girl's athletics in the large schools at that time. She later became active in the Future Teachers Club and looked forward to a career in education. In the summer, she worked as a lifeguard at the Muscatine pool. Her life was cruising—until Jake Moore asked her to the Wilton High "Spring Fling," where she met Paul Maas.

Paul Maas was a typical farm boy. Born on November 25, 1950, he was the son of George and Madge Maas. George was a tall, muscular man who loved the cattle business. He wore blue jeans, button-up shirts, cowboy boots, and always wore a cowboy hat. He was proud to be a cattleman, and he let everyone know it. He promoted beef wherever and whenever he could. He was also a gentleman, never using foul language or telling off-color jokes around women.

Madge was a small lady with a perpetual smile. She stood about five-four and was in good physical condition. In fact, George always loved to kid her about being stacked. She was also one of those people who could eat anything and never put on weight. Madge was a bundle of energy and could outwork most people. She managed her family, including George, with great efficiency.

Paul had a sister named Susan. She was four years older and had the easygoing temperament of their father. She attended Drake University and eventually became a high school teacher in social studies. She and her husband, Jeff, lived in Waterloo.

Being born in November, Paul was almost always the oldest student in his class. He spent some time in a one-room country schoolhouse until the district consolidated in 1960. Paul rode a bus to Wilton from then on.

Being tall and lean in small town America—and especially being six feet tall by the time he was in eighth grade—meant a boy played basketball. It didn't matter whether he had any talent or desire. He just played. Paul had topped out at six-four by his sophomore year and was moved up to varsity. The problem was he only weighed 175 pounds dripping wet, which meant that when he got into shoving matches with other centers, he generally lost the battle.

Paul's greatest loves were his vocational agriculture classes and FFA. He loved working with animals and crops. He was chapter vice president his junior year and headed for the top job during his senior year. Many girls wanted to date him, because he was not only good-looking, but he never put anyone down. He talked to everyone and was one of the most popular boys in school.

"Never think you're better than anyone else," Paul's dad always told him.

The junior class elected him class president, and he could easily picture himself as senior class president and homecoming king. He was also cruising toward his senior year—until that Wilton High "Spring

Fling," which he attended with a girl named Kelly and met Sara Jane McWilliams.

Sara danced with the handsome young man named Paul during a mixer dance. Paul lived just outside of town. He was a good dancer and flowed easily with the music. He couldn't seem to stop staring at Sara as they danced at arm's length.

"Are you from Durant?" he asked. "I haven't seen you before."

Durant High was Wilton's arch rival, and if Sara had been from Durant, it would have been like dancing with the devil.

"No," she replied sweetly. "I'm from Muscatine. I'm here with Jake Moore. I know him from my church youth group. He's a nice guy."

"Yeah, I know Jake, too," said Paul. "We're in vo-ag together. What's your name?"

"Sara McWilliams."

"I'm Paul, Paul Maas. You've sure got pretty hair."

"Thank you," she replied with a touch of embarrassment.

After finishing the dance, Paul smiled at Sara and said, "Thank you for the dance." Then he returned to Kelly.

Sara thought she'd never hear from Paul again, but the very next day the phone rang.

"Hello?" she said.

"Is this Sara McWilliams?" asked the voice on the other end of the line.

"Yes, who is this?"

"This is Paul Maas—the guy you danced with last night. I've been trying to find your number. I couldn't get hold of Jake, so I just started calling all the McWilliams in the Muscatine phonebook. Are you busy tonight? I was wondering if you'd like to go to a movie."

Sara was dumbfounded. "Well, tomorrow's a school day, so it would have to be the early show."

"That's fine," Paul said.

"I'll ask Mom if it's all right," said Sara. Then she held her hand over the phone and yelled, "Mom, may I go to a movie tonight with Paul Maas? You know, the guy I danced with last night. I told you about him. Remember?" After her mother had given the okay, Sara said, "Mom says okay."

"Great," Paul replied. "I'll pick you up at six-thirty. The first show starts at seven. Tell your mom, you should be home by 9:30."

At six-thirty on the dot, Paul arrived in his Chevy pickup. Sara's mom answered the door.

"Good afternoon, Mrs. McWilliams. My name is Paul Maas. Maybe you've heard of my dad, George Maas. He's one of the county supervisors. I've come to take Sara to the movie, *State Fair,* the new version with Pat Boone in it. We'll be home right after the show."

Sara's mother was thoroughly charmed by the tall young man in the long-sleeved dress shirt, blue jeans, and cowboy boots. A moment later, Sara came through the door from the living room, wearing a white blouse and straight red skirt that accented her height.

"Hi," she said sweetly, "I'm ready to go."

Paul looked at her and said with a smile, "Boy, you look great!"

That was the beginning of their romance. Paul was so polite that it took six dates before he asked if he could kiss her, and even then it was just a peck. Sara was surprised, but she enjoyed the kiss immensely. He was much different from the others she'd dated. In fact, she really liked Paul Maas.

They dated all that summer. Sara went to the county fair to watch Paul show his FFA heifers. On judging day, Sara even helped wash them. She got soaked when one of the heifers decided not to stand quietly and the water sprayed all over. Luckily, Paul had warned her to bring a change of clothes.

She went to the restroom and came back in a white blouse and blue jean shorts. She looked as if she was all legs. Her part-time job as a lifeguard had given her a gorgeous tan. The day was hot, but Paul's animals showed well, receiving two blue ribbons and a red.

On Saturday night, Paul had two surprises for Sara. The first was that he was going to attend Muscatine High that fall. Second, while taking a ride on the Ferris wheel, he asked if they could go steady—which Sara answered by throwing her arms around him and saying, "Yes!"

Fall semester started out great for Paul. He fit in at MHS quickly, and even though all the girls were gaga over him, he only had eyes for Sara. As the year went by, Paul took Sara to the homecoming dance, the Christmas Fling, the Sweetheart Ball, and the Senior Prom. He tried out for the basketball team and made it. His playing time was limited, but he didn't really care. Basketball had always been just something he did because he was tall and enjoyed the game.

One game, he went in for an injured teammate and brought Muscatine from behind by scoring twelve points in two minutes. They won the game, and Paul was the school hero that night.

Paul also excelled in FFA. He and four others went to the state contest on the parliamentary procedure team, where they received a gold rating. Meanwhile, Sara became the president of FTC, and she sometimes helped in the elementary classrooms. Soon graduation was upon them and they began thinking about college. Paul had only one school in mind, Iowa State University in Ames. Sara chose Northern Iowa in Cedar Falls.

While at college, they kept in touch, but they also dated other people and participated in student activities. They saw each other on holidays and dated during the summer. Sara kept her job as lifeguard and manager at the Muscatine pool, and because the pool closed late, it meant dating after 9:00. This suited Paul fine, since he worked until dusk most nights anyway. Sara also had either Saturday or Sunday off every other week. They scheduled dates around her work.

After graduating from ISU, Paul returned home to farm with his parents. Sara taught fourth grade in the Lone Tree school district, living with her parents until she found a small house to rent. Paul helped her paint and clean the place before she moved in. They dated throughout the year, and Paul was always patient and polite. He even helped Sara with school projects, including visiting her class one day to explain how corn and soybeans grew.

In February, the principal came to Sara's classroom and asked if she and Paul would chaperone the FFA Sweetheart Ball. She called Paul and he said he'd enjoy being one of the "old guys" who stood around the edge of the dance floor.

Spring was soon blooming everywhere, and when Paul finished planting corn in May, Sara brought her class out to the farm for a field trip. Paul had some calves ready for everyone to pet. He enjoyed telling the students and their mothers about the farm. Paul's mother had baked some cookies and had Kool-Aid ready, and they made it a memorable field trip.

School was out in late May and Sara began working for the park system organizing youth programs, but she was a regular at the Maas farm every weekend. She rode with Paul as he cultivated the corn and beans, and he taught her how to drive the 620 John Deere with its hand clutch. He even let her cultivate solo one afternoon. She impressed Paul's dad with her ability to guide the tractor down the row and not plow out any corn.

One day when Paul needed to bale hay, Sara volunteered to cultivate on her own. She spent the entire day in the field, coming in only at lunchtime. Madge drove some snacks out to the field in the afternoon to check on her.

"You're getting good at this, ya know?" Madge said with a smile. "You'd better watch out or it might become a full-time job."

"I wouldn't mind that a bit," Sara replied.

On the last day of baling, the men found themselves a person short, so Paul's first thought was to ask Sara to help, but George wasn't convinced. Finally he relented, saying, "Alright, if she's willing, I guess we could let her try."

Paul called Sara, and she began driving the tractor right after lunch. It took just two trips around the field before she was driving as if she'd been doing it all her life. She never missed the hay and let the clutch out with the smoothness of butter. By the end of the day, George was ready to hire her full-time, claiming that she drove better than most men—even if she was a city girl.

One day, when George, Madge, and Sara were sitting alone at the kitchen table, George said, "You know, Sara, if I had my way, you'd be a permanent part of this operation already. I'm going to talk to Paul about it. He's in love with you anyhow."

"George, you hush up," Madge scolded. "Don't go embarrassing the girl. Sara, you pay no attention to him. He's always saying things he shouldn't."

"Well, I'll tell you this much," George said. "I never saw anyone take to driving a tractor like Sara does. She's better than Sue ever was, and I always try to give credit where credit is due."

Smiling broadly, Sara said, "Thank you, Mr. Maas. I like driving the tractor. It gives me the feeling that I can help and I like being outdoors."

On July 4th, Sara attended the Maas family picnic. Sue and her family arrived from Waterloo, and when she heard that Sara had been driving the tractors, she said, "Wow! They never let me out there unless they were desperate!"

They all attended the town parade and watched the fireworks from the park by the river. On the way back to Sara's house, she told Paul she was going to be taking a short vacation with her parents. They were going to see her brother, Bill, in Kansas City. They'd return on the eleventh, and as soon as they got back, Sara's dad wanted to paint the house. As they pulled up to the house, they found Mr. McWilliams standing in the front yard, looking up at the second floor peak.

"What are looking at, Mr. McWilliams?" Paul asked.

"Well, I was going to paint the house as soon as I got back from Kansas City. I want to do it while the plant is shut down, but I don't know how I'm going to get up to that peak. I don't do too well with heights," he replied.

"I'll check my calendar," said Paul, "but I don't think I'm doing anything special the Tuesday after you get back. How about if I come and do the high spots? We've got a forty-foot extension ladder and I'd be glad to help."

"That would be great!" John replied. "I could use some young legs and arms. I'll have everything ready on Tuesday morning."

"Well, you two will have to paint by yourselves that day," said Sara. "I have to teach that morning and then I'm going with Tammi to hunt for her attendant's dresses in the afternoon."

"That's all right, Sugar," her father said. "Paul and I can do it ourselves."

Sara smiled, lowered her voice, and said, "Well, I suggest that you wait until Mom leaves. You know she's always afraid of someone falling."

When Tuesday arrived, Paul showed up with the ladder tied on the top of his pickup. Sara's mom had just left for work and John was waiting in the driveway. Paul leaned the long ladder against the house, then climbed up and started on the west side of the house.

At 11:30, John said, "Hey, Paul, let's take a break. The sun will be off the east side after lunch so we won't be so hot. Let's grab a bite and continue then."

"Sounds like a good plan. Say, I wanted to ask you something about Sara anyway, when she wasn't here."

They went inside, and as John scrounged in the refrigerator to find some leftovers, he asked, "What was it you wanted to ask me?"

Paul paused, cleared his throat, and said, "Well, Mr. McWilliams, you know that I like Sara very much, and I know she feels the same about me, so I'd like to ask her to marry me, if you'll give your permission."

John smiled as he pulled some chicken out of the refrigerator and approached the kitchen table. "Well, it a serious step, so I assume you've given it a lot of thought."

"Yes, sir," Paul said, studying John's face.

John broke into a wide smile, held out his hand, and said, "I'd be proud to have you as a son-in-law, so you definitely have my permission. When are you going to pop the question?"

Paul sighed with relief and said, "Probably next week. I'll take her to the Eagle's Nest for supper, as soon as I see what her schedule is."

After lunch, they both began painting again. They were already cleaning up when Emma arrived home. She looked up at the high peak, but only shook her head. She was just glad she hadn't been there to worry.

After they had put everything away, the three of them were sitting on the front porch with iced tea when John finally broke the news. "Paul here is going to ask Sara to marry him next week!"

"Oh, Paul, that's wonderful!" Emma said, giving Paul a sincere hug. "I think the two of you are well matched! Congratulations!"

"Thank you," said Paul, "but now I'd better be getting home. Please don't tell Sara about any of this, okay?"

"Don't worry, Paul," said Emma, "I can keep a secret. But I'll have to watch John."

"Don't you worry about me," John said, giving his wife a playful look. "My lips are sealed."

Ten days elapsed as Paul harvested the oats and baled the remaining straw. Sara was busy finishing summer school classes, so there was no time for them to get together.

Finally, on a warm late-July afternoon, Paul called to ask if Sara could come to the farm. Sara replied, "Sure, but what should I wear? Are we going to be working?"

"Not this time," Paul said evasively. "I thought we might go out for dinner. I've never been to the Eagles' Nest, and I hear it's nice. Why don't you wear your yellow dress, the one with the short jacket? If you can stay overnight, I thought we could leave early for the fair tomorrow. Shorts and tennis shoes would be fine for that."

"Sure, I can stay over. I'm just cleaning house. I'll see you this afternoon."

Sara put on her yellow knit dress, looked in the mirror, then twirled from side to side letting the pleated skirt swirl. To complete the outfit, she put on her red strap sandals.

When Sara arrived at the farm, no one seemed to be around. Even Paul's parent's car was gone. Knowing the house was always unlocked, she went inside and took her overnight bag and other clothes to the guest bedroom.

Then she used the bathroom and returned to the kitchen. She turned on the fan and sat in front of it. It was a hot day and the breeze felt good. She looked around the kitchen, which was antiquated, but serviceable. Cupboards went all the way up to the nine-foot ceiling. The counter top was laminate but dated. It had been a great kitchen in the 1940s, but it needed some serious updating. She wondered if it might be her kitchen someday.

Her eyes fell upon a small box on the counter and a note beside it. In Madge's handwriting, it read: "I decided to go with your dad. Don't forget the box."

Sara resisted taking a peek, but it looked like a ring box. Was that why Paul had asked her to come to the farm? If it was, she was going to have to act totally surprised when he popped the question! She walked out into the backyard, where there was a rope swing in the old oak tree.

"That looks like fun, but I don't want to get dirty," she thought.

The swing's seat was covered with dust, so Sara scanned the yard for something to cover the seat. She spotted some towels hanging on the clothesline. She unpinned one, draped it over the seat, and started swinging.

A few minutes later, she heard the familiar pop-pop of the old John Deere. Soon Paul turned into lane. Sara watched as he pulled the tractor into the machine shed. He reappeared, walking fast and talking to himself, not even noticing Sara on the swing or her car in the shade of the trees.

Through the backdoor he hurried, still talking to himself. He looked nervous. She jumped out of the swing and by the time she walked into the kitchen, Paul had gone downstairs to shower. She smiled as she sat in front of the fan, listening to him sing some old country song.

What happened next surprised them both.

Paul never suspected anyone was in the house. He was used to showering and dashing quickly upstairs, covered only with a towel. When he appeared at the kitchen door, he was naked except for the small towel. His leg was completely exposed on one side, he looked at her in shock.

"Wh—when did you get here?" he stammered.

"About thirty minutes ago. I thought I'd come early and talk to your mom, but since she wasn't here, I made myself at home. I've been swinging in the backyard for about fifteen minutes," Sara said with a smile.

As nonchalantly as possible, Paul sauntered over to the counter to somehow hide the box. He opened the cupboard above the sink and pulled out a glass. Then, with one hand still gripping his towel, he turned on the faucet. He noticed some birds at the feeder in the backyard.

"Hey! Sara, come and look at all these goldfinches!" he said, trying to distract her attention.

Sara walked over to the window and stood beside Paul. While she was looking out the window, he reached out to slide the box behind the toaster, but as he straightened back up, he whacked his head under the open cupboard door. As he reached up toward his aching head, the towel dropped to the floor.

As Sara turned to see what had happened, she saw Paul, now completely naked, rubbing his head. When he realized the situation, he put the glass down quickly and picked up his towel. Then he plopped into the closest chair, covering his legs with the towel.

"Are you all right?" Sara asked, trying her best not to laugh. "Let me see your head." She felt the top of his head where a big welt was forming. "We'd better put something cold on it."

She found a damp washrag and ran cold water on it. Folding it neatly, she then placed it on his head.

"There, is that better?"

"Yeah," Paul said. "Thank you."

Then, smiling slyly, Sara added, "The next thing I should do is help you with your towel, since you aren't completely covered."

Paul turned bright red and said, "Uh, if you'll excuse me, I think I should probably go get dressed."

"Why?" she said with a giggle.

"Because I have something *else* I want to show you," he said, turning to go.

"Well, I don't know," she teased. "I've seen quite a bit already. Are you sure my heart can stand any more?"

"Wait here," he called as he ran up the stairs. I'll be right back."

Sara sat in front of the fan and waited, and when Paul finally returned, he said, "I'm sorry, but we'll have to come up with a Plan B. I called the Eagle's Nest and found out that they're closed for remodeling. You did bring your clothes for the fair, right?"

"Yes," Sara replied.

"Well, why don't you change into them now, because that pretty yellow dress might get dirty where we'll be going."

She went to her room and changed. When she returned to the kitchen, she saw that the ring box was gone, but she didn't say anything about it.

"Come on, let's go," Paul said, holding out his hand.

"Where to?"

"You'll find out."

He ushered Sara out to the pickup, then they headed toward the back pasture. After bouncing across the field, Paul turned the pickup toward a sand dune that had been left by an ancient glacier. Because it only grew small trees and buckthorn brush, it was fenced off from the rest of the field.

They got out of the truck and climbed the dune hand-in-hand. At the top was a small clearing where Paul had placed a park bench. Paul spread a blanket on the ground. Then they kicked off their sandals and stood barefoot in the cool sand. It was quiet and a slight breeze was blowing over the crest of the dune, rustling the leaves in the trees gently.

Paul turned to Sara and said, "I've always loved it here. I used to play here as a kid, and when I got older, I came up here to get away and think. That's when I brought the bench up here. This isn't how I planned it."

"Planned what?" Sara asked innocently.

Paul pulled the blue box from his shirt pocket and opened it. Then he got down on one knee and said, "Sara Jane McWilliams, will you please accept this ring as my formal proposal of marriage? Would you be willing to spend the rest of your life with a farmer? Will you try to love this place as much as I do?"

"Yes, yes, and again yes," Sara said, tears filling her eyes.

Paul slipped the ring onto her finger. It didn't fit exactly, so she had to hold the ring on with her thumb as she jumped into his arms and kissed him. They held each other tightly, then Sara pulled him down onto the blanket and unbuttoned his shirt, but he stopped her as she began to slide it off his shoulders.

"Now, there's one other thing I need to tell you," Paul said. "Do you remember the six guys I lived with at college? We called ourselves the Plowboys, and we created our own little fraternity. The frat guys always pinned their women, so when Jerry was about to get engaged to Sandy, we decided we should give a special pin to the lucky or unlucky women who said yes to us.

"We went to the jewelers in Dogtown to look for something, and we finally decided on ear pins. They're supposed to go on ears, but we thought we'd pin them to the girl's clothing, preferably an undergarment."

"Okay, but what has that got to do with me?" Sara asked.

"I'm getting there," Paul replied. "I called Jerry yesterday and asked if everyone had followed through on our pact, and he said they had, as far as he knew. They'd all clipped the pin on their fiancée's bra, except Harry, who pinned his on Kelly's underpants—he didn't tell Jerry if she was wearing them at the time or not."

As Sara laughed, Paul reached into his pants pocket and pulled out the pin. "I'm the last one in our fraternity to get engaged, so here's my pin. You can wear it wherever you want."

Sara looked down at the ground and pretended to be hurt. "Oh, no, you don't, Paul Mass!" she said. "I expect to receive my pin the same way all the others did. You have to finish the job."

Sara pulled her pink top over head, exposing her pink bra. Then she took Paul's reluctant hand and made him attach the pin to it. He started to pin it on the fabric between her breasts, but she stopped him.

"Right here will be fine," she said, pointing to the top of the cup. "It's okay. You won't hurt me." She then pulled her shoulders forward to give him more room to work.

Sara didn't put her top back on as they leaned back to watch the sunset from the top of the dune. She removed Paul's shirt so she could feel his warm skin next to hers.

"Can we start to plan the wedding for next year?" she asked as golden hour glowed all around them, bathing the land in unbelievable beauty.

They chose late July for three reasons. One was because it would be a year after their engagement. Second, all the planting and spraying would be done and hay would be put away so Paul would be available for a honeymoon. And third, Sara had already signed a contract to teach one more year at Lone Tree. She'd have to hope for an opening in Wilton or Muscatine next year. If all else failed, she could substitute.

Paul's parents were building a new home in Wilton, and their wedding would probably hurry them along. When they had finished moving, Paul and Sara could live in the family farmhouse.

The next morning, Sara waltzed into to the kitchen, humming happily.

"My, my, you're chipper this morning," Madge said. "What could make you this happy?"

Sara held out her hand to show the ring.

"Gee, where did Paul get the money to buy such a big stone?" Madge said in mock astonishment. "He's always telling me how broke he is." Then she enfolded Sara in a warm hug and added, "Welcome to the family, Sara. George and I have been waiting for this moment for a long time. When George proposed to me, I didn't have a clue what I was getting into, but all those years of hard work have been a pleasure for me. Farm life gets into your blood, and I wouldn't change a thing. I hope you'll be able to say the same thing in twenty years."

"I just know I'm going to love it," Sara said. "I'm looking forward to being a farm wife."

Madge smiled at her, nodded her head, and said, "Yes, Sara, I think you're going to do just fine."

Chapter Six
The Big Itch

School started the week before Labor Day, and Sara faced a new classroom of children full of boundless energy. She and Paul were asked to chaperone another dance, but this time they surprised the students by dancing. In fact, when the DJ played a favorite old swing number, the floor cleared to watch Paul and Sara dance. They put on quite a show, moving like a couple who had been dancing together for years. Everyone clapped when the number was over, and they graciously bowed as they accepted the applause. Everyone agreed that Miss McWilliams and Mr. Maas were the hit of the dance.

The fall harvest went well. Sara stayed overnight on weekends to help. She learned to hitch wagons and pull the loads back to the farmstead, where Paul's dad unloaded the wagons while Sara returned to the field for another load. She also rode in the combine cab with Paul when time allowed.

Sara and Madge hit it off from the start. She helped with lunches and dinners. Madge taught her how make delicious pies with flaky crusts. One afternoon, Paul called on the CB to say that he needed some tools to fix the combine in the field where he was harvesting soybeans.

George and Madge were just on their way out the door for a meeting, so Sara said, "You two go ahead. I can take the truck out."

"That would be great," said Madge. "Paul will be surprised when he sees you, but you might as well get used to it. This happens all the time to farm wives."

Sara hurried out to the pickup and drove to the shop to grab the tools Paul had asked for. She was glad they were right on the workbench as he had told her, because she didn't have a clue what she was looking for.

Bouncing across the end rows, Sara could see the combine sitting in the middle of the field. Paul had all the doors on the machine open. It looked like a giant wounded bird in the late afternoon sun. Paul was surprised to see her instead of his dad, but after Sara explained the situation, he just smiled. It would take a little longer to explain what she needed to do, but they could replace the roll pin together.

Crawling under the combine, Paul said, "When I tell you to turn the wrench, you pull it to the right. I have to line up the shaft and the sprocket on the other side. When say I stop, you hold it tight and steady. Understand?"

Sara nodded and said, "I'll do my best."

Lifting and twisting the shaft under the combine, Paul kept up a constant chatter. "A little to the right…oops, too far…back up a little… stop right there…now hold it!"

Sara heard pounding, a few moments of silence, several more pounds, then more silence, until Paul finally called out, "OK, we got it! Good job!"

Sara let go of the wrench and as she turned, a gust of wind shook the combine door and sent a shower of soybean dust cascading from the door ledge, covering her from head to toe. Sara screamed and coughed as Paul scrambled from underneath the combine. When he emerged, he saw Sara shaking her hair furiously and jumping up and down to shake off the dust. She was a sight!

Peering through the dust-covered eyelashes, Sara saw Paul smile, then he laughed out loud.

She gave him a playful shove and said, "What is this stuff? It's itchy and sticks to me like glue."

"It's just bean dust," Paul replied. "It's tiny hairs from the pods.

They're charged with static electricity and they'll stick to anything. They've got sharp edges, which is what makes you itch."

"Well, it feels like the insulation that fell from the attic when my dad and I installed a vent fan in the bathroom," said Sara. "That stuff itched like crazy, but this stuff is worse."

Reaching into the back of the pickup, Paul grabbed an air hose, attached a blowgun, and blew the dust out of her hair. "Don't rub your eyes," he said, "and when you get back to the house, take a shower—and wash out your eyes. I wouldn't be surprised if your eyes are mattered shut in the morning, though. Man, you're a mess!"

He raised the back of her sweatshirt and blew the dust from her back. Then, he handed her the hose. "You'd better do the front. I'll get some shop wipes from the cab for your face."

When she caught a glimpse of herself in the pickup's rearview mirror, even she had to laugh at herself.

Sara pulled her sweatshirt over her head with her back to Paul while he reached into the cab and got the wipes. He also pulled out one of his old t-shirts and handed it to her. "Here, you can put this on after we get you cleaned off."

The breeze felt good on her sweaty, dusty skin. She wiped the rest of her body as Paul cleaned her back. She surmised that desperate situations called for desperate moves, and she didn't really care what Paul might see. She had never been this itchy before. She unhooked her bra so he could clean the dust trapped underneath. Then she unhooked the button of her dust-filled jeans and slipped them off.

"Well, this could be fun!" Paul joked.

"You've seen me in a swimsuit, silly," Sara giggled.

Sara felt completely comfortable standing in front of Paul nearly naked. The thought of what fun going further might be crossed both their minds, but she grinned as she reminded him, "Some things are worth waiting for, Mr. Maas."

They were alone, with no one around for miles, and Sara was standing in front of her fiancée in her underwear. It wasn't exactly forbidden at that time for two people to be partially undressed in front of each other before they were married. After all, it was the '70s and Sara had always dreamed of a wedding night that would be absolutely amazing. She and Paul had talked about waiting a number of times. Even so, she loved the feeling of his warm hands on the small of her back.

She reached for the t-shirt and held it over her breasts as she slowly turned around. He looked at her and thought he was the luckiest man alive. He wrapped his arms around her and pulled her close, feeling the softness of her breasts against his chest. Sara looked up and kissed him passionately. She could wrap her arms around his neck since she was so tight against him. She got chills as he slowly ran his fingers down her back. Holding each other in the warm moonlight, there was nowhere in the world they would rather have been.

It wasn't the first time Paul had seen a woman in just her underwear—he'd been to college—but this was the woman he was going to marry next summer, the woman of his dreams. He desired her so much at that moment and he could tell by the way she was pressing against him that she felt the same. As much as he hated to do it, he kissed her again, and led her back to the driver's side door of the pickup.

"Wow, it's going to be a long wait until next summer," he said, trying to lighten the mood, "but it will definitely be worth every second."

She pulled on the t-shirt, climbed into the pickup and fired up the engine as Paul turned back toward the combine to finish the last section. Then she headed back to the farm and hurried into the house in just her underwear and the t-shirt. There were no lights on in the house, so George and Madge apparently hadn't returned.

As she ran downstairs and took off the rest of her clothes, she paused a moment to think about what had happened, and it made her smile to know that next year there would be no reason to stop if the same situation arose. They'd be a married couple—and she couldn't wait! She turned on the hot water, stood under the shower, and opened her eyes, just as Paul had instructed.

When she finally stepped out of the shower, she reached for a robe or dry towel, but found none, so she decided to do what Paul had done the summer before and tried to wrap herself up in a too-small towel before heading for her bedroom. Madge apparently didn't believe in large towels.

She tossed her dirty clothes beside the washing machine and headed upstairs, stopping briefly on the landing to look out and see the combine lights blazing amid a cloud of dust in the field. She ascended the last three steps to the kitchen, peeked around the corner, and when she saw that the coast was clear, she sped through the kitchen and bounded up the stairs to the guest bedroom. Then she flopped onto the big bed, thinking, "This is great. It's exhilarating—and such freedom. I think being a farm wife will be just fine!"

She put on her pajamas and fuzzy slippers and went back downstairs, where she waited in George's big recliner until he and Madge returned. They came in talking and laughing, so she knew they'd had a good time. They were surprised to see her sitting there, but they laughed when she told them about the events of the night—although she left out the braless and partially naked part.

Madge stayed to talk while George went into the den to watch the news. "What a great story! I hope it didn't discourage you from being my new daughter-in-law. I know there were many times when I couldn't believe what I'd just done after helping George with some project or other." Then she smiled and asked, "Are you going to bed now?"

"No, I'll wait up for Paul."

"Fine, but I imagine he'll be pretty late," Madge said. Then she called out, "Come on, George, let's go to bed. Sara's going to wait up for Paul."

Sara soon found out why Madge had been smiling. Paul wouldn't come in till after midnight. She did a load of laundry, then curled up in George's chair and fell asleep until Paul finally walked through the back door.

"Hi, hon," he whispered as he kissed her forehead. "I need to take a shower, but this time I'll take some clothes downstairs with me."

When he had showered and returned to the kitchen in knit shorts,

Sara handed him a piece of cake and a glass of milk. "Did you get the field done?"

"Yes, I did," he said with a smile, "thanks for your help. Are you sure you still want to be a farmer's wife?"

Sara replied, "Yes, and yes again!" As she bent down to kiss him on the forehead, her pajama top draped down just enough for Paul to catch a quick glimpse. She was wearing nothing beneath her pajamas. Waiting was definitely getting harder!

Sara yawned and said, "Now, Big Boy, I think it's time we both go to bed. We've got a big day tomorrow, right?"

"Big Boy" was her nickname for Paul, and it fit him well.

Sara put the dishes in the sink while Paul locked the back door. Then they turned off the lights and reluctantly headed toward their own beds.

With harvest completed, Thanksgiving dinner was spent with Sara's parents because her brothers were there. Bob, Shelly, and their children had arrived from Kansas City on Wednesday and would visit Shelly's parents on Friday. Tom, Kris, and their kids came in from Des Moines, but they stayed at a nearby hotel where the kids could swim. When Paul arrived, everyone was waiting, and Sara introduced him to Emil Baumgardner, the much talked about neighbor from across the ravine.

After a huge dinner, the men retired to the family room to watch football. When the game was over and it was time to leave, Emma handed out leftovers to everyone. Paul was staying over because he had agreed to go shopping with Sara on Friday. Sara and Paul offered to walk Mr. B home, and as they walked across the ravine, they talked comfortably. Sara even followed Mr. B into the house to make sure he was okay before she'd return home. It was obvious that he was special to her.

At 6:00 the next morning, Paul's alarm went off on the coffee table by the sofa in the basement family room where he had spent the night. He'd slept on that sofa before, but it seemed more comfortable this time. He climbed the stairs to the kitchen, where he found Mrs. McWilliams, dressed in pajamas and a housecoat, busy fixing breakfast.

"Do you want two eggs or one?" she asked.

"Two would be fine," Paul replied.

"Sunny side up or over easy?"

"Over easy, I guess."

"Coffee or milk?"

"Milk, please!" said Paul. "Boy, you ask a lot of questions early in the morning, Mrs. McWilliams."

"You can call me Emma," she said with a smile. "After all, you're almost family." As she set a plate down in front of him, she added, "I want to tell you that John and I are very pleased that you and Sara are getting married. Ever since she first met you, you're all she's talked about. She loves the farm and the animals. I hope you'll be patient and teach her how to be a farmer's wife."

"I will, Emma. I promise," replied Paul.

"You know, I even envy her a little," Emma added with a smile. "God has blessed both of you. I just know you're going to be happy for a long time. Now eat up, 'cause you're going to need your strength today. Sara has been up for an hour, getting ready. You've hooked up with a real livewire, you know."

"Don't I know it," Paul agreed. "Oh, and thanks for the kind words—and the warning."

Just then Sara popped through the doorway, all dressed and ready to go. "You'd better hurry up and get dressed, Big Boy. The mall opened ten minutes ago. I've got a huge list of things to get, so let's get rolling!"

Paul hurried to finish his breakfast and then went back downstairs. In less than fifteen minutes, he was showered, shaved, and ready to go. In spite of his hurrying, he found Sara was already waiting in the pickup when he emerged from the downstairs family room. .

"Good luck, Paul!" Emma called after them. "Sara, don't you go wearing him out on his very first shopping spree."

Sara seemed to have an endless supply of energy. While having lunch at McDonald's in the mall, she told him they would probably be done shopping by four, but it was nearly five by the time she finally announced that they could finally go back home. Paul could only shake his head in amazement.

They ate supper with John and Emma that night. Paul announced that he should probably head for home. "Why don't you come out and bum around with me tomorrow, Sara?" he asked. "My folks are going to Waterloo to visit Sue for a delayed Thanksgiving. So we could meet for lunch and you could help me work with the cattle. I'll even take you out for supper afterward."

"Okay," Sara said. "I'll pick up some Maid-Rites for lunch on the way. How many do you want?"

"Two will be fine," Paul said. Then the thanked Emma and John for their hospitality, kissed Sara goodbye, and said, "I'll see you tomorrow."

Chapter Seven
—Hot Turkey, Cool Christmas—

When Sara arrived at the farm the following morning, Paul was just coming outside. "Go on in. I'll be there in a minute. I've just got to check out something in the barn!" he shouted.

When Paul returned, they had Maid-Rites and fries while Paul laid out what they were going to do the rest of the afternoon. Sara went into the half bath in the hall and changed from her sweats to flannel-lined jeans. Then she put on Madge's hooded sweatshirt, chore coat, and stocking cap. Paul found her some gloves which fit fairly well. Sara pulled on her boots and then they headed outside.

First, they ground two big bales in the tub grinder for the feeder calves. Then Sara climbed up into the haymow and tossed down several small bales of straw. Paul loaded them into the skid loader bucket and divided them between the three loafing sheds. They scattered the straw in the sleeping areas. The chore soon became a straw fight as they happily tossed chunks of straw at each other.

Finally, Paul took Sara out to check the lick tanks for the stock cows. He explained that the cows were winter pastured in the harvested cornfields and the lick tanks gave them extra nutrients. Paul loved to see Sara taking in every word, and she loved being there with him and learning his ways.

"Do you still want to go to dinner?" he asked.

"No, not really," she replied. "It means we'd have to clean up and get dressed. I'd have to redo my hair. Let's just stay here and make some pizza, okay?"

"That's fine with me. I'm sure we can find some in the pantry."

When they got back to the house, they went to the basement to take off their work clothes. Sara hung Madge's sweatshirt and jacket on a hook, took off her boots, and she headed upstairs while Paul finished with his coveralls and coat. He put their gloves overhead on a hot air duct so they'd dry, and then went up to the kitchen. By the time he got there, Sara had changed back into her sweats.

Paul searched the pantry and found a pizza mix. Sara mixed the dough while he scrounged for toppings. After turning on the oven, she spread the dough on the pan and added bacon bits, black olives, hamburger, part of a chicken breast, and plenty of cheese.

"Why don't we eat in the den?" Paul said. "There's a good football game on, and when that's over, there are some Christmas specials."

Sara agreed and Paul set up some TV trays in the den. Twenty minutes later, they settled in with their pizza to watch the game. Paul suggested she stay over and head home the next morning. Sara claimed she had lesson plans to do and needed to finish what her class was doing for the winter program.

"I also need to clean house, wrap presents, and best of all, sleep in!" she added with a laugh.

Paul countered that it was getting too late for the forty-five-minute drive home and there was a 30 percent chance of snow. "Besides, your house will be cold—and I'll let you sleep in tomorrow morning while I do the chores. I'll let you leave right after lunch, I promise," he said, looking a bit like a pouting little boy.

"No, I've got to go," Sara said, going to the hall coat closet and pretending to get ready to leave. Then she reached down, grabbed her duffle bag, ran back into the den, and gave Paul a warm kiss, saying, "I thought you'd never ask—but if I'm staying here, I'm going to take a shower right now and change into my pj's. I don't want to smell like a cow all night."

"Great!" said Paul happily. "I'll pop some popcorn while you take your shower. When you're done, give me a holler and I'll take mine. If you smell like cows, I must, too, and I want to shower upstairs because it's too cold downstairs."

"Deal!" said Sara.

Paul got out the old popper, put in some oil and popcorn, and waited for it to heat up. He was just finishing a batch when Sara called that she was out of the bathroom. He bounded up the stairs, grabbed his sleeping shorts and a t-shirt, and dashed into the shower while Sara dried her hair with Madge's hair dryer in the master bedroom.

Soon they were sitting close beside each other in front of the TV. This time they sat on floor cushions. Sara said she was cold, so Paul slid the pocket doors to the den shut and turned on the space heater. Sara put a small pillow on Paul's lap and laid her head on it, her feet pulled up, facing the heater.

She looked up at Paul and said, "Hon, did you enjoy yesterday?"

"Yeah, sure I did," he said without looking away from the game.

"Will you take me shopping again?"

"I don't know, maybe," he said with a sly smile

"Good. Now will you do something for me?"

"Of course."

"Will you turn off the TV and talk to me?"

"Okay," he said, flipping off the TV with the remote. "What do you want to talk about?"

The room was quiet except for the wind outside. The small table lamp was the only light and the red glare from the heater gave the den a toasty feeling.

Sara finally said, "Well, to start with, what did you do in the summer when you were a kid? In the city, I had all kinds of playmates. I could walk to any of my girlfriends' houses and the park was only three blocks away. On warm days, somebody's mother would take us to the pool. I had a season pass. I could ride bikes with my friends, and my brothers always had some of their friends hanging around, so we were never bored. What did you do by yourself with no one close by?"

"I was never bored," Paul said. "When I was real young I played in the yard and garden with my farm toys, but I wasn't allowed outside the fence unless someone was with me. Mom was in the garden a lot so I helped her some. One time I had a little garden of my own, with peas, beans, carrots, and one tomato plant. I was so proud of my first peas. Mom cooked them special, just for me.

"When I was seven or eight, I'd bum around with Dad. I had to be ready when he wanted to go to town. I was always barefooted and never wore a shirt, so when he was ready to go I had to get on my shoes and a shirt in a hurry. We always had fun. Dad liked ice cream, so we always hit the ice cream shop before we came home.

"I tried to help in the shop and I rode with him to check the cows. By the time I was nine or ten I could go to the creek and the pond by myself, so I played in the creek and built mini-dams. I fished, but I wasn't allowed to swim in the pond without having someone else there. Sometimes my sister would take me to the pond. She'd lie on the beach and sunbathe, while I played in the sand or waded near the shore.

"She sometimes brought her friends along, and as long as I didn't bother them, I could tag along. She had one friend I really liked. Her name was Joyce. She wasn't the sunbathing type. She liked to swim, and she taught me not to be afraid of the water. She'd take me out in the deep part and make me float and tread water. I learned a lot from her. Of Sue's friends, she was my favorite. "

"Okay," said Sara, "and what else?"

"A few other boys from down the road came over sometimes, but they lived four miles away and came from a big family, so they always had someone to play with. At thirteen, I'd sometimes start on the cultivator in the morning and drive until dusk. I'd listen to the radio and I got a good tan—at least above the waist. Since I didn't want to look goofy at the pool, I'd take my pants off when I was working the ground beyond the creek. After getting a couple bad sunburns, I finally got smart and wore my swim trunks plus I learned to take some suntan lotion along."

As Sara laughed, Paul said, "All in all, I don't think I ever was bored. Tired, maybe, but not bored."

"I wish I could have been here then," Sara said thoughtfully. "You know, hon, my leg's burning up. Could I switch to your other side? You'll have to slide down a bit so I can get my legs stretched out."

As Sara scooted around his feet, Paul watched intently as her top began to work its way up her back, baring her back and stomach. She placed the pillow on his right side and again put her head in his lap. Paul gently began to caress her hair with his right hand while he touched her exposed stomach with his left. In the warmth of the room, bathed in pale light, they were lost in a world of their own.

Sara looked up and studied Paul's handsome features.

"What are you looking at?" he asked.

"I'm just looking at your face," she replied.

"Well, what do you see?"

"I see a man with hazel eyes and mousey brown hair, a man with a pleasing smile, a man who loves animals and has a passion for farming. I see a man who will love me for the rest of my life and will be a good father to our children. Lastly and most importantly, I see a man I'm madly in love with."

Paul smiled warmly and Sara pulled his t-shirt out of his shorts and said, "Take it off." "Why?"

"Because I want to see something."

As he removed his shirt, Sara knelt straddling one of his thighs. She took her index finger and started to count.

When she had finished, she announced, "Twenty-five chest hairs! Are there any on your back?"

"I don't know. I've never looked," he said with a smile.

"Well, lean forward and let me see," she said. He leaned forward to let her look. "Nope. But you ought to see my dad. He's as hairy as a bear. Mom makes him wear a shirt to bed because he tickles her too much."

Paul looked at her slyly and asked, "How many hairs do you have on your chest?"

"None!" Sara said, giggling as she peeked down the collar of her shirt.

"Let me see."

"Really?"

"Sure, there's no one around."

He quickly unbuttoned her top and folded the sides back. He pretended to check her chest while he put his hands around her waist and began to massage her lower back.

"You're fabulous," she cooed. "You give great massages."

He brought his hands up and massaged her neck, and she leaned back, letting his hands work. Slowly, he slipped the pajama top from her shoulders. She let it fall down her arms and onto his legs. His hands followed down her spine to the small of her back. She rose up on her knees, her navel at the level of his lips. Pausing momentarily, he felt for the elastic waistband of her pajama bottoms and eased them down to her knees.

He placed his hands on the back of her thighs and pulled her body close to his face. As he rubbed his nose in her belly button, she giggled. She sat back on her heels and ran her hands slowly down his chest. She was sitting almost naked in front of him. He stared at her, mesmerized by the soft red glow of the heater reflecting off her soft curves. She reached down and unbuttoned his shorts and let herself in.

A few seconds later, she said breathlessly, "I think we'd better slow down, don't you?"

Trying to regain his composure, Paul sighed, "Yeah, lemme go to the bathroom for a sec."

As Sara rocked back on her heels and pushed herself up with her hands, her pajama bottoms fell to her ankles. Paul picked up his t-shirt from the couch and started to stand, but his shorts caught on the sofa cushion and they dropped to the floor. For a few seconds they stood naked in front of each other—they started to laugh. Paul bent down to retrieve his shorts. As he was coming up, Sara was reaching down and they bumped heads, making them laugh even harder.

Sara reached out and put her arms around Paul's waist. He place one hand on her back and one hand on her rump. They pressed together, tightly holding each other, skin touching skin, but only for a moment, and let go. Paul turned and dashed upstairs.

When he returned with another pair of shorts and t-shirt, he found Sara sitting on the couch, dressed again.

"Come sit next to me," she said sweetly, as if nothing unusual had happened, "and we'll finish watching the game."

Paul sat down and put his arm around her. She put her head on his shoulder. It had been a long day and they were exhausted. When the news came on, the weatherman predicted strong winds and blowing snow overnight, but the skies were supposed to clear by noon. Sara was glad she had decided to stay overnight. In the morning Paul was up and outside before Sara woke up. She had breakfast on the table for him when he came back in.

"Good morning, hon!" she said cheerfully as he sat down.

After picking at his food for a few moments, Paul said softly, "Look, hon, about last night—"

Sara put a finger to his lips. "We got a little carried away, that's all—and you want to know something else? I'm not complaining one little bit."

They ate breakfast and read the paper. Sara fixed sandwiches for lunch and announced she needed to head home. She promised she'd call as soon as she got home to let Paul know she'd gotten there safely.

December was hectic. Sara had to control her excited students while getting them ready for their winter program. The end of the semester would be right after the Christmas break, and she didn't want to leave everything until after the holidays.

Paul spent his time readying the equipment and barns for the rest of the long Iowa winter. There were crop information meetings to attend; and seed, fertilizer, and other supplies to order for the next year. He also had some special shopping to do for Sara.

On Christmas Eve, Paul went to Sara's parents' house. It was just the four of them. They had an evening meal of oyster soup, and opened presents. Sara's present to her "Big Boy" was a 35mm camera, since photography was Paul's only hobby. Paul gave her a mint green skirt and cardigan sweater with a crisp white blouse. He said he thought the color would look good on her.

Sara went into the bedroom, and returned to the living room to model the gift. Paul had been right. It fit perfectly and the color looked great on her. Paul took photos of her with his new camera, claiming she should be a fashion model. After the gift exchange, the four of them went to the late service at First Church.

Paul stayed overnight, and on Christmas morning, they drove to the farm. Sue and her family had arrived the night before. The gift unwrapping was bedlam as Sue's three kids excitedly opened their presents. Sue and Jeff had brought gifts for the kids from home plus Grandma and Grandpa Maas added several more. Paul gave Sara another gift that morning—a dark blue pantsuit and pale blue sweater. Her long legs accented the beautiful lines of the fabric.

When it seemed all of the gifts were opened, Madge reached behind the tree and pulled out two presents marked: "To Sara, Our New Addition." Everyone watched as Sara opened the boxes. The first contained a pair of insulated rubber boots, accompanied by a note that read: "These are to keep your feet dry while walking through the cow poop in the barnyard and for keeping your feet warm while shoveling the back sidewalk. Farmers can shovel tons of snow and ice from the feed bunks and alley ways, but they seldom see a reason to clear the back sidewalk. Wear them with my love, Madge."

The second box was bigger, and inside were insulated coveralls, a hooded sweatshirt, three pair of gloves, and a green Pioneer seed corn stocking cap. The note in the box read: "Wear these to keep warm while helping Paul pull calves at three in the morning."

Everyone laughed until they had tears running down their faces. It was a wonderful day, and nighttime came quickly. When they asked if Sara would like to stay over, she happily agreed, but she'd have to sleep in Paul's bed, since Sue and Jeff were in the guest room. Paul would bunk in the den with Seth and Noah, Sue's oldest boys.

It took about an hour to get everyone settled in. After Sara had crawled into Paul's bed, she had trouble sleeping, especially since she could hear Paul and the boys talking and laughing downstairs in the den. She could smell Paul's body on the sheets and blankets, which made her wonder what it was going to be like to sleep next to each other every night. It was her first Christmas with Paul and his family, and she would never forget one moment of it.

During the long winter, Paul and Sara saw each other often. They sometimes had pizza at home and sometimes ate at the Catfish House restaurant near Sara's house. In February, they chaperoned the FFA dance again. March began with a huge snowstorm, closing school for two days. Sara was actually snowbound in her little house for two days, but late in the second day, she finally made it over to her parents' house. Paul came in for the evening, but couldn't stay long. The snow had caused lots of problems with the cattle and he was very tired.

Finally the long winter ended, spring blossomed, and school let out for the summer—and Sara was glad. Now she could put her entire focus on the wedding—her dress, the bridesmaids, the church, the reception, and about a thousand other details that needed to be worked out.

They had to attend marriage counseling with Pastor Tom. The pastor was amazed at their maturity and surprised because they were the first couple he'd counseled in a long time who hadn't been intimate before marriage. Pastor Tom told them how unusual it was in the today's world and that they could be proud of themselves. Paul and Sara gave each other knowing glances, realizing how close they had come the previous Thanksgiving weekend.

Chapter Eight
Cool Waters

The Friday before the wedding was a scorcher of a July day. Temperatures were well into the nineties with high humidity. Sara came out to drive the baler to help bring in the last of the straw. Paul hired some high school boys to load and unload. They finished baling around six o'clock. All that was left was a partial load to get into the barn. George had to go to a cattlemen's meeting and decided to leave. All the boys were anxious to get to town and cruise around, so Paul paid them and let them go.

He turned to Sara and said, "We can unload the last load ourselves, can't we, hon?"

Paul climbed into the mow, and when he gave the signal, she plugged in the electric motor on the elevator. Paul watched as she placed bales on the elevator. She looked cute in her blue sleeveless blouse and blue jeans, her brown hair ponytailed under her green seed cap. She carefully placed each bale and watched it ascend up the track. Finally, the last bale disappeared into the haymow. She hopped off the rack and unplugged the machine.

"Last one!" she hollered.

Paul slid down the rails on the conveyor. He was soaking wet. The sweat made his skin shine. There were pieces of straw sticking to his skin and his jeans were soaked to his knees.

"It's very hot up there!" he exclaimed.

"I've been thinking," she said. "Why don't we have a picnic out by the pond?"

"Sounds great, but I've got to cool off first. You could make some sandwiches while I shower. It should be cooler out there."

Sara made the sandwiches and packed some leftover cake. She got the iced tea from the refrigerator and filled the thermos. Instead of covering the basket with a dish towel, she grabbed two bath towels from the wash basket. They might make a good cover for the picnic table, in case, it was dusty.

When she was just about done, he appeared from the basement.

"Are you ready to go?" he asked. "The new pickup is hooked to the trailer, so we'll have to take the old one. It hasn't got a reverse, so we'll have to watch where we park."

They hopped into the old pickup and headed for the pond, which was big by farm pond standards. It was fed by three tile lines and a spring, so it stayed fairly clean. There was a small sandy beach and a diving dock that reached out beyond the duckweed and moss. An old picnic table sat in a grove of willows, an idyllic place on a hot summer evening. The breeze off the water was refreshing. They sat in the shade and ate their supper.

"I'm still cooking inside. I think I'll take my shirt off," said Paul. "Do you mind?"

"Heavens, no. Not at all," replied Sara. She liked looking at his shirtless body. "Why don't we take a walk around the pond and see if that cools you off?"

They repacked the picnic basket and started around the edge of the pond. They stopped at the diving dock and looked at the inviting water.

Sara said, "We could go swimming in our underwear. That would cool you off completely. There's nobody around to see us anyhow. How about it?"

"I'm game if you are," Paul replied with a smile, already beginning to strip down to his undershorts.

He ran out on the dock, but before he leaped in, he threw in the inner tubes that always hung on the posts. He took one big step and cannon balled into the water. When he emerged, he gazed back at the dock and saw Sara still standing there. She picked up his shorts, folded them, and placed them neatly on the dock. She placed his sandals next to them. She hung the towels that covered the basket on one of the dock posts. Then she knelt down and removed her shoes and socks.

"Okay, close your eyes, and no peeking!" Sara warned.

He pretended to shut his eyes, but he really just squinted and watched as she removed her blouse and laid it on the dock. She unbuttoned her jeans and slid them off, leaving just a pale blue bra and blue panties with lace side panels. It was a sight he'd never forget. After she glanced at Paul to see if he was peeking, she stepped back and then bolted forward, executing a perfect dive over his head. When she surfaced, she swam out to the center of the pond, did a swimmer's flip and swam the backstroke back to Paul. Finally, she stopped on the opposite side of the tube and smiled at him.

"Where did you learn to swim like that?" he asked in astonishment.

"You knew I spent two summers as a lifeguard at the Muscatine pool. Many times the AAU boy's team would practice there before and after hours. I'd come early or stay after to swim with them, and I could beat most of them. Coach Johnson always said he wished I was a boy because he needed me on the team, but there are no girls' sports in the big schools. I learned to dive from the state champ, Jim Krause. Did you like my dive?"

"Yeah, I'd like to see you do that again."

"Maybe in a little bit. I want to cool off first. Let's go."

"I can't swim like you, but I'll try to keep up."

They swam – but in truth Sara swam and Paul just paddled along. When they finally rested at the tubes, Sara decided to try another dive. This time when she reached the top of the dock, she struck a sexy pose, swiveling her hips as if she were a stripper.

Paul watched with glee and quietly said, almost embarrassed,

"Take it off, take it all off!"

Sara looked at him for a moment. She looked away as if she was checking the surrounding pasture. She made sure no one was around and studied the situation. Then, giving him a smile, she reached back, unhooked her bra, and let it slide away. Next, she hooked her thumbs on each side of her underpants, slid them down, and stepped out. She stood unashamed in front of Paul's searching eyes for a brief moment. Then, taking two big steps, she dived over him again, surfacing about ten feet away, and again swam to the middle of the pond. She did her swimmer's flip and breast-stroked back to him.

"This swimming in the nude is great! You should try it. I've never experienced it before. You feel so free."

She helped Paul free himself of his undershorts and tossed them up onto the dock. Taking his hand, she led him out into deeper water.

"You're safe with me," she assured him. "You're swimming naked with a naked lifeguard, remember?"

They rested by floating in the tubes for an hour until Paul complained his skin was getting wrinkly.

"You go first. I'll throw the tubes up. I don't think you have enough energy left to do it," Sara said, giggling.

Paul climbed onto the dock and caught the tubes. This time it was Sara's turn to watch. Paul was dark brown to his waist, then almost as white as snow down to his feet.

"Now, that's what I like to see—my man naked."

She lay back, closed her eyes, and floated on her back in the water. Paul watched from the dock, thinking she was as lovely as a mermaid. Watching her swim with nothing on was great.

Sara opened her eyes and saw Paul gazing at her. She smiled, then sculled over to the ladder and climbed onto the dock. Paul handed her a towel. They put on just their outer clothes. Sara didn't button or tuck her blouse in her jeans. She just tied the ends in a loose knot in front.

Paul slipped on his sandals and picked up the basket. Sara decided to go barefooted as they walked back to the truck through the dewy grass. She took the basket from Paul and walked behind the truck, placing it in the truck bed. She was about to open the door when she noticed Paul standing in front of the hood.

"Hon, come here," he called. "Let's watch the moon come up over the horizon."

Sara stood in front of him and leaned into his chest. He put his arms around her midsection and she held on to his hands, as his thumbs caressed her stomach below her blouse. They watched as the yellow moon rose over the hill. Sara let go of his hands to brush the damp hair from her face, he surprised her by moving his hands up under her shirt.

She placed her hand behind his head and brought his lips down to hers for a passionate kiss lasting several seconds. Paul let his hands slide down to her jeans. He unbuttoned and unzipped her jeans and slid them down her legs. She flipped them over in the grass with her foot. He turned in front of her and pinned her against the front of the truck. With one hand he untied her blouse, letting it fall open. She could feel him pressing against her as they kissed. She could feel how excited he was, and that excited her.

All she could think of was her desire for more. It seemed so right. She sighed passionately as he nibbled on her ear. All she could hear was his breathing growing heavy with arousal. She reached down and unzipped his shorts. They fell to the ground. After all, they were adults, not children. The night was warm and the moon was shining brightly. They had just been swimming nude. There was no one within miles. He put his hands on her waist and lifted her off the hood. She braced herself on his shoulders and looked down as he carried her to the passenger side of the truck. Setting her down on the seat, he cupped her cheeks in his hands and kissed her passionately. He backed away and looked deeply into her eyes. She was moving her eyes up and down his body.

"What you looking at?" he asked.

"I'm just checking out the merchandise before I sign up next week. I didn't get a good look last Thanksgiving. That was just a peek."

"Oh, man, you're making this very hard!" Paul whined. "And in more ways than one."

Sara laughed and said innocently, "Who, me? What did I do?"

Paul answered, "You are amazing in every way."

"Now, what are you doing?" she asked as Paul seemed to be looking for something as he lifted her shirt.

"I thought I saw a blemish awhile back. I just wanted to check it out. I don't want to sign up without checking for damaged merchandise either."

"Did you find anything?"

"Yes," he teased. "What's this little round scar on your hip? I spotted it when you dove over me."

"Oh, that, it's a scar from my smallpox shot when I was little."

"I guess I'll accept it."

Sara slapped him playfully. They were about to continue their romantic encounter when the pickup shook violently. Startled, they looked around, but saw nothing. It happened again. This time Paul spotted an old stock cow rubbing her rump on the pickup bumper. He hollered at her, but the cow just raised her head, stared at him, flicked her ears, and ignored him. Paul walked to the back of the pickup and chased the old cow over the hill. Sara enjoyed seeing her naked man in sandals chasing a cow over the hill, and she laughed until tears ran down her face.

"I think we'd better go back to the house," Sara said when Paul finally returned.

"I suppose," Paul conceded. The romantic mood was definitely broken.

Since the cow's scratching had rolled the pickup against the fence, they had to push the truck backward because it had no reverse. When they reached the gate, Sara hopped out to open it, but she had trouble unhooking the latch. When she finally got it, Paul jokingly honked the horn as she swung it open, making her jump with surprise. Sara stuck her tongue out as he started to drive through. Then she undid her jeans, bent over, and mooned him as he went by. He was still laughing when she climbed back into the cab.

"What's the matter? Haven't you ever been mooned before?" Sara asked with a smile.

"As a matter of fact, I've never had the privilege," he said. "You're just one big surprise after another, aren't you?"

With that she unbuttoned the one button holding her blouse together and threw it open. "This is what women do in New Orleans to get attention during Mardi Gras," she announced. "I hope I've got your attention!"

"My, my, you're a wild one tonight, Sara Jane!" Paul exclaimed.

"Yeah, and I'm going to get worse after next week. Just you wait and see."

"I can hardly wait," he said, almost clipping a corner post with the pickup because he was so mesmerized by Sara's open blouse.

As they approached the outbuildings, they saw that the house lights were on and Madge's car was in the driveway, so Sara quickly buttoned up her blouse. After parking the truck, they gathered up the towels and basket and headed to the kitchen. They found Madge putting food in the refrigerator.

"What are you doing, Mom?" Paul asked.

"Well, I was out here this afternoon and found nothing in the cupboards or frig. I was going to town for groceries anyway, so I thought I might as well get some for you, one more time. Next week it'll be Sara's job, not mine. What have you two been up to?" she asked.

"I was so hot after baling that Sara suggested we go down to the pond and have a picnic. And then we decided to go for a swim in our underwear. Sara's a great swimmer. You should see her dive."

Madge looked at Paul and said, "Why, Paul Maas! I thought I raised you better than that. How dare you go swimming with a girl in your undershorts? If it would have been your Dad and me, he would have had me skinny-dipping before I could say Jackie Robinson! There's nothing like a dip in the pond in your birthday suit with your sweetheart!"

Paul's jaw dropped. He couldn't believe what his mom had just said. Sara looked at Madge and burst out laughing. Madge hadn't been born yesterday and there wasn't anything she hadn't tried.

"I hope he kissed you on the butt. George was always a chest guy," Madge joked, looking at Sara.

"Mom!" Paul exclaimed.

"No, he didn't," Sara replied in mock disappointment," but maybe next time." Then she added, "Madge, I don't want to be rude, but I feel I have pond critters crawling around in my hair. If you'll excuse me, I'd like to take a shower."

"Sure, go ahead," replied Madge. "I've got to be getting home anyway. You're staying over, aren't you?"

"Yes, but I have to leave early in the morning. I have my last wedding dress fitting at Mary Bourn's in Tipton. Would you like to go along?"

"Sure would. I'll leave something for George to eat. When are you leaving?"

"I've got to pick my mother up at 8:30. If we leave Muscatine at nine, we should be in Wilton at 9:30 and make it to Tipton about ten, don't you think?"

"I'll be ready," Madge assured her.

"Paul, I'm going upstairs and get some clothes. Do you need me to get something for you?" Sara asked.

"Sure, my sleeping shorts and a t-shirt. They're hanging behind my closet door."

"I know where they are. I'll be back in a jiff."

As Sara disappeared upstairs, Paul and Madge finished putting the groceries away. When Sara returned, she tossed Paul's clothes to him and started down the basement steps, calling, "See you in the morning, Madge."

"Okay, sweetie."

By the time Sara had returned to the kitchen, Madge was in her car saying goodbye to Paul. Sara stepped out the back door and waved. Paul turned and looked at her standing in the doorway. She had her hair wrapped in a towel and was wearing a short green-and-white candy-striped robe.

"I'll be on the front porch brushing my hair when you get done showering," she said.

"Okay, I'll be right out," he answered.

Paul hurried downstairs and showered. He flipped off the kitchen light as he walked toward the front porch. He opened the screen door and saw Sara standing in the moonlight combing her hair.

He whistled and said, "You look like some kind of goddess. I never saw anything so lovely."

"Why, thank you, honey," she replied.

Just then the phone rang.

"Now, who can that be?" Paul grumbled.

He disappeared into the house and answered the phone. When he returned, Sara asked, "Who was it?"

"Just Mom. She wanted to make sure I put the milk in the refrigerator."

While he was gone, she had removed her robe and was wearing just her pajamas—or what might be called pajamas. The top was a mint green camisole that barely covered her torso. Paul could see her rib cage peeking out from the bottom. The bottoms of the pajamas were candy-striped short, short hipster panties with little white ruffles across the hips. There was a lot of Sara showing in between. Neither piece left much to the imagination.

"The robe was too hot. Do you like my pajamas?" she asked coyly, the full moon revealing her every curve.

"Yeah, I like them a lot. Where did you get them?"

"I saw them two weeks ago when I went shopping with Tammi. I was going to save them for our honeymoon, but tonight seemed more appropriate. They don't cover much, do they?"

"No, but enough."

He sat in the swing and watched as she continued to brush her hair. Each time she raised her arms the top exposed more skin. Her nipples made little bumps in the fabric as it hung over her breasts.

"If we go to the backyard, will you swing me?" she asked.

"Sure, let's go."

Sara skipped like a nymph around the house to the old oak tree. She sat in the swing with her head back as Paul pushed her back and forth. The moonlight filtered down through the leaves, filling the grass with dappled shadows. Paul watched Sara's hair flow in the breeze. Her long tan legs stretched out in front with each push. Finally, she said, "I really should go to bed. I've got a busy day tomorrow. You want to see me jump out?"

Before he could answer, she slid out of the swing seat and high into the air. When she landed, she came down awkwardly on one leg, sending her tumbling into the grass.

"Are you all right?"

"I guess I'm a little out of practice. I used to do that all the time when I was a kid."

Paul shook his head and helped her up. He gently brushed the grass from her backside. He didn't have the heart to tell her that she had grass stains on her new pajama bottoms. They turned and walked hand-in-hand toward the front porch. She stopped at the first step, turned toward Paul, and kissed him.

"I still think we'd better go to our separate beds," she whispered, "but I'm so looking forward to next week."

"Me, too," Paul said softly. "I'll be ready."

Sara grabbed her robe as she went into the house and Paul locked the screen door behind them as he went in. Upstairs, they met in the hallway between their bedrooms.

"Next week, we won't have to go to separate bedrooms," Sara said happily. "I'm going to sleep right on top of you. It's going to be great." Then, changing the subject, she asked, "Are you going to be able to help me move my stuff from Nichols? Dad said he could do it on Tuesday."

"I'll set aside Tuesday to help," Paul replied. "If it's sunny, I'll bring a barge wagon and a tarp. If it's rainy, I'll clean out the livestock trailer. We can put all your boxes and furniture in the dining room for now. You can hang your extra clothes in the master bedroom closet. That's where they'll be later anyway."

They went to their respective bedrooms and Paul turned on his fan. The humming soon put him to sleep. About three in the morning, he was awakened by a clap of thunder. He got up and checked the sky. A thunderstorm was approaching from the west. He shut his windows and hurried downstairs to shut windows and to close the front door.

Back upstairs, he peeked into Sara's room to see if she had closed her windows. She hadn't, so he tip-toed in and pulled them closed. Sara never moved. She must have gotten warm because she had ditched her covers. Paul looked at her for a moment, then reached down and pulled the sheet over her. He kissed her forehead, and she smiled, but didn't wake up.

He returned to his room, but just as he had drifted back to sleep, the weather radio blasted on and woke him up. He hurried into Sara's room, saying firmly, "Sara, wake up! There's a tornado warning! We have to go to the basement."

Sara looked up and asked sleepily, "Why?"

"When there's a tornado warning in the country, you have to take notice. We always head to the basement right away," Paul explained, pulling Sara out of bed and shoving her slippers into her hand.

"Wait! Can't I put my robe on?" she complained.

"You can put it on in the basement. I'll carry it," Paul said. "Now get going."

They flew down the stairs barefooted, ran through the kitchen, and descended the basement stairs. Paul guided Sara to the southwest wall. The wind was picking up. They could see leaves and limbs flying around outside through the small window. The rain pounded the walls and the lights flickered briefly, and went out. All they could hear was the wind as it whistled around the corners of the house. As they crouched on the floor in the darkened room, Paul held Sara close.

In about ten minutes, the storm subsided. Sara didn't know whether to laugh or cry. She decided to giggle.

"What's so funny?" Paul asked.

"I can see the headlines now. Man found in basement with his fiancé, wearing only their night clothes. He was wearing shorts and she was in almost nothing pajamas. Rescuers said it was quite a sight."

Paul started to chuckle, too, as he fumbled around the basement for a flashlight. Then he led Sara back upstairs.

"I'll go out and check the cattle yard gates and buildings. You stay here and wait before you go back upstairs, okay?" he said. "Oh, and another thing. Draw a pitcher full of water before the cattle start to drink. They'll drain the supply tank in a hurry once they get started."

Sara nodded and headed for the kitchen sink. Paul put on his boots and raincoat and headed out. About ten minutes later, Sara heard him kick off his boots and shake out his raincoat. He found her sitting on the couch with a blanket wrapped around her body.

"I think we should stay in the den," she suggested, "in case there's another storm."

"Okay, but I've got to put on some dry clothes," Paul agreed. "I'll be right back."

"You don't have to for me," Sara teased. "Just come back."

He returned in dry clothes and stretched out beside her, his feet resting on the two footstools. She put her head on his shoulder and they talked a bit, but they were both soon sound asleep again.

When the old clock in the hall banged out six, Paul awoke with a jerk. The morning sun was filtering into the room. He tried to wiggle out of Sara's grasp without waking her, but she woke up anyway.

"What's up?" she asked.

"I'm going to check outside. I want to know if the power lines are down here at the farm or somewhere else. I'll be back in a few minutes."

"Can I come with you?" Sara asked.

"Sure."

"I'll go upstairs and change with you. Well, not with you, but at the same time. Oh, you know what I mean."

They headed upstairs and changed into regular clothes, but neither of them closed their door. Next week they could change together and not in separate rooms. She put on the same jeans she'd worn the day before, but found a clean checkered blouse to wear.

They met at the landing by the kitchen door and headed outside. The sun was shining through the receding storm clouds. The thunderheads were still towering to the east. The sky seemed extra blue, as if it had just been washed, and the bright sunshine made the wet grass extra green. The air smelled fresh and cool. Sara held Paul's hand as they walked across the farmyard.

They found little damage. There were buckets and pieces of paper all around and small branches covered the lawn. A small door on the barn was hanging by one hinge. The hayrack they had left by the bale elevator had blown across the yard and was pressed against a lilac bush. A blue plastic tarp had been deposited in a tree, though they had no idea where it had come from. They circled around the barns and then returned to the house.

"I guess it will be cold cereal and orange juice for breakfast," Paul announced. "We can't cook anything. The power lines must be down somewhere. We might be out for a few hours."

A moment later, the phone rang. It was George, checking on the damage.

Paul said, "Everything's okay here. The corn is leaning, but it should come back up, but tell Mom the sweet corn in the garden is flat. We haven't got any power. How about in Wilton?"

Paul listened to his dad's answer, then turned to Sara and said, "Mom wants to know if you're still going to Tipton."

"Yes," Sara replied, "but I might be a little late because I'll have to go to Muscatine and get ready."

"She'll be waiting. The power's out in Wilton, too."

Paul hung up, then turned to Sara and said, "Dad said there was a bad storm in northern Cedar County. They think it might have been a small tornado. There was a lot of hail damage, too. We're lucky we only had minor damage. If we had electricity, we could turn on the TV."

"Well, we can't do that, so let's eat breakfast so I can get going," Sara said.

After breakfast, Sara went upstairs and retrieved her skirt, blouse, and overnight bag. Just as she was coming down the steps the power came back on. The lights flickered, the refrigerator shook to life and the pump in the well started. The pipes rattled as the air was forced out. The kitchen sink faucet sputtered and spit. Sara had forgotten to shut it off when she drew the drinking water. Paul flicked on the TV and watched as the weatherman described the damage in Cedar, Clinton and Jackson Counties. The rain was now east of the area and clear skies were supposed to prevail for the next five days.

After getting the weather report, Paul returned to the cattle lot to feed the steers. The silo unloader was working again because the power had returned. He was thankful he didn't have to fire up the generator.

Sara changed her mind and decided to get dressed here at the farm. She returned to her bedroom and started to change.

She was about ready to put on her skirt when Paul burst into her room, saying, "Honey! I need you to help me free a steer caught in the feed bunk. Oops! Sorry! I didn't know you were changing."

He had caught her in her underwear.

"Sure, I'll just put my jeans back on," she said.

She followed Paul downstairs wearing only her jeans and bra. He handed her a flannel shirt hanging by the back door and they headed for the barn. The steer had somehow gotten his foot stuck between the braces of the feed bunk and was struggling to get up.

Paul handed Sara a long wrecking bar. "When I pick up the bunk, you need to jam this bar behind the brace and pry it off," he said. "As soon as the brace is free, the steer will be able to get up. Ready! On the count of three!"

When the count reached three, Sara jammed the bar into the brace when Paul lifted the bunk. She pulled with all her might and pried the brace off. The steer broke free, but not without a lot of pawing and splattering, covering Sara with wet brown cow manure. Her clean jeans were clean no more, and the flannel shirt gapped down and a big gob of manure dropped inside. Another splatter had landed in her hair and was running down her neck. She looked at Paul, and though he smiled, he didn't dare laugh. She gave him a scowl, but burst out laughing herself.

"Look at me!" she exclaimed. "I'm a mess!"

She reached up inside the shirt, wiped off a small handful of manure, and flipped it to the ground. She was going to have to shower and wash her hair again before she could go to Tipton. Paul helped her out of the cattle yard and back to the house. This was only the first of many times her life would be interrupted by a farm emergency.

"Will you call my mom and tell her I'll be late? See if she'd be willing to drive out here, too. That would save a lot of time," Sara said as they walked into the house. "Then you'd better call your mom. Then call the Tipton Bridal Shop and explain what happened. They'll understand if you call. I'm going down to take another shower."

Paul was sitting on the kitchen stool when she emerged from the basement wearing only a towel. "I wondered what you'd be wearing when you came back up," he said, smiling.

Sara returned his smile and said, "The first thing I'm buying when I live here will be bigger towels. These things barely cover anything. Apparently your mom didn't believe in large fluffy towels."

"I know," Paul agreed, thinking back to the night he had asked Sara to marry him and his small towel experience.

She hurried upstairs, dressed quickly, and returned, saying with a chuckle, "I guess I'd better get used to these quick changes, huh? Is my mom coming out? If she is, I still might be on time."

"Yeah! She understood and had no problem with coming out. She should be here any minute."

"Are you going to church with me tomorrow?"

"Sure am. I'll be there at 9:00. Are we going out for lunch afterward?"

"We can. Is there anyone in particular you'd like to ask along?"

"No."

"I'll ask my folks then, okay?"

"Sounds good to me."

Emma arrived. Sara met her at the door. The two of them got into Sara's car and started down the drive. Paul waved goodbye, and he thought, "What a great partner she's going to be. Most women would be upset with what had just happened, but she thought it was fun!"

Chapter Nine
We've Only Just Begun

"Is there anything more I have to do before the wedding?" Paul asked before he headed home Sunday evening. "I've got a fairly full next week. Monday, the courthouse for a marriage license, Tuesday, we move you over to here. Wednesday, I get your car serviced. Thursday, haircut and check on rehearsal supper. Friday, rehearsal and supper, and Saturday, wedding. Is that all?"

"Sounds like you've got it down pat, Big Boy," Sara replied cheerfully. "Now get going. Like you just said, we've got a big week ahead. "

The week went by quickly and it was time for the rehearsal at the church—but Paul was late. The stock cows decided to have soybeans for lunch, so the fences had to be fixed before he could leave the farm. Everyone kidded him the rest of the evening, especially Sue. She figured he had gotten cold feet. The rehearsal dinner was in the ballroom at the Eagles Inn, and George made sure everyone had plenty of prime rib from his own herd. He wanted everyone to know he was a cattleman.

The wedding day arrived. July 26th was a warm day, but cloudy. Sara was beautiful in her gorgeous white gown with long sleeves, designed to hide her long arms. Her father proudly walked her down the aisle, and just before the vows were to be recited, Sara walked over to her mother and gave her a big hug and a kiss.

"Thank you, Mom, for everything," she whispered.

She returned and gave her father a kiss on the cheek. Everyone chuckled because he took out his handkerchief and wiped off her lipstick. John turned and proudly gave his daughter's hand to Paul. Sara took Paul's hands as they exchanged vows.

He looked directly into her eyes and repeated, "I, Paul, take you, Sara, as my wedded wife, for better, for worse, in sickness, and in health, till death do we part."

Sara followed with, "I, Sara, take you, Paul, as my wedded husband, for better, for worse, in sickness and in health, till death do we part."

They placed their wedding rings on each others' fingers.

Just as they went forward to kneel at the altar, the sun burst through the clouds and shown gloriously through stained glass windows above them, making a luminous halo around the pair. Pastor Tom took it as a sign of God's blessing on their marriage.

Pastor Tom helped them up from the altar. He turned to the audience, and announced, "I am proud to present to you, Mr. and Mrs. Paul Mass. You may kiss your bride now, Paul."

Paul proudly kissed Sara and walked her down the aisle as everyone cheered and smiled. The reception line formed and everyone shook hands and gave their congratulations. As the crowd left, each person was given a pale blue, silver, or white balloon to be released when Paul and Sara appeared at the church door.

Paul and Sara were supposed to get into a limousine and head to the reception, but when they walked out the door, George had replaced the limo with a brand new 4430 John Deere tractor and a freshly-painted white hayrack. The rack was covered with white carpet and contained a love seat for the newlyweds and padded white chairs for the rest of the bridal party. There was a white staircase so the bridal party had no trouble climbing onto the hayrack. On the back of the hayrack was a big sign. It read: JUST MARRIED PAUL & SARA MAAS. Cans and old pans were strung out behind, making a tremendous racket as the party slowly drove away. The balloons soared into the sky. The local John Deere dealer, Lyle Coats, drove them all around town.

At the reception, the DJ was great and Sara and Paul wowed everyone with their dancing. Sara found out that her father- in-law could also cut quite a rug, for he and Madge did a swell Texas two-step.

When the song "Rockin' Robin" was played, Paul showed his new wife he wasn't as shy as he let on while the crowd cheered and hooted. When the reception was over at midnight, Paul whispered, "Let's spend our first night together back at the farm. Mom and Dad are moved to Wilton. The house is ours. We can start our honeymoon tomorrow," he whispered in her ear.

"Great idea," Sara replied with a beaming smile.

When they got to the house, Paul announced he needed a shower after all of the dancing. Just before they went inside Paul swept Sara up into his arms and carried her across the threshold. They were going to start off on the right foot. He helped Sara out of her wedding dress in the living room, then said, "Go upstairs and shower and put on that yellow dress I've always loved, would you, Mrs. Maas? I'll meet you in the kitchen."

Standing in front of him with nothing on, Sara started to help Paul remove his tux. She bent down and untied his shoes, unbuckled his cummerbund, undid his bow tie, and took the studs out of his shirt. Then she slowly unzipped his trousers and with one quick pull she had him in his shorts.

"Why don't you shower upstairs with me?" she asked, smiling broadly. "It's our house now and we're a married couple, Mr. Maas!"

"I think I could do that Mrs. Maas," he said, pulling her close. "I need a back scrub tonight anyway."

They showered together, and retired to the master bedroom, but Sara didn't put on the yellow dress. Instead, she pulled Mrs. B's old wedding nightgown out of its yellowed box to wear. Mr. B had given it to her just three days before the wedding.

"Where's the yellow dress?" Paul asked.

Sara explained the significance of Mrs. B's nightgown. "You remember Mr. B, don't you?" she asked. "I thought I'd continue the tradition. I even snipped a piece of it and pinned it to my wedding gown so I'd have something old." She walked over to him and gave him hug. She said, "But if it's really important to you, I'll put on the yellow dress."

Paul smiled, held her at arms length, and said, "No, hon, it's okay. I understand."

Sara put her arms around his neck and Paul held her close. He ran his fingers over her athletic body, feeling every curve and every muscle. Sara brought her hands to his hips and pulled him even closer. She felt him becoming aroused, but this time she didn't have to pretend she didn't notice. The breeze from the fan gently blew Sara's hair forward around her face, framing her face like a halo.

"The gown fits you perfectly. I'm glad you put it on—and it's a nice tribute to a great lady. Wear it on every one of our anniversaries. It will make each one special."

"Do you want to go to the dune?" Sara asked

"Sure," Paul said with a nod.

Sara slipped into sandals while Paul grabbed his shorts from the laundry basket. They found two old blankets and headed downstairs. Climbing into the old pickup, they drove through the moonlight toward the dune.

Sara kicked off her sandals and left them in the pickup as they raced each other to the top of the dune. They spread out the blankets they brought. Paul embraced Sara pulling her close. She succeeded in untying his shorts and pushed them down. He looked at her and started to unbutton the nightgown. He was so excited his fingers wouldn't work. Sara quietly undid the top button, then the second. He finally calmed enough to undo the last button. Slowly he slipped the shoulder straps off her shoulders and down her arms. The gown fell. They stood naked, holding each other in the silky moonlight.

Paul whispered, "I think it's nice that we waited for this moment."

"I do, too," she replied, remembering how they almost hadn't waited the week before at the pond.

Paul bent over and observed her breasts closely, then said with a chuckle, "Still no chest hair."

"There'd better not be, Big Boy!" she said, gently slapping his face.

He took her hands in his and held them out, scanning her body up and down.

"Do you like it?" she asked.

"Yes, most definitely."

"Well, I hope so. It's a little late to back out now."

"I want to touch every square inch of you."

Paul turned her around and told her to close her eyes. He placed his hands in the small of her back and slowly traced up her spine with the back of his hand. He followed her shoulders and the back of her neck. He stroked her hair with his fingers. He spun her around again so she was facing him. He gently brought his fingers to her face, feeling her eyebrows, her nose, her lips, and her chin. He continued down both sides of her neck and along her shoulders. Very slowly, he stroked her arms and hands, touching each finger before he returned and slowly caressed each of her breasts. He made a special emphasis of very lightly kissing her areola and nipple as he cupped each breast. Then his hands went down her sides to her waist and to the back of her hips. He knelt and slid his hands down her long legs and caressed her ankles. He pulled her down on the blanket, where his hands began massaging one of her feet as she stretched out.

"Your feet must be killing you after wearing those shoes you wore today," he whispered.

His fingers followed the curves of her feet and back down to her heels. Sara tried not to cringe while being tickled as his rough hands ran down the inside of her foot. Paul then sank down on the blanket and lay next to her. With soft kisses, they enfolded each other in a loving embrace, savoring the erotic anticipation of really being with each other for the first time.

When they had finished, Paul said breathlessly, "So this is what they call lovemaking. I've never felt such a rush! Waiting until we were married made this the most amazing experience—and the beginning of a whole new world."

"That was absolutely wild, Big Boy," Sara cooed. "Where did you learn to do that thing with your hands? It drove me crazy. Every nerve in my body was tingling! I felt like I was going to jump right out of my skin. I'm glad I saved myself for you." Then she smiled wickedly, pulled him above her again, and said, "Let's do it again!"

"Well, maybe in a few minutes," Paul replied. "Let me catch my breath real quick."

They snuggled close together in the moonlight and were soon fast asleep. When they awoke, the morning sun was peeking through the trees. They wrapped themselves in the blanket and kissed.

"Good morning, Mrs. Maas," Paul whispered.

"Good morning, Mr. Maas," she replied tenderly. "Our first morning as man and wife."

Paul stood and then pulled her up. Before they dressed, they embraced briefly as the morning sun warmed their bodies. They were a man and a woman starting out together. They were God's creation. They looked over the waving cornfield and pledged to God that they would be good stewards of His land. He would be the center of their lives and their family. It was a moment with God they would never forget. Until death would they part, and not sooner, was their solemn vow.

They returned to reality and got dressed quickly, since George was supposed to be doing the chores while they were on their honeymoon. They drove back to the farmhouse and fell into bed, but they were awakened at eight by the crackling and pinging of gravel. George and Madge were driving up the lane. They stumbled downstairs to greet them.

"I thought you'd be gone already," George said as he walked into the kitchen.

Madge laughed when she saw that Sara was in her nightgown and barefoot. Paul was in boxer shorts.

"Silly us," she said. "Maybe we should have waited a little longer to show up this morning."

Madge herself was barely dressed. She had on some old tennis shoes, shorts, and one of George's long-sleeved shirts with snaps instead of buttons. She must have decided in a hurry to come to the farm with her husband.

"No, that's fine, Mom," Paul replied sleepily. "We'll be leaving in about an hour."

"Yeah, I can see you're both ready to hop in the car and take off," George teased. "Well, don't worry about a thing. We'll take care of the farm while you're gone."

Sara watched through the window as George and Madge went outside and headed down the pasture road in the old pickup. When Madge got out to open the gate, Sara was surprised to see that she had ditched the shirt and was wearing only an old thin t-shirt and shorts. She could also tell that Madge had no undergarments on. Were they planning to go for a swim? The thought made her smile.

Her thoughts were interrupted as Paul said, "Well, hon, we'd better get going. We have a long ride ahead of us."

"Where are we going?"

"Egg Harbor in Wisconsin, to a place called Honeymooner Heaven, right on Green Bay. Some of Sue's friends went there and liked it. It's a ten-hour drive from here."

"Well, let's get out of here before your folks get back," Sara suggested.

"Right!"

They packed up Sara's car and were on their way in thirty minutes. Sara's hair was still a mess, but she didn't care. It would be windblown from the ride anyway.

When they finally arrived at Honeymooner Heaven that evening, the owner showed them to their cabin on a small inlet. There were only four units in this isolated grouping, but there was a big motel on the other side of the hill with a large beach and a pool. The owner said if the bay got rough, Sara and Paul were welcome to use the motel pool.

The cabin had a kitchenette, a living area with a sofa, chair, and small TV, a bathroom, and a bedroom with a queen-sized bed covered with a white quilt. It would be perfect for their week-long honeymoon.

They soon found out the other three cabins also contained newlyweds. One couple, Jean and Tom, were from Milwaukee; Teresa and Jack were from Chicago; and Anne and John were from St. Paul. John was a Vietnam veteran who had lost his leg in the war, but it didn't seem to bother him. He was now a high school teacher. Sara and Paul spent time exploring the area with Anne and John. On Washington Island, John proved he could ride a bike as well anyone.

The week flashed by and on Friday night, all four couples went to a fancy restaurant in town. It was a perfect ending to a great week.

When Paul and Sara returned to their cabin for the last night, they couldn't sleep. "Let's go sit on the porch," Paul suggested.

"That's a great idea," Sara agreed.

Sara put on her mint green pajamas with the brief top and green candy-striped hipster bottoms that Paul liked and Paul threw on his new knit sleeping shorts. They sat in the rocking chairs on the porch, listening to the waves lap against the shore. Sara suggested they go for a walk and sit down on the beach one last time.

"What if someone sees us in our pajamas?" said Paul.

"Don't be such a prude," Sara chided. "There's no one here except three other honeymoon couples, and I think they'd understand."

Grabbing a blanket, they started off, making their way barefoot along the beach. They found what they thought was the ideal spot, spread out the blanket, and sat holding each other, watching the moonlight dance on the waves.

"You wanna go for swim?" Sara asked.

"Sure, I'll go get our swimsuits," Paul replied.

"Who needs suits? We're going skinny-dipping."

"Right here?" Paul asked, his voice rising.

"Why not?" she said, already slipping out of her pajamas. "There's no one around, and as soon as we get away from the shore, nobody can see anything."

"Okay, I guess."

"Come on, chicken!" said Sara, splashing into the surf before Paul had even stood up.

With her naked wet body gleaming in the moonlight, she came running back, grabbed Paul's hand, and led him into the water. Soon they had waded out to a sandbar, where they sat naked in the sand, watching the sparkling water dance all around them.

Paul pulled Sara close, kissed her passionately, and whispered, "I want you, right here."

Now it was Sara's turn to be surprised. "We can't do it here," she said. "Let's head back to the shore."

"Okay," Paul said, "We'll make love on the beach. Like you said, no one is around."

"Okay, Mr. Maas," she said with a laugh. "Why not?"

When they got back to the blanket, Paul pulled Sara to him, but she stopped him. "This time I get to give you the back massage."

Paul rolled over and Sara placed her hands in the small of his back. She massaged his entire back, applying extra pressure where she knew his muscles needed it. Then she had him roll over and she began running her hands over his chest, combing the twenty-five hairs between her fingers. She moved her fingers to his face, where she gently traced his eyebrows, his nose, and his lips before gliding her hands along his arms and hands.

She kissed him gently, then slid her hands down his stomach and onto his hairy legs. Never taking her hands from his body, she knelt at his feet. She caressed each foot and toe, just as he had done to her on the dune.

Finally, she lay back on the blanket while Paul propped himself up on one elbow. She pulled him over to her. They made love sweetly, passionately, not caring if anyone saw. The whole world had been reduced to just the two of them and the love they shared.

It was on their way back to the cabin that they discovered they hadn't been alone. Anne and John had apparently had the same idea. Sara and Paul could hear them giggling and splashing somewhere out in the water. John's artificial leg and shorts were lying in the sand, along with Anne's robe and nightgown. Skinny-dipping seemed to be on their agenda that night, as well.

The next morning, all four couples met on the beach to say their goodbyes. Later everyone departed for their homes. Even though the honeymoon had been delightful, Paul and Sara were happy to be home. The trip had been long and tiring. Immediately, they collapsed exhausted in their big bed. They had barely shut their eyes when they heard a loud bang from outside!

Peeking out the bedroom window, Sara saw the yard was full of people banging on saw blades and buckets. Some of them were setting off fireworks.

"What's going on out there?" Sara asked.

"It appears that we're being shivareed," Paul said with a tired smile. "We're going to have to go downstairs and let them in, and then feed them."

"But we just got home!" Sara said, panicking. "There's no food in the house."

"Don't worry, hon," Paul reassured her. "It's just an old tradition. They've brought ice cream and pie with them. All we have to do is get a pot of coffee going."

As Sara threw on her biggest, thickest robe, Paul opened the window and shouted that they'd be right down. Then they went out onto the porch and stood smiling sleepily as the revelers chanted, "Kiss her, kiss her, kiss her!"

Paul obliged by taking Sara into his arms and kissed her deeply. Then they invited everyone in for coffee. Madge and Emma had provided the ice cream and pie, and Sara's old friend Tami and her husband had come from Davenport to share in the fun.

The crowd stayed until well past midnight, and Sara would never forget her official welcome to the community, entertaining guests in her pajamas and bathrobe.

Morning came much too early the next day. Although Sara unpacked and washed some clothes, they did as little as possible that day. When Paul came in at noon, he looked as tired as Sara felt.

"Let's lock the door, unplug the phones, and go take a nap," he said sleepily.

"That is one of the best suggestions I've ever heard," Sara quickly agreed.

They trudged upstairs and collapsed into bed, sleeping in their underwear. At about 4:00, Sara awoke, poked Paul, and told him she was going to take a shower.

"Would you like to come along?" she asked.

"Another great suggestion," Paul said, glad that his folks and installed an oversized shower so there was plenty of room for two.

He followed Sara into the shower, where they scrubbed each other's backs—and Paul didn't miss the opportunity to bathe Sara's front. Sara returned the favor, loving how excited Paul got when she was near him. She covered his chest and stomach with suds, and as she moved down his legs she could see that he was paying full attention to her every move.

When she had finished, she pressed her body against his and said coyly, "There, I think we're done."

"Nope, I don't think so. Now your body is full of suds. You'll have to wash off again."

He moved aside, allowing to Sara to move under the water spray. When there was no trace of soap left, he put his arms around her and gave her a slippery hug and kiss.

"There, now you're done."

He turned off the water and they dried each other with the large, fluffy towels Madge had given them as a wedding present.

"Let's go out to eat," said Sara. "I'm too tired to cook."

"How about Happy Joe's?" Paul suggested. "But before we go, can we spend a little more time in bed?"

"Sure," Sara said with smile. "I wouldn't want to waste a body I just washed—and it looks like you're ready for a little more action."

After they had their pizza, they stopped by Sara's parents' house to tell them about the honeymoon. Sara and Paul headed back to the farm early and were in bed by 9:00. The next day would be the first real day of the rest of their lives.

Chapter Ten
Hi-Lo-Hi

A week after Sara and Paul returned home from their honeymoon, they finally had time to sit and write thank-you notes until their hands cramped. Paul suggested, since it was the end of the summer, they go to the state fair. Sara had been to the fair with her folks when she was younger, but all they did was tour the Varied Industries building and the midway. Paul assured her that this time she'd see the real fair.

They left early so they could have a full day at the fairgrounds. When they arrived, they headed straight for the Cattle Barn. While walking down the aisles, Paul stopped to talk to some of the breeders. He was looking for new bulls and the fair was a good place to check some out. He also was interested in artificial insemination and the availability of semen.

Outside the cattle barn, Paul led Sara to the Dairy Bar, where they sold the best ice cream and milk shakes in the Midwest. Then they headed for machinery row and the 4-H Building. They ate lunch at the Beef Barn and then rested in the shade at one of the stage shows.

Paul showed Sara the Ag Building with its butter cow. Next they headed for the Pioneer Building where Sara took second place in her first cow chip throwing contest. By then it was getting late and Paul said they should start for home, but Sara wasn't ready to leave.

"Can't we stay a little longer? We haven't even ridden any rides yet. I know you are tired; but the real fun is still out there. We haven't seen the fireworks, and I've heard they're wonderful."

"It will be pretty late when we get home, but anything for you, sweetheart." Paul said with a smile.

"How about staying over until tomorrow? Can't we call your dad and see if he'll check the cows? He just has to push buttons to feed the steers."

Paul could see he was losing this battle, so he found a phone and called home. His dad said he could do the feeding in the morning, but he had a meeting at one the next afternoon. Paul assured him they'd be home before noon.

"Dad says we can stay, but remember that we are farmers and we can't rely on other people to do our chores," he reminded Sara. "Now let's go ride!"

They rode some of the thrill rides and watched the fireworks from atop of the double Ferris wheel. The last ride Paul took his new wife on was the famous boat ride in the "Old Mill." They left the fairgrounds about eleven and drove for an hour and a half before stopping for a bite to eat at a McDonald's.

"Let's keep going," Sara said. "I'll drive part way. We can be home by 2:30. It'll save us some money."

The next morning, Paul called his dad early and told him he'd feed the cattle. He also got the mower conditioner ready for the next day. He wanted to get things done so he could quit early and spend a relaxing evening with Sara. Sara dashed into town to visit her mother and check with the school system about openings. She returned home before three.

Sara gave up on finding a full-time teaching position and applied as a substitute. In a school system as large as Muscatine, subs were generally busy. Two weeks after school started, she got her first call to teach fourth grade, her favorite grade. The other teachers soon found out that Sara was an excellent teacher and she was soon in demand by the system. When teachers returned to their classes, the students were always on schedule and wished Mrs. Maas would come back.

Late September meant harvesting. Sara pulled home the silage wagons, unhooked them at the barn for George to unload. She would hitch to an empty one and head back to the field. One day she unhooked a full load in the farm yard. As soon as she turned around to look, the wagon started to roll backwards down the slight slope of the farmyard. She jumped out of the cab and grabbed the wagon tongue and tried with all her might to stop it. Her feet slid in the loose gravel. As Sara tried to readjust her feet she stumbled and fell on the sharp stones, cutting and bruising her hands and knees. The wagon continued on. All she could do was watch. It rolled down the drive towards the old abandon hog house. The wagon snapped off the corner post like it was a matchstick. It continued to rumble into the pens and gates, finally stopping against the building. The building shook and a cloud of dust plus several sparrows came flying out of the broken window. Sara sat in the drive and started to cry. By this time, George had finished unloading. He heard the smashing of wood and a loud thud as the wagon hit the hog house. Around the silo he came running and saw Sara sitting in the middle of the drive.

"Sara, Sara, Are you all right?" he screamed when he was running to where she was sitting.

"Yes, I'm fine. A little scratched up and bruised." She replied as she tried to stand up.

"What will Paul think?" she wailed.

"I'll tell you what he'll say. We can always fix a wagon or a fence easier than bones. Good thing you didn't get in behind it. Now you go into the house and clean your hands and get some different jeans on. I'll go out to the field and get Paul. We'll get this wagon back on its wheels in no time. Now don't you fret. Everything will turn out fine." George assured her.

When Paul came in he headed right for the house.

"Are you all right?" he asked. He checked her scratched and bruised hands. He poured some hydrogen peroxide on the wounds and wiped her tears.

He gave her a hug and told her how the same thing happened to him. The only difference was there were hogs in the pens. They headed for freedom as soon as the gate was destroyed .It took several minutes before they were all corralled. Never again did she let a wagon free without blocking a wheel. She soon became a valuable asset to the operation and she loved every second. Paul claimed she was even better than his dad. George almost agreed. He did relent that she was much prettier.

After the silage cutting was finished, it was time to get ready for soybeans. One Friday night, one of the teachers, Ann Foreman, called for Sara's help. Her mother was in the last stages of cancer. She was given just a few days to live and Ann wanted to go to Omaha to be with her. She asked if Sara could teach her class for about two weeks.

"I'll ask Paul," Sara said. "He's right here."

When Sara asked her question, Paul replied, "We'll be doing soybeans. Dad will be able help me. It doesn't take more than one other person to harvest beans. I think you could substitute if you want to."

"I'd be glad to help," Sara told Ann. "Can I meet with you before you leave? I'd like to know what you expect."

"Great," Ann replied. "How about meeting at Mulberry School at nine in the morning?"

"Sounds good to me. See you then."

The next Monday, Sara started teaching. She left every morning at 7:30 and retuned about 4:00. If she had time, she'd fix a sandwich for Paul and George. Madge had usually been there first, but the men didn't mind the extra attention. The first week went by fast.

Ann called from Omaha to say, "My mother's still hanging on. Can you sub a third week?"

"Sure," Sara replied. "Things are going well here. Take as long as you need."

The second week also went well, but during the third week things began to fall apart. On Wednesday, Sara had an angry mother approach her to complain that her little Ben was being bullied on the playground. Sara assured her she'd check on Ben more often. On Thursday Ben received a bump from one of the boys, and Ben's mother was back again. This time she was furious, and Sara had to get the principal. It was agreed that Ben would stay in during recess and Sara would have to babysit Ben during her lunch hour. Sara thought it was unfair, but it solved the problem temporarily. Now she'd have to do her grading at home on her own time.

Paul was also having a rough week. On Wednesday, he discovered one of the biggest steers had swallowed some metal or other sharp object. He called Dr. Johns, but there was little he could do. He checked the steer and found his temperature normal, so he told Paul the best thing to do was to butcher the steer immediately.

Dr. Johns called the locker and explained the situation. Although they didn't normally kill on Wednesdays, they said they'd make an exception for Paul. It would cost an extra $75 for the set-up. Paul agreed to bring the steer in right away. At least, he could salvage the meat. Dr. Johns gave the steer a sedative. After a short struggle, he and Paul got the big animal loaded into the livestock trailer.

When Paul got home, it was already 1:00 and nothing seemed to go right after that. The beans were tough and he plugged the header twice. It had been a rough day, but he knew it would be better when Sara got home. He was mistaken. She had had a very frustrating day, also. The two ate supper quietly and retired to the den. Sara graded papers, while Paul read the grain reports. They figured there couldn't be two bad days in a row.

Thursday didn't start any better. George came in from checking the stock cows and reported one of them had wrapped some barbwire around her foot, cutting her hoof. They'd have to bring her in to the barn, call Dr. Johns again, and have him dress the wound, which meant another late start. It was noon before the doctor left and the cow was isolated in the hospital pen.

Paul hurried inside to grab a bite to eat. All he could find was peanut butter and some old bologna. It would have to do. When he was finished, he left everything on the table. Sara would understand.

Outside, he climbed into the combine, turned the key, but nothing happened. The starter just clicked. He must have left the key on the day before and run the batteries down. He'd have to get the charger and hope to recharge the batteries quickly, but nothing goes quickly when you're in a hurry. Paul put the charger to the starting mode and waited.

When he finally got out to the field, it was already two in the afternoon, but his troubles weren't over yet. A wagon in the field had a flat tire which would have to be changed. Thank goodness, Paul had a collection of spares for the wagons, but it was 4:00 before he finally started combining. At 10:00, he headed in from the field, tired and dirty.

Sara came home at four and found dirty dishes on the table. The kitchen floor was tracked with dirt. There was a big greasy handprint on the refrigerator. She was in no mood to clean house after her terrible day at school. What was Paul thinking? She cleaned up and waited for Paul to come in. Instead of eating with him, she made herself a sandwich and started on her schoolwork.

When Paul burst into the kitchen, he saw nothing to eat.

"Woman! Where's my supper?" he bellowed.

"In the fridge," she snapped back, "and I'm not your woman! Get your woman to fix something for you. This one's tired and doesn't like to clean up disgusting messes when she gets home."

"Well, I'm tired and hungry. I need something to eat," Paul complained.

Sara stormed into the kitchen, slammed some dishes on the table, pulled some leftovers out of the refrigerator, and started to reheat them on the stove.

After pushing the food in front of him, she said, "I'm not your woman and I'm not your cleaning lady. I'm your wife, and don't you forget it! Don't ever call me that again! I'm going to bed. You'd better clean up and put dishes in the dishwasher. Goodnight!"

"Boy, you're bitchy tonight," Paul said testily.

"I'm not your bitch, either. She's outside in the doghouse. Why don't you go sleep with her?" Sara said as she stormed out of the kitchen and headed upstairs.

Paul had never seen her so angry. He quietly put the dishes away and even wiped the table. He showered downstairs, not wanting to make too much noise. When he was ready for bed, he crawled in slowly and turned off the light. The next morning, Sara had calmed down, but was still upset. Paul didn't say a word. Anything he might say would be wrong. Sara left for school at 7:30, leaving Paul all day to recover and regroup.

When Sara returned from a better day at school, she found a bouquet of her favorite daisies sitting on the kitchen counter and a note from Paul that read: "Sara, I'm sorry for what I said. You're everything to me but never just my woman. You're my friend, my lover, my partner, and my wife. I could never imagine living without you. Please accept my apology. I'll never use the word woman or bitch in that context again. If you accept my sincere apology, please come to the field and eat with me in the combine cab. You'll find some sandwiches in the fridge. Love, Big Boy."

Sara melted as she read Paul's apology. She realized they'd both had frustrating days. Things were said that shouldn't have been said. It also wasn't fun worrying about Paul all day, hoping he wouldn't have an accident because he wasn't thinking clearly

Just then, George walked in and asked, "Can you handle the hauling in? I'll finish the chores? Mrs. Schroeder has passed away. Madge and I need to go to the visitation."

"Sure," answered Sara.

She and Paul needed some time together anyway. She went out to the field, and Paul was delighted when he saw her get out of the old pickup, carrying a small basket of goodies. He climbed down from the combine cab.

"You're just wearing a t-shirt. What's the matter? Are you that hot?" Sara asked. She was wearing a hooded sweatshirt. She didn't want to get dumped on again.

"The AC is on the fritz," Paul replied. "I had dad call the repairman. They think they can get here tomorrow morning, so today all I have is the fan."

"How about some supper, Big Boy?"

"Great! I sure am hungry," Paul said happily. "Did you find the sandwiches?"

"Yes," Sara said with a smile. "It is pretty warm out here, isn't it? Especially when I'm wearing this hoodie. I just didn't want to get a shirt full again."

When Sara unzipped the sweatshirt and took it off, she revealed she was just in a t-shirt, her nipples made little bumps under the fabric.

"You're only wearing a t-shirt. What's the matter? Are you hot?" Paul kidded her.

With a quick step and a leap, she threw her arms around his neck and kissed him.

"I'm sorry! I couldn't concentrate at all in school today," she said. "Let's never argue like that again, okay? I love you, Paul. Will you forgive me? And to answer your question, yes, I'm hot. Hot for you."

With the argument over, Sara hopped back into the pickup to go get the 4430. She'd unload until Paul quit, and the prospect of some lovemaking later made the night go faster for both of them. It was Friday, so they could be together all day on Saturday.

Ann's mother finally succumbed to cancer, and after the funeral she returned to Muscatine. She told Sara her mother had died in her sleep one night while everyone was trying to arrange their schedules for another week. It seemed as if she knew it was time for her to go. When Ann and her sister returned to say goodnight, she was gone. It was a peaceful way to die after all the suffering she'd gone through.

"Ben's mother really caused a fuss. She thought her little Ben was being bullied. I think he's overprotected. She's watching all the time."

Ann shrugged her shoulders and stated, "There's one every year. I'd heard about Ben's mom from the teachers in the lower grades. I knew she'd be in sometime. Too bad it had to be on your watch."

Finally the beans were in and the switch to corn harvest began. Paul needed help hauling corn from the Becker place, so Sara decided to put a hold on teaching for a while. She'd pick and choose her teaching jobs until the corn was in.

She and George worked well together. If he was available, he'd help hitch the wagons. They finished on November twelfth. Fall tillage would then continue until the ground froze. Paul and George worked on weaning the calves and Paul had many things to finish up before winter. George was tied up with county business, since he'd put many things off until after harvest. That left Sara the sole driver for the chisel plow, but it was a job she liked. It gave her time to plan, clear her head, and think about the future and her life on the farm with Paul.

It was late afternoon when she pulled in from the last field. The fall tillage was done ahead of time. Thanks to Sara's many hours in the tractor. She didn't like the thought of fixing supper. She was planning to tell Paul they were going out. As she walked out of the machine shed, she noticed Madge's car in the drive. In the kitchen, she could see Madge working away.

"Now what's she doing?" Sara wondered.

Madge was always one to surprise people. Sara loved her mother-in-law because of all the energy she possessed and she hoped she could be as good a farm wife as Madge.

"Good evening. Did you get everything plowed?" Madge asked when Sara walked into the kitchen. "I thought you might need a night off from cooking. I had this casserole and it was too big for George and me. Paul and George had a meeting with the tax man, and they just left you out there to fend for yourself. I scolded them for that. I hope you don't mind me being in your kitchen."

"No, not at all," Sara replied. "I didn't want to fix supper anyway. Thanks. I forgot about the tax man."

"Well, wash up and sit down. I'll go and get the men. I want to talk to them anyway," Madge said with a smile.

Sara went upstairs to the bathroom to change. She combed her hair, washed her face, and put on some lipstick. When she returned to the kitchen, Paul and George were sitting at the table.

"Hi, hon. Boy, you sure do clean up well!" Paul teased. "You'd never tell you've been in a tractor all day. Thanks for finishing up. It's been a long time since we got all the fall tillage done. I think I'll hire you for another year."

"Sit down," Madge told Sara. "I'll serve tonight."

After a short prayer, everyone dug into Madge's tater tot casserole, followed by homemade pumpkin pie.

"Okay, Madge. What are you buttering us up for?" George asked.

"Well, I've been working in this old kitchen for many years. Today I pulled on one of the drawers and the front came off in my hand," Madge explained.

"That's the one my dad fixed just last week, along with that cupboard door," Sara added apologetically.

"That's just what I mean," Madge said. "Sara, you need a new kitchen. These two men have no respect for a hardworking woman. They go out and buy a fifteen thousand dollar tractor and think nothing of it, but they think all they have to do for their wives is provide a warm house and comfy bed. They don't consider our working conditions at all. I worked in this antique kitchen for forty years, never realizing what I was missing until we moved into our new house. This kitchen was built back in the twenties, and it needs an update. Sure there's a dishwasher, but it's on the wrong side of the room, and the refrigerator is thirty years old. We got it when Sue was born. You just worked for several weeks helping with the harvest. You cook, wash clothes, clean house, and even teach. Girl, you're some kind of a superwoman. Don't let these men get away without some kind of a reward."

As Madge finished her tirade, she slammed her hand on the counter to make sure they were paying attention, making the edge pop off. She laughed and added, "See what I mean?"

There was a stunned silence as Sara looked around the kitchen. It did need an update, but she could live with it. The sink was an old cast iron double bottom with no garbage disposal. The cupboards were huge, going clear to the ceiling. Even tall Sara had to get a stepstool to reach the top doors. The countertop was a marred green laminate with a metal edge running around it. Pieces of the edge were missing in spots, and there were a couple brown rings scorched in the surface from too-hot skillets over the years. The stove was placed okay, but it wasn't self-cleaning and one of the burners was lopsided. The dishwasher was a portable model and had to be attached to the sink faucet. Many times washing by hand was faster.

The kitchen was the most used room in the house, and most meals were eaten there. When friends visited, they sat at the kitchen table. Salesmen were entertained in the kitchen, whether they were selling seed, fertilizer, or animal feed. It was a place to get warm on a cold day. The smells of freshly baked bread or cookies always attracted the men from outside. When kids arrived home from school, the kitchen is where they snacked and told Mom about their day.

Paul looked at Madge and said, "Now, Mom, We'll get a new kitchen sooner or later."

"See, he's trying to back out already," Madge replied. "Don't let him do it, Sara."

"Okay," Sara said, seeing that Madge was determined to have her way. She decided to let Madge stay in control of the conversation.

"Okay, Madge, calm down," said George. "We'll see that Sara gets a new kitchen." Then he looked at Paul and said, "When I get to town tomorrow, I'll contact Dan Duncan about where he buys his cupboards. He does a lot of kitchen remodeling. I bet you and I can remove the old ones and save some money."

"My dad could install the new cupboards," Sara volunteered. "He's done that many times for other people on his days off. He and Paul could get it done during the winter."

"Now we're getting somewhere," Madge said happily. "Let's not let up on these guys. Tell them it has to be done before next spring. I'll ride George and you take care of Paul."

"It's a deal," Sara answered with a laugh.

Her tirade finished, Madge asked sweetly, "Now, does anyone want more pie?"

After Paul's folks left, Sara told Paul, "I want you to know I had nothing to do with the idea. It was your mom's all the way. I'm just as surprised as you are."

"I know," Paul said with a broad smile. "Mom's been that way as long as I've known her. When she sets her mind on something, there's no changing it. But she's right. You deserve a new kitchen before we have any kids."

As she looked at Paul with a smile, she thought, "Kids? This was the first time he's ever mentioned children. I wonder where he came up with that idea."

The next morning, Sara looked in the phone book for kitchen cabinet and remodeling companies. She called the school system to tell them she was available to teach again. She also called her dad to tell him he'd been volunteered to help install the new kitchen.

"Sure," he said. "The plant will be on shut down for two weeks in February, so I can get the cabinets installed then. If we run out of time, I'll take a day off to help finish and install the countertop. I'm sure you can find someone to install a new floor. You are getting a new floor, aren't you?"

"I guess," Sara replied. "I never thought of it, but it would be the right time to replace it. Wow! We've got a lot of work to do!"

"You sure do, Pumpkin."

When Paul came in for lunch, Sara suggested they go to town and shop. They spent all afternoon at flooring stores and the lumberyards, but they couldn't find what they wanted for the cabinets in Muscatine. The next day they headed out again for the Quad Cities. After shopping all day, they decided on simple birch cabinets. The sales rep said she'd come out in two days to measure and design the kitchen. Time was short because of the holidays, but the rep said she'd make sure the cabinets arrived before the end of January. She also suggested doing the floor first.

"I guess we'll be eating meals in the den for a while," Sara said.

"Heck, no," the rep said. "Make Paul take you out every night. It may be your only chance to claim that privilege."

Thanksgiving came fast, and this was the year for Sara's brothers to come for Christmas instead of Thanksgiving. Because she and Paul were the only ones living close, they worked out a plan to have a small brunch with Sara's parents and Mr. B and then go to Paul's folks' house in the afternoon. Paul's sister and her family would be down for the weekend.

The first thing Sue said when they arrived was, "I hear you twisted enough arms to get a new kitchen! Good for you! I think I helped destroy the old one a couple of times. The big scratch on the end of the counter was mine. I tried to ride my new bike inside instead of waiting to go outside."

"Now, Sue, leave her alone," Madge said. "It was all my idea. Sara wouldn't have said a thing if I hadn't exploded over the broken knife drawer."

"I was just kidding," Sue said. "That kitchen was built back in the dark ages. What kind of plans have you made? I hear your dad's going to install the cupboards."

Sara explained they were going with birch cabinets and a mottled dark green countertop. She also said they had picked out a light green-and-gray floor tile because it wouldn't show dirt as much. They would paint the walls a light yellow to make it cheery.

"Sounds wonderful!" Sue said. "Jeff and I waited until we had two kids, which was a mistake. You need a good kitchen with kids. I had to move the microwave every time I wanted to warm a bottle. By the way, when are you and Paul going to start a family?"

"My land, Sue," Madge said with a laugh. "They only got married in July."

"I guess that's true," Sue said thoughtfully. "It feels like I've known you forever. You're like a kid sister to me." She paused, then added, "Well, have you two thought about it?"

Sara smiled and replied, "We've discussed it a couple of times, but we've decided to wait till next year—and thanks for the compliment about being your kid sister. I'm honored."

Sara loved how Sue always said what was on her mind, and knowing how Sue felt about her made Sara feel like a real member of the family.

Chapter Eleven
A Bump in the Road

With Thanksgiving over, Christmas was right around the corner. Paul busied himself getting the livestock equipment and barns ready for winter. There were always automatic waters needing new heating elements or thermostats. He cleaned the shop and made sure the shop heater was ready. Burned out light bulbs were replaced, loose doors tightened, and tractors needed to be fine-tuned before the cold weather set in. Sara was teaching full-time as a substitute. Paul promised Sara he'd go shopping with her, but the only time they had together was on weekends. Even the long Thanksgiving weekend proved unsuccessful for shopping, but they thought there would still be time for shopping before Christmas. On Thursday after the Thanksgiving break, Sara stopped at her mom's for a chat after class one day and noticed that her mom seemed nervous. They talked about Emma's cooking job at the nursing home and how each of the residents was doing, then Emma sighed and said, "Sara, I've got something to ask you."

"Sure, Mom," said Sara. "You seem upset. Is something wrong with Dad?"

"No, it's not your dad. It's me. I've had this lump on my breast for about six months. I thought it might go away, but it's getting bigger."

Sara panicked. "Mom, why haven't you gone to the doctor? This could be serious! Have you told Dad?"

"Of course not."

"Why not? He should know."

"He's so busy. I didn't want to bother him."

"It's only 4:00," said Sara, dialing the phone. "I'm calling Dr. Barnes right now to set up an appointment. I'll go with you." When a receptionist answered, she said, "This is Sara Maas. I'm calling for my mother, Emma McWilliams. She needs to see Dr. Barnes as soon as possible. What times do you have open?"

"I have a 10:00 and a 2:15 open tomorrow," the receptionist replied. "I also have most of Monday open. What seems to be her problem?"

"She just told me she's had a lump on her breast for six months and I'm concerned. We'll see you tomorrow at ten," said Sara, hanging up the phone. Then she hugged her mom and said, "It'll be alright, Mom. I'll stay here till Dad gets home from work and we'll tell him together. I'll call home and leave Paul a message so he doesn't worry."

When Sara's dad arrived, they sat him down to tell him. He was grateful Sara had already set up an appointment and said he'd take the next day off work.

"You don't have to that. I'll take Mom this time," said Sara. "Let's see what the doctor says and go from there. You might want to take time off later."

The next morning, Sara and Emma were at Dr. Barnes' office early, anxious to hear what she would say. After Dr. Barnes examined Emma, she said, "Emma, I think you should have a mammogram taken on Monday. There's definitely something there. I'll see if I can get you into the university hospital for some other tests we aren't able to do here. I'll be right back. Sara, you help her get dressed."

When Dr. Barnes returned, she had an appointment set up for Tuesday morning with Dr. Zhou at the women's clinic. "She's one of the best in breast cancer research," Dr. Barnes said. "It was a miracle there was an opening with her this soon."

"Are you sure all this is necessary?" asked Emma. "The people at the home depend on me."

"Emma, if I didn't think this was necessary, I wouldn't put you through all these tests. We have to find out what that lump is. It's probably just that, a benign lump. They'll just remove it and you can go on as if nothing happened. But if it isn't, we want to be sure we catch it before it is too late."

"Thank you very much, Dr. Barnes," said Sara. "We'll be there early on Tuesday."

"Good," replied the doctor. "I'll have Ellen make copies of your records, Emma. Sara, can you pick them up Monday? Also, be sure to take the mammogram photos with you."

"No problem."

After stopping at the Maid-Rite restaurant for sandwiches, Sara and Emma returned home. They had to plan the next week. Emma called the nursing home to tell them of her tests and to let them know she wouldn't be in. Sara called the school system and told them she'd be unavailable. When John came home, he let the plant know he was taking Tuesday off. Everything was in place. The waiting would be the hardest part.

"How's your mom?" Paul asked when Sara got home.

"She's going to Iowa City for tests on Tuesday. Dad and I will go with her. We'll know more then."

"Well, do whatever you need to do. I'll be fine," said Paul, giving her a hug. He could see she was worried.

Because Sara surmised there would be more than one day at the hospital, Sara fixed several casseroles and sandwiches on Saturday and put them in the freezer with directions written on each one. She'd found out in her short time as Paul's wife that he was only a pizza and hot dog chef. Sunday, Paul and Sara went to church and everyone was curious about Sara's mom. Several women offered advice and words of encouragement. They said they'd start a prayer chain on Tuesday morning. Sara was pleased that Paul's church family, which was now also hers, was so concerned.

Tuesday morning, Sara and her parents arrived at the hospital.

Check-in seemed to take forever, since there was a lot of paperwork involved. It took about two hours for Emma to be assigned a room. But once she was settled in, lab workers were there in minutes, taking blood samples, blood pressure, and EKG readings.

Dr. Zhou finally arrived and introduced herself. She was a small woman with jet-black hair. She moved with an air of authority, and when she spoke, everyone jumped. On the other hand, she was very pleasant and had a warm bedside manner.

She examined Emma's breast thoroughly, then said, "Emma, I'd like to get a biopsy as soon as possible. I'm taking a vacation in two weeks, and I'd like your results before then. Could you stay overnight? We need to make sure everything else is okay. If everything checks out, we can schedule surgery for Thursday. If the lump is benign, we'll remove it and you can go home in a just few days. If it's malignant, we would have to consider how far along it is and whether it has reached the lymph nodes. What do you think?"

Emma looked at John and Sara and said, "I don't know. We all have jobs and my daughter lives on a farm. Do we have—"

"Thursday will be fine, Dr. Zhou," Sara interrupted. "You go ahead and schedule the procedure. We'll be here."

"Okay," said the doctor. "I'll call the surgical floor and see what time is available. A nurse will inform you of the time. I'll see you tomorrow, Emma. Don't worry, we'll take good care of you. You might have trouble sleeping tonight, so I'll prescribe a sleeping aide for you."

Fifteen minutes later, a nurse returned and said the procedure would be at seven on Thursday morning. Prep would take about forty-five minutes and the surgical procedure would take about an hour if everything went well.

Sara and her dad decided to find a motel close by and reserve a room for an overnight stay on Wednesday night. If the weather changed they wouldn't have far to drive. They left Emma at seven that evening and headed home. She dropped off her dad and made sure he was all right before heading home. It was late when she finally pulled into the drive. She found Paul waiting with a pizza in the oven. He was happy to see her.

He was concerned about Emma but was glad she could get in so soon. Sara was exhausted, so they had their pizza in the den, and Sara was soon sound asleep on the couch. She had a big day ahead. On Wednesday, she and her father would head back to Iowa City and help Emma prepare for Thursday's surgery.

Paul helped her upstairs, and as they approached their bedroom, Sara stopped and said with a touch of weariness, "I have to pack some clothes for tomorrow and Thursday. I'll probably have to pack Dad's, too. He's helpless without Mom. It will be a long day on Thursday. I should call Bob and Tom and tell them what's going on. I don't think it's necessary for them to come. I'm sure the surgery won't be life-threatening."

It was late at night before Sara had finished packing. In the morning, Sara kissed Paul goodbye and headed to Muscatine to pick up her dad. In Iowa City, they went to the motel and checked in. When they walked into Emma's room, Dr. Zhou was there, accompanied by a tall young man.

"Good afternoon," the doctor said with a smile. "This is Dr. Lars Anderson, my associate. He'll be assisting me tomorrow. I have five surgeries scheduled for tomorrow, so Dr. Anderson will finish your mother's procedure if it runs late. He'll be with her all of the time. I'll come and see you right after we're finished."

Nurses were in and out all afternoon, assuring John and Sara that everything was going well. They returned to their motel at ten. Sara knew it would be difficult for her dad to sleep, so she had brought his sleeping meds.

They were up and dressed at 5:00 in order to be at the hospital on time the next morning. They had their rolls and coffee and headed out. When they arrived, Emma was already receiving calming medication, and at seven the surgical team came to take her. Sara and John went to the family room to wait. Pastor Fred from Muscatine Christian church arrived at 9:00 and was a great comfort. He'd been with many families during such events. He asked Sara how she was and that they missed her. He was glad she was active in Paul's church. He told her he realized you can't serve two churches. The surgery went longer than expected, but Dr. Zhou finally came to talk to them.

"The surgery went well," she began, "and the good news is that the tumor was benign. The not-so-good news is that we had to remove more tissue than planned, since there were actually two tumors. Emma will be in recovery for at least two hours. Dr. Anderson is finishing the surgery. I'd like to keep her here for two more days. I think she can go home by Saturday. She should see Dr. Barnes early next week. If there are any complications, don't hesitate to call me. The reception desk can page me. Emma should rest for two weeks. She'll be very sore and she won't be able to lift anything heavy for a month. Do you have any questions?"

"No, not right now. Thank you, doctor," said John, relief showing on his face. "I appreciate your concern. As long as I get her back, that's all I care about."

Dr. Zhou smiled and assured him by saying, "I believe your wife will be fine, as long as she receives regular check-ups."

As Dr. Zhou left the room, Sara said, "I'll call Paul, then Tom and Bob. Tom wanted to come, but I talked him out of it. I'll call the nursing home, too. I'm sure they'd like to know about Mom. I think we should stay over one more night, don't you, Dad?"

"Absolutely," John said.

Just as Sara walked out of the door, she met Tom in the hallway.

"I thought I told you it wasn't necessary for you to come," said Sara.

"I know, but you're not the boss, Sis," Tom replied. "Bob will be here this afternoon. I talked to him this morning. You care for Mom and Dad all the time, so we thought we'd help this time. You can take care of Mom while Bob and I help with Dad. How's Mom doing—and Dad?"

"Mom's not back from surgery yet. There were actually two tumors, but they were both benign. She'll just need some time to recover. The doctors had to remove most of her right breast to get it all, but she'll be fine in a couple months. I've got some calls to make. You stay with Dad in case Mom comes back before I do."

Tom surprised his father and the two of them waited for Emma's return. Sara was entering the room as Emma was wheeled in. Two nurses got her tucked into bed, and as soon as they left, John pulled up a chair beside the bed. Emma was groggy, but she smiled weakly and said, "Hi, honey."

"Why don't you and Tom get something to eat? I'll sit with Mom," John told his children. "When Bob shows up, I'll go to eat with him. I'm sure he'll be hungry after the long drive."

"I'm hungry," said Sara. She could tell her dad wanted some time alone with his spouse. "Come on, Tom. Let's go to the cafeteria and get something to eat. We need to talk anyway."

Bob arrived from Kansas City around 4:00. By that time, John was ready to get something to eat. Bob said hello to his mom. The two of them stayed until Sara and Tom returned. As they stood around her bed, Emma told them in a faint whisper that she was glad to have her family with her.

Bob bent over, kissed her on the forehead, and said he'd see her in the morning. Then he hugged Sara and said, "Thanks, Sis. You're wonderful."

Finally, he turned to his dad and said, "Well, Dad, let's go get something to eat. It's been a long day for both of us. I need a break and I'm sure you do."

Bob and Tom stayed with their parents on Friday while Sara went to Muscatine to get the house ready for Emma's return. She contacted some of Emma's friends, who said they'd be glad to check on her several times a day. The church women would also send some food over.

Emma was dismissed from the hospital Saturday morning. Bob and Tom helped get their mother settled in at home. Tom went back that evening, but Bob said he'd stay until Sunday. It would give Sara a chance to sleep in her own bed.

When Sara got home, Paul met her at the door with loads of questions. She told him all the details, then Paul filled her in on what had happened on the farm. They talked and laughed for almost an hour. They acted as if they'd been apart for a long time, and it would be nice to sleep together again.

On Monday, Sara received a call from the school district asking is she could sub again. There were many teachers out and they were desperate. It was December 15th, only ten days till Christmas, and Sara hadn't even started shopping. Emma was counting on her to do her shopping, too. Sara made out some lists and took a chance that Paul would be able to help. He agreed, but he warned her he was going to buy each item the first time he saw it instead of shopping around for the best price. He spent two days at the malls and when Sara got home from school, he had every gift sitting on the dining room table.

"Great job, honey!" Sara would say. "Now I know who to call on next year!"

They spent their evenings wrapping presents. Actually, Paul did most of the wrapping while Sara prepared for the next day at school. By Christmas Day, everything was ready.

Sara's brothers were coming, and Emma had recuperated enough to enjoy the hustle and bustle of the grandchildren. Kris and Shelley brought food from home and Sara cooked the turkey. Emma, with the help of her daughters-in-law, made her famous pumpkin pie. It was a joyous celebration, made even better since Grandpa John had found a neighbor who showed up dressed as Santa. He came right after dinner and amazed the little ones, who couldn't believe Santa had made time to stop in and see them. Christmas was on a Thursday, which made for a long weekend. No one had to hurry home. Kris and Shelly would have their family Christmases on Saturday.

On New Year's Eve, Paul and Sara attended a party at Tammi's. They played cards until 11:50, then all started watching the clock. Food and drinks were served and at precisely midnight as the old clock struck for the final time in 1975. Sara and Paul kissed each other.

Tammi sidled over to Sara and asked, "Are you pregnant yet, Sara?"

"No," Sara answered.

"You do know how to do it, don't you?"

"Yes, I'm pretty sure I do," Sara replied, blushing.

"Well, it's about time! I had my first one in just seven months," said Tammi. Then she looked at her husband and said, "We'll never be able to do that again, will we, Howard?"

"We're going to wait for a while," Sara said, giving Paul a big hug.

At 1:00 in the morning, the party broke up and Paul and Sara headed home.

"What do you think about having children, Big Boy?" Sara asked.

"I think you answered Tammi right," Paul replied. "I think next year suits us."

Sara taught steadily until semester break. When she had time, she cleaned out the top cupboards. She'd have to find places for all the stuff until the new cupboards were installed. Most was just piled on the dining room floor. Paul and George started dismantling the kitchen on January 20th.

The floor installer was scheduled for the 25th and the old cabinets weren't easily removed. In some places the plaster came off the walls with the wood. The walls would have to be patched before the new cupboards could be installed. Luckily, all the patches were behind the new cabinets, so matching the plaster wasn't an issue. Among the items found behind the old counter were four tickets to Holiday on Ice.

"Remember when we lost those tickets?" George asked Paul. "Boy, was your mom mad at me! I can't wait to tell her we finally found them."

The floor was installed on time, but in late January there were still no cupboards and Sara was getting nervous. One Saturday, she and Paul painted the ceiling and masked around the woodwork. Sunday afternoon, they primed the walls, and Sara started painting them on Monday since there was no school. She was interrupted by Paul needing help to repair the silage unloader.

The next morning she was up early and almost had the first coat on when the phone rang. It was the cabinet company, needing directions.

They'd be there in an hour.

When they finally arrived, the deliveryman asked, "Where do you want the cupboards?"

"In the garage, I guess," said Sara.

"I'd be glad to put them in the garage, but I'd suggest you put them in the house," the deliveryman said. "It's easier to work with warm cabinets, and we'll carry them in for you."

"Sounds good," agreed Sara. "We can put them in the dining room, but I'll have to move some things around."

"That's okay," he replied. "We'll start getting them ready on the truck. Is there anyone who might help with the bigger pieces?"

Just then, Paul arrived in the pickup. "Yes, my husband is here now," Sara said.

She put the lid back on the paint can and started to move boxes of dishes and pans into the living room. A few minutes later, the deliverymen and Paul started bringing in the boxes, and soon the dining room was full. They put a couple in the living room and left three of them in the kitchen. Sara figured she could work around three boxes.

When all the boxes were in, they had Sara open one to make sure they were right. They joked that they probably should have done that earlier. It would have been sad to have to load everything back into the truck. After the deliverymen left, Paul announced that he had to go out to bed down the cattle. Sara told him she was going to finish her painting.

"How about going out for supper?" he asked as he approached the door.

"No," she replied. "I've got about twenty minutes to go. Then I'd have to clean the brushes and myself before I went anywhere."

Paul smiled and said, "Okay, here's Plan B. I'll call Casey's for pizza. By the time I change my clothes and run into town, you can be done and showered. We'll eat in the den—and I must say, you look cute in those paint clothes. By the way, I think the Cyclones are on TV. We can watch the game in the den while we eat."

Sara smiled back. Was Paul's comment about being cute indicating some later action on or was he just being nice?

"Okay, make it sausage and pepperoni."

Paul ordered the pizza, changed his clothes, and headed for Casey's. By the time he returned, Sara had finished painting, showered, and was sitting in the den in her pajamas.

"I've been reading one of your women's magazines," said Paul as they ate. "It said that if you've been on birth control and decide to have children, you shouldn't expect immediate results after stopping the pill. It can take several months. Maybe we should consider it. It might be a while before we get any results. I think you should quit the pill, what do you think?"

"You read my magazines?" Sara said in surprise. "Yes, I think that sounds great!"

"Super! I can't wait to start!" he said with a twinkle in his eye.

"I'll let you in on a little secret," Sara said in a hushed tone. "I stopped taking the pill two weeks ago."

"Well, let's finished this pizza and get started," Paul said happily. "On second thought, let's forget the pizza until later."

"Right here? Right now?" she asked.

"Sure," said Paul, starting to unbutton her pajama top.

Sara whispered in his ear, "Remember what happened in this room about a year and half ago?"

"I sure do!" said Paul. "How could I ever forget? But that was just the preview. This, my dear wife, is the main feature."

Sara and Paul held each other close on the floor and finished what they'd started the previous year. They forgot all about the TV or pizza—

and the Cyclones actually won that night.

By Friday the painting was finished and everything was ready for John to begin installing the cabinets. John and Emma both came out on Saturday. Emma claimed she didn't want to miss the fun.

Sara and Emma opened boxes while Paul and John studied the plans. On Sunday, John got a call to do double overtime at work and he couldn't refuse, so Paul and Sara placed the lower cabinets in their specific spots, hoping it would meet with John's approval. Work went quickly and the countertop was ready to be measured by Wednesday.

Paul and John finished hanging the cupboards on Friday, so all that was left to do was wait for the countertop. It was nice not to have anything extra to do on the weekend. Everyone needed a break. John went back to work during his plant's shut down because his department was doing a major renovation and he needed to help. He promised her that as soon as the countertop came in, he'd help install it.

Thursday morning the countertop company called for directions to the farm. Paul and George helped unload the pieces. They had just gotten it placed on the cabinets when John made his appearance. He shoved it against the wall. He was amazed at how straight the wall was. There would be very little adjustment needed. He told Sara he could be there at seven in the morning and to call the plumber to install the sink and dishwasher right after lunch.

On Friday, the plumber finished the hook-ups and everything was in place. John returned Saturday morning and installed the last trim pieces. Sara's new kitchen looked fabulous. Monday was Presidents Day, so Sara invited both sets of parents to the farm for a celebration lunch of homemade pizza—made in her new oven. Madge said she couldn't believe it was the same room she had cooked in for so many years. The only thing left to do was to make window treatments, and Emma volunteered to help Sara sew whatever she wanted.

Chapter Twelve
Old Blue Wins One

March was the start of calving season. When compared to an average Iowa spring, that March was miserable, snowy, and wet. It took a lot of bedding to keep the calving barn dry. Paul set up several pens in the back to isolate the new mothers from the rest of the herd and checked the barn before going to bed and again first thing in the morning.

One night he went to check and didn't come back right away, so Sara got worried and went out to check. She found Paul lying just outside the man gate.

"Paul! What happened?" she screamed as she ran to him.

"I'm alright, I think," Paul answered. "Old Blue and I got into a fight and I lost. I got between her and her calf. I almost made the gate, but my arm got stuck between her head and the fence post. I don't think it's broken, but it sure does hurt. "

"Do you think you can get up?" Sara said, reaching down. "Here, take my hand I'll help you up. We'd better get you to the emergency room."

He took Sara's arm and pulled himself up, his face grimacing with pain as she brushed off the straw and dirt with her gloved hand.

"Well, maybe I should get checked out," he said weakly. "Old Blue caught me in the ribs with that stub horn of hers. Help me get to the house. Maybe I'll feel better if I can sit down."

With his good arm around Sara's shoulder, Paul hobbled across the farmyard to the backdoor. In the kitchen, Sara grabbed a short stool. As he sat down, the pain in Paul's chest shot through the rest of his body.

He gritted his teeth and said, "Help me get out of these boots and work clothes and we'll go, okay?"

"Sure, honey. Are you sure that's all Blue did to you? I see a hoof mark on your back. Did she step on you?"

"I don't know. It all happened so fast. When she knocked me down, all I could think of was rolling under the fence. If she stepped on me, I don't remember it."

"You stay here while I change."

Sara hurried upstairs and changed into clean jeans and a knit top. Grabbing her fleece jacket from the hall closet, she hurried to the kitchen.

She helped Paul with his jacket and told him, "I'll bring the pickup around. I think it will be easier for you to get into. Don't move. I'll be right back."

Outside, Sara started the pickup and looked over at the passenger side. She'd have to clean off a spot for Paul to sit. The seat was covered with wrenches, empty pop cans, candy wrappers, and various receipts. She wondered how he managed to keep any kind of books with all those papers in the truck cab, but this wasn't the time for a lecture, so she just brushed everything onto the floorboard. The only items she tried to collect were the receipts. She stuffed them into the glove compartment. Sara jammed the pickup into reverse and backed out of the shed, throwing gravel as she went. As she approached the house, she half expected to see Paul standing by the gate, even though she had told him not to, but he wasn't there. He must have been hurting worse than she'd thought.

She hurried in the back door and found Paul patiently waiting on the stool. He smiled through his pain and said, "I figured I'd already gotten one female mad at me tonight. I didn't need two."

Sara helped him outside and into the pickup, then closed his door and scampered around to the other side. As they tore down the driveway, Paul said, "Slow down, honey. I'm not dying. We'll make it to the hospital in plenty of time. We don't need a speeding ticket, too."

Sara parked the pickup in front of the emergency door at the hospital, and hurried around to Paul's door. As she opened it, two emergency room people came rushing out to help, one of them pushing a wheelchair.

"My husband got stomped by a cow," Sara told them. "I think he broke something. He's in a lot of pain."

They helped Paul out of the truck and settled him into the wheelchair. Then they wheeled him directly to the emergency room while Sara parked the pickup. She hurried to admissions and filled out the admitting forms. When she finally caught up with Paul, he was already in a hospital gown and lying on a gurney. He smiled as she came in and she lifted the covers.

"Well, they did leave your socks on," she said in a feeble attempt at humor. "I guess you're covered."

"Are you Mrs. Maas?" a nurse asked as she stepped in from behind the curtain. "We're going to have to take some x-rays. Your husband might have some broken ribs and a cracked bone in his wrist. He definitely has a large bruise on his back. Dr. Jones will be in shortly to talk to you."

Two technicians arrived and wheeled Paul away. Twenty minutes passed before they brought him back. One of the men said, "The doctor will be in shortly to discuss the results."

There was no one else in the emergency room, so Sara found it hard to understand why it took another twenty minutes for the doctor to appear. She held Paul's hand until Dr. Jones finally arrived, carrying a clipboard.

"Paul, you have two broken ribs, a hairline crack in a bone in your right wrist, and a big bruise in the shape of a hoof on your back," the doctor explained. "We'll tape your ribcage to prevent the ribs from moving. You'll have to wear a protector for three weeks to avoid further injury. The wrist will be in a hard cast for two or three weeks, then we'll see if a soft cast will do for a couple more weeks. Your back will be sore for awhile, but I'll prescribe some pain medicine and sleeping meds. I want you to see your family doctor in three days." Looking first at Paul, then at Sara, he asked, "Any questions?"

"I guess not," Sara replied. "We're in the middle of calving season and this should prove interesting. I guess I'll have to learn how to check cows, too."

"Just be careful," Doctor Jones said with a smile. "We don't want to see you in here, too."

Sara and Paul finally arrived back home at six in the morning. It had been an all-night affair. George came to the house, wondering where Paul was. Sara met him at the door and led him into the den where Paul was reclining in his chair.

"Hi, Dad," Paul said as George looked on in shock. "I got the short end of the stick when I tried to move old Blue's calf. She mauled me a bit."

"How long are you going to be laid up?" George asked.

"Three to four weeks."

"This is going to present some problems, but nothing that can't be overcome, right, Sara?" George said. "I'll just have to come around more often. I'll bring Madge with me and the three of us will get the chores done." Noticing how tired Sara looked, he added, "Why don't you get some rest and I'll check the cows? I'll be back around eleven with some lunch and we'll plan our strategy."

As promised, George and Madge arrived with lunch and a casserole for supper. At the kitchen table they planned their day.

"Madge and I will be here early every morning to do chores. We'll stay most of the day. Sara, do you think you can check the cows at ten? If you have a cow start to calve, call me or Dr. Johns. Don't try to pen a cow up without help," George ordered.

Sara agreed. She'd have her hands full with Paul for a while.

"I've been trying to get Paul to sell old Blue for two years. I hope he listens to me now. She has a mean streak. As far as I'm concerned, she's hamburger," George said firmly.

The calving process went well for two weeks with no major problems. By the last week in March, only six cows still hadn't calved. Paul was feeling well enough to assist with chores, opening gates, operating the skid loader, carrying bales one-handed, and instructing Sara on what to do.

One Thursday evening, Sara decided to take a shower before the news. When she came downstairs in her pajamas, Paul said he thought he'd check the cows by himself, but there was no way Sara would let him go out alone. She put her coveralls on over her pj's and they went out together.

Upon entering the barn, they heard a low moan coming from the far corner of the barn. A black cow was in labor and the calf's head was already sticking out.

"We'll have to get her into the calving pen, and call Doc."

The cow was easy to pen. She wanted to get the birthing over. As Sara waited in the barn, Paul headed back to the house to call the vet. When he returned, he was carrying an armload of old rags and towels.

"Doc is at Van Heusing's," Paul said. "He'll be tied up for a couple hours. Dad's at a night supervisors meeting. Do you think you can pull this calf?"

"I—I can try," Sara replied. "What do I have to do?"

"First you have to push the head back into the cow and then find the front legs. Then you'll tie twine on each foot and pull them out first."

Just then the poor cow let a desperate moan. She again tried to push the calf out, but it was stuck.

"We can't wait for the vet," Paul said. "If we do, we'll lose the calf and maybe the cow, too."

"I can do it," Sara said resolutely.

She pulled her arms out of her coveralls and tied the sleeves around her waist. She slipped off her pajama top and put on an old t-shirt from the rags Paul had brought.

"Okay, I'm ready," she said, taking a deep breath. "What's next?"

"Lubricate your arms with this salve," said Paul, handing her a plastic bottle. "Then start pushing the head back into the cervix. I'll hold her tail and lean into her side so she can't move. Once you've got the head back in, feel around with your fingers until you find one of the calf's legs. Then slip this twine over the hoof and try and pull the leg out ahead of the head. When that's done you have to do the same thing with the other leg. If we're lucky, we can pull both legs out. The head will follow, and the rest of the calf will slide out."

"Wait a minute. I'd better take my rings off," Sara said. "I don't want to lose a diamond ring inside a cow. Where should I put them?"

"Put 'em in my breast pocket. It has a zipper," said Paul. "Just don't forget to take them out before you wash these overalls."

Sara lathered up her arms and started to push the slimy black head back into the mother. It was difficult because each time she shoved in, the cow tried to shove out. With one big push, using both hands, she finally forced the head back inside. Then she felt inside until her fingers wrapped around a little hoof.

Paul handed her a piece of twine, and with her free hand, she slipped the twine in, using her other arm as a guide. Thank goodness her mom had taught her how to tie knots and make loops for knitting. Her arm was in almost to the elbow. She slipped the loop over the hoof and dewclaws and pulled it tight. Then Paul took hold of the string and helped pull with his good hand. The first little leg popped over the aitch bone.

"Good. We're halfway there. I'll hold on to this one while you see if you can snag the other foot," Paul instructed.

Sara slid the second piece of twine in and looped it over the second hoof. "Great job!" Paul said. "Now put this pipe in the loops of the twine and pull both legs at the same time."

The first tug revealed two little black hooves. Paul latched on with his good hand and pulled down as Sara tugged with all her strength. She even put her foot on the cow's rump to give her more leverage. Dripping with sweat, some of Sara's hair had escaped from her green stocking cap and was plastered on her forehead. Finally, the head began to appear, and as soon as its chest cleared the birth canal, the calf flopped out onto the straw.

"You saved a calf, Dr. Sara!" Paul said excitedly. "Congratulations!"

Looking at the calf lying still in the straw, Sara asked, "Is it dead?"

"No. I can see his heart beating," Paul replied. "He just needs a little air. Clean the mucous out of its mouth and nostrils. Hold his head in one hand and open the mouth with your other hand. Then put your mouth as close as you as you feel comfortable with and blow air into his lungs."

After Sara had done as she was instructed, the calf gave a kick and shook its head.

Paul said, "Perfect! Now help me get him up front." As he lifted one of the calf's rear legs, he added, "Oops! I guess we have a she instead of a he."

They dragged the calf up to the mother's head. Paul released the cow and she began to lick the afterbirth from her calf. The cow's rough tongue stimulated the calf and the calf tried to stand on her feet. Sara took some of the old towels and wiped as much of the moisture and slime off her arms as she could. Sara took her disgusting wet t-shirt off.

"Yoo-hoo!" they suddenly heard someone call from the front of the barn. It was Dr. Johns. "Anybody here?"

"Over here, Doc!" Paul hollered as Sara quickly untied her coveralls and pulled them over her shoulders, pulling the zipper as high as she could. She didn't have time to retrieve her pajama top. She left it hanging on the gate.

"Looks like you've got everything under control here!" Dr. Johns said, leaning against the pen.

"Sara did all the work. She was terrific!" Paul replied proudly.

"I've always thought women do a better job at pulling calves than men. They have smaller arms and hands." Looking at the calf, Dr. Johns added, "It looks like the little girl needs some help getting started. Sara, if you wouldn't mind, could you do it? That way I won't have to clean up afterward, since it's already been a long night. I'll coach from here."

"I don't mind," Sara replied. "Just tell me what to do."

"Get the calf between your legs and hold him up."

"Okay," Sara said, following the vet's instructions.

"Good! Now with one hand, grab one of the mother's teats and squeeze from the top to the bottom. You'll get some milk to come. Then with your other hand pull the calf's mouth right up to the bottom of the teat and give her a face full of milk. She'll start licking the milk."

Again Sara did as the vet had told her. "Now put the teat right in her mouth and stroke the underside of her throat. She should start nursing."

When she placed the teat in the little heifer's mouth and stroked the area under her neck, she immediately started to suck. Within minutes, she was nursing vigorously. Sara stepped back and smiled.

"Well, I think I can go home now," said Dr. Johns. "Paul, I think that woman is a keeper. Great job, Sara!"

As the vet walked away, Paul shut the gate on the calving pen. Then he turned to Sara and said, "Let's call it a day, but I'm afraid you're going to have to shower all over again."

"That's okay," Sara said, still smiling. "It was worth it. Boy! I hope Doc didn't see my pajama top hanging on the fence. That could have been am embarrassing moment. I won't forget this for a long time. How's your arm?"

"It's fine. Now let's get going. You grab your pajama top. I'll catch the lights if you'll get the door."

They walked back to the house arm-in-arm. Sara put Paul's cast in a plastic bag. She helped Paul remove his body wrap, as he called it, and got into the shower to bathe him. She gently toweled him off, trying not to put too much pressure on his sore ribs. After drying herself, the two of them fell into bed. It had been a long night. It was a good thing that Sara didn't have to go to work in the morning.

Paul had his cast removed the first week of April and got his soft cast, but he worried that he would not be ready for the spring rush. He needn't have worried. The April rains spaced themselves every two or three days, keeping everyone out of the field and giving Paul and George time to catch up.

They decided not to convert to thirty-inch row spacing and stay with the standard forty-inch spacing for another year, even though there was a decisive yield advantage to narrower rows. Because of Paul's injuries, it would have been difficult to change the equipment. All the tractor's wheels would have needed to be readjusted to accommodate the narrower setting. It also would have meant a major investment in new machinery. The planter was only the start. Cultivators and a different corn head would also have to be purchased.

With the planter issue settled, they busied themselves getting the equipment ready and the lots cleaned. Usually some of the manure hauling is done during the month of March before the frost leaves the ground, but that year, because of Paul's injury, all they could do was to pile it outside the lot. That meant there were four days of manure hauling to be done before any tillage could be started.

The third week turned dry and work was started. Paul bought a new manure spreader from the John Deere dealer, with the stipulation that he could continue to use the old one until he finished cleaning the lots. On Friday, Sara, George, and Paul started hauling. Sara drove the 4430 and the new spreader, George took the 4020 and the old one, and Paul drove the skid loader.

They put the cows and calves in a small pasture close to the barn. The cows enjoyed the freedom of the pasture and it allowed Paul to work without the cattle getting in the way. Madge knew the importance of getting the lots cleaned, so she fixed lunch, returned to Wilton for the afternoon, and then brought supper out in the evening. Sara told her she could stay, but Madge always had an excuse for going back home. Sara decided that Madge felt uncomfortable in the old house with the new kitchen because it was no longer hers. She was thankful Madge let her do what she wanted with the house.

By Monday, the job was done. All the lots were clean, including the feeder lots at the Becker place. Disking and field finishing could finally be started. On April 25th, Paul pulled the planter from the shed, and by nightfall twenty acres had been planted. The weather stayed dry for two weeks and the men put in long days. Sara substituted three days a week, but on her days off, she relieved George in the field. He spent those days doing chores around the buildings. He was happy for the break from tractor driving. The long hours of driving always caused him severe shoulder and neck pain.

Chapter Thirteen
A Family Begins

On May 5th, Sara got another call from Anne Baxter, asking for help. This time it was Anne who had been diagnosed with breast cancer and was going to need surgery and chemo treatments. She asked if Sara could take over her class until the end of the school year.

"Since planting is almost finished and we won't be baling hay until June, I don't see why I can't, Anne," Sara replied. "But I'll ask Paul when he comes in anyway. How are you holding up?"

"I'll know more tomorrow," Anne replied tentatively. "The surgery is definite, and next comes the radiation and chemo. My doctor gave me lots of encouragement. She seems to think we caught it in the early stages."

"Who's your doctor?"

"Dr. Zhou."

"That's who my mother had. She was great. You'll have the best of care. We'll be praying for you, so take care of yourself and don't worry about the kids."

"Thank you so much, Sara. Could we meet in my classroom tomorrow? The children already know you, so I think the transition should be easy," Anne said with a sigh of relief.

"See you tomorrow," Sara replied. "Don't you fret. We'll get along fine."

When Paul came in from the field and Sara had explained the situation, he said, "Sounds like a no-brainer to me. Dad and I can finish planting and spraying. Maybe it will work into a full-time position someday. It sounds like Anne is the one we should worry about."

"Thank you, hon," said Sara, giving him a hug. "I knew you'd understand."

The next morning, Sara visited Anne and the kids. She started teaching the next day. She stopped at her mom's after school on Wednesday because it was Emma's day off.

As they sat drinking coffee on the front porch, Sara asked, "How are you feeling, Mom?"

"I'm fine. How about yourself? " Emma replied.

"I'm fine, I guess," Sara said tentatively.

"What do you mean, I guess?"

"Well, I've had a little nausea in the mornings lately and my breasts are very tender. I don't want anyone to touch them. I also have a funny feeling in my stomach area."

"That's interesting." Emma asked with a smile. "How long since your last period?"

"Let me see. I guess I skipped April, and I barely had one in March, and I can't remember February, since I've been so busy with school and the farm."

Emma took her daughter's hands, looked her in the eyes, and said, "My dear daughter, I think you're with child." The word *pregnant* wasn't in Emma's vocabulary. "You have all the symptoms. I think you should give Dr. Barnes a call."

"Really, Mom? Do you think I might be pregnant?"

"Definitely."

"Oh, Mom! This is exciting!" Sara exclaimed. "Dr. Barnes' office is still open. I'll give her a call."

Sara rushed to the phone and dialed. When Dr. Barnes herself answered, Sara said, "Dr. Barnes! I wasn't expecting to hear your voice. Where's Mary?"

"She had to leave because she has a sick child and Lana's with a patient, so I'm the only one left to answer the phone. Who is this?"

"I'm sorry. This is Sara McWilliams Maas. I need to schedule an appointment."

"Okay. What seems to be the problem, Sara?" the doctor asked. After Sara had described her symptoms, she said, "I think your mother may be right, but we have a problem. I'm leaving for a few days and won't be back until next Tuesday, so I think we should skip the first step and go right to the next. I'll call my friend and associate, Dr. Julia Giles. She's an OB/GYN. All the women I've sent to her have been very happy. If you've got a minute, I'll call her office and let you talk to them."

Sara waited on line for a minute, a voice said, "This is Dr. Giles' office. Lori speaking. Dr. Barnes tells me you want to make an appointment. This is Sara Maas I'm speaking to, isn't it?"

"Yes," Sara answered.

"I have openings on Friday at 11:00 or 4:30," said Lori. "Otherwise it will have to be next week."

"Friday at 4:30 will be fine."

"Good, I'll put you down. Dr. Giles would like the father to come to the first appointment, too, if that's possible. She likes the father to be involved right away."

"I'll try to get him to come. We're farmers and this is a busy time."

"I understand. Maybe we should pray for rain on Friday," Lori joked.

"Yeah, maybe. Either way, I'll see you Friday at 4:30," Sara said with a laugh.

Sara promised to call her mom as soon as she found out if she was pregnant, then headed home. As she pulled into the farmyard, she noticed the shop lights were on. When she swung the car in front of the shop door, George came walking out.

"Is Paul around?" Sara asked.

"He's spraying at Becker's," George replied. "He'd like to get done before it rains tomorrow, so he might be late. Can I help you with anything?"

"Not really, Dad," said Sara. "I just need to talk to Paul. It can wait a little while."

Sara returned to the house, changed her clothes, and started fixing supper, hoping Paul wouldn't be too late. Sometimes she had to warm his meal three or four times before he came in.

It was nine o'clock before she saw him pull into the driveway. He poked his head inside the kitchen to let Sara know he was headed to the basement for a quick shower. It was no longer a shock when he returned naked. He just walked by and headed upstairs, but before he got out of range she gave him a pat on his bare behind.

"I still like to see my man with nothing on," she said as they both laughed. "Don't cover up too much. I've got something we have to discuss when you get back."

When he returned, he was wearing only a t-shirt and boxer shorts. He claimed he didn't want to excite her too much.

"Hon, I have an appointment with Dr. Giles on Friday, and I was hoping you could come with me," she began as he sat at the kitchen table. "It sounds like it'll be raining anyway."

"Okay," said Paul, a confused expression, "but who's Dr. Giles? I haven't heard of him."

"It's a she, and Dr. Giles is an obstetrician," Sara replied, watching to see if that hint would register. When Paul showed no sign of understanding, she said excitedly, "Paul. I think I'm pregnant! And Dr. Giles wants both of us to come to the first appointment."

"You're pregnant?" Paul said with a huge smile. "Really? Whoopee! I'm going to be a dad! You betcha I'll be there. What time on Friday?"

"4:30."

"Are you sure?"

He stood, enfolded Sara in his strong arms, swirled her around, and quickly set her down again, saying, "Sorry. I suppose you should take it easy. We don't want anything to upset the apple cart."

"Don't worry, hon. I won't break," she assured him. "In fact, I'm not completely positive. That's why we're going to see Dr. Giles. She'll have the final say."

Neither of them could sleep that night, and Thursday seemed to drag on and on. It did rain early on Friday morning, eliminating any field work. Sara's class had art during the final period on Friday, so Sara asked Mrs. Braun if she could dismiss the class directly from the art room instead of sending them back to her room. That way Sara could leave early to make her appointment. Mrs. Braun heartily agreed, so at 3:00 on Friday, Sara headed home, took a quick shower, and was drying her hair when Paul arrived.

Paul announced, "I'm showering, too. I don't want to smell like cows the first time we meet the doctor."

"Okay, but hurry," said Sara. "We don't want to be late."

Paul playfully grabbed the towel Sara had wrapped around herself and took it with him toward the shower, leaving her standing nude in front of the big mirror.

"Save that for tonight, Big Boy," she said with a playful smile. "There's no time for messing around right now."

After his shower, Paul asked, "What should I wear? Jeans or khakis?"

"Khakis and a nice shirt. No t-shirt," Sara ordered.

It had started to rain as Paul let Sara out at the door of Dr. Giles' office building. She walked into the office while he parked the car.

"I'm Sara Maas. I have an appointment with Dr. Giles," Sara told the woman behind the counter.

"Yes, Mrs. Maas. Please have a seat and fill out these insurance forms. A nurse will be out as soon as possible. We're running a little late. Is your husband with you?"

"Yes, he's parking the car. He'll be right in."

A few moments later, a damp Paul walked in and sat down beside Sara. There were four other women in the room, each obviously pregnant. He felt like a fish out of water. He looked for a magazine to read, but there were none he was interested in—only *Woman's Day, Parents, Family Circle,* and *Family Life*—so he just sat patiently while Sara filled out the forms.

It was only twenty minutes, but it seemed like an hour before a nurse finally emerged through a swinging door and called, "Mrs. Sara Maas?"

Sara got up and asked if Paul was to come also.

"Yes, by all means," the nurse replied. "My name is Cassie. I'm Dr. Giles' nurse. Please follow me I'll take you to one of the examining rooms."

Paul and Sara followed Cassie down the narrow hallway, and Paul again felt out of place, since he seemed to be the only man there, and all the women except the staff members were in varying stages of pregnancy. Cassie stopped Sara at the weight scale. She wrote down her weight and height.

"We'll need a urine sample, too. You take this little cup and head down the hall to the restroom. Leave the cup on the shelf when you're done. I'll take your husband to the examination room."

Sara continued down the hall while Cassie took Paul to the little exam room. It was a typical room with an exam table, two chairs, and charts hanging on the walls. It had a small sink with a cabinet above it. There was one window with no shade or blind that faced the outside into a wooded ravine.

"You just make yourself as comfortable as a man can be in here," Cassie said with a smile. "I know you feel strange. My husband only came with me once and refused to come again. I'll see if I can find your wife. She doesn't know where we are. I'll be right back."

She came back with Sara in tow. "Here you go," Cassie said cheerfully. "Sara, sit up here on the table. I have to take your blood pressure, pulse, and temperature."

While making small talk, Cassie asked Sara, "Do you know Anne Baxter?"

"Yes, I substitute teach for her. Why do you ask?"

"Anne's my sister. I thought your name sounded familiar. She told me how good you are. She was so glad you could help. This is a trying time for her."

"Oh, my goodness," Sara said in surprise. "How's Anne doing? I think of her all the time."

"She's doing great," Cassie replied. "They think they caught it in time. She lost a breast and has to go through chemo, but she'll be back teaching by fall."

"That's great news," said Sara. "I'll tell the children on Monday. Tell Anne they miss her."

"I sure will," Cassie replied.

"Now slip out of all your clothes and put on this gown. The doctor prefers the ties in the front in this office. Since you haven't got socks on, put on these footsies. I'll be back in a few minutes. Just leave the door open a crack when you're ready. Don't worry about the window. It's one-way glass. The doctor likes lots of natural sunlight. I tell everyone that, in case they're nervous about it."

In spite of Cassie's assurance, Sara still glanced at the window several times as she got undressed. Paul helped by hanging her clothes on hooks, and held up the hospital gown for her to slip into.

When she turned her back toward him, he said, "Hon, you look radiant today. I've never seen you so happy."

She slipped her arms into the gown and began to tie the cords.

"This thing would be short on a tall midget," Sara joked.

Sara sat on the examining table and told Paul to open the door. In a few minutes Cassie returned with a clipboard and asked a few more questions about Sara's health, then said, "I'll check to see what is keeping Dr. Giles."

There was a commotion in the hall. They could hear two women talking. Dr. Giles, a woman in her late forties, finally entered the room, followed by Cassie. She said, "Hello! My name is Julia Giles, but you can call me Dr. Julia."

She looked over at Paul and then at the chart she was holding. "Paul, I'm glad you could come today. I like to have husbands see what their wives have to go through. Too many men don't realize the changes a woman's body goes through when she's pregnant. Well, let's get the mystery solved. Sara, lay back, put your feet in these stirrups on the end of the table, and let me take a peek." Holding up a metal instrument, Dr. Julia then said, "I'm going to place this in your cervix so I can see what's going on. We keep them in the refrigerator for all our patients." Noticing the look of horror on Sara's face, the doctor smiled and quickly added, "No, I'm just kidding—but it *will* be a little cold. Paul, why don't you hold her hand, since this is her first experience with this?"

Sara did as she'd been instructed and as Cassie placed a small sheet over Sara's legs, Dr. Julia sat on her little stool and disappeared under the sheet. Paul saw Sara wince as the doctor inserted the instrument.

It was over in about thirty seconds.

"Well," the doctor said with a smile, "Congratulations, Mr. and Mrs. Maas. You're going to be parents. Everything looks fine. Let me check a few more things out and then you can get dressed. Sara, sit up on the end of table. I want to listen to your lungs."

As Sara sat at the edge of the table, Dr. Julia listened to Sara's lungs. "Everything sounds good. Now just lay back and I'll do a breast examination."

"Breasts are a bit tender, huh?" Dr. Julia said as she noticed Sara frown. "Sorry. I'll try to be gentle. Are you going to breast feed your baby? You know, God gave women breasts for one purpose and one purpose only—to feed babies."

"I guess so," Sara replied. "We haven't talked about any of that stuff yet."

"Of course," said Dr. Julia. "Well, you get dressed and we'll talk in my office, okay?"

"Okay. Thank you," Sara replied.

Cassie stayed behind after Dr. Julia had left the room. "When you're dressed, I'll show you to the doctor's office. It's just two doors down. We'll be seeing you again in about two months—and don't worry. By the time you finally deliver the baby, getting undressed and wearing these little gowns will seem like second nature." Before she left, she added, "Nice to meet you, Paul."

Paul watched as Sara slipped off the exam gown. He'd seen her nude many times, but this time she looked so vulnerable, yet so contented. He guessed it was the old cave man instinct, but he suddenly felt the need to protect her.

In Dr. Julia's office, the doctor explained the changes Sara's body would be going through and how they might affect Paul. The due date was November 12th. Then she gave them some brochures to read when they got home.

Finally, she looked at Paul and said, "I know one question most guys want to know but are afraid to ask. Can we still have sex? The answer is yes, you can as long as Sara's comfortable with it. There will come a time where it will no longer be easy for her, but she'll let you know, not me, okay? Go home and read everything I gave you—and enjoy your first pregnancy. Lori has already left, so call Monday and set up your next appointment."

Sara and Paul each shook the doctor's hand and headed home to tell the world.

"Boy, I hope I don't have to go through that again. I mean, I didn't mind going with you, but all those *women*. I really felt out of place. It was worse than shopping for your underwear," Paul exclaimed while driving.

Sara laughed. "Well, honey, it wasn't the most pleasant experience for me either. It was my first time, too."

Sara's first call was to her mother. Emma was filled with joy, since she'd been the first to know. She also promised to tell Mr. B the next time she saw him.

Paul called his parents next, and Madge was only mildly surprised, since she thought Sara had been acting differently. When she heard the due date, Madge laughed.

"Poor planning on your part, son" she said. "That means Sara won't be able to help with the harvest. I suggest you check the calendar before your next one. All you have to do is count ahead nine months, just like those old black cows." Then she added, "Oh, and I've been meaning to tell you. Sue called and she's due in August. I guess I'm going to be a grandma twice this year."

On the last day of school, Sara told the students Mrs. Baxter would be coming in that day and she'd be wearing a baseball cap. When Mrs. Baxter arrived, she removed the cap to reveal her bald head. She told the students it was the medicine she was taking that had caused her hair to fall out. The students were full of questions, which Anne answered the best she could. Sara thought Anne was very brave to come to school and talk about her cancer.

It was July 25th and their wedding anniversary, so Sara put on Mrs. B's nightgown. She walked into the den where Paul was watching TV, danced around him like a belly dancer, and bent over to kiss him. As she did, the gown revealed her ever-enlarging breasts. They hadn't had any sexual activity for at least four weeks.

She pulled Paul out of his chair, took off his shirt, and undid his shorts. He lifted the gown over her head. Her protruding belly wasn't huge yet, but it definitely was no longer flat. She patted his chest, leaned into him, letting her body press against his.

"I think we'd better try this upstairs in bed," Paul told her.

"Good idea! I'll race you," said Sara, pushing Paul back into his chair as she ran toward the stairs. Paul caught her at the bedroom door. He led her to the bed and lay down on his back and Sara climbed on top of him. She tried to get into position, but it wouldn't work. Her large tummy kept getting in the way and she couldn't move as easily as she liked. They tried several maneuvers, but nothing seemed to work. Finally, she flopped down beside him and started to giggle.

"Rule number 26 in the farm wife's handbook," she announced. "Don't try to have sex when you're five and half months pregnant. It just doesn't work. Period!"

They laughed until Sara had to race to the bathroom before she wet the bed. Apparently, sex would have to wait for a while.

By the end of October, Sara was starting to get miserable. Everything she did was a chore. Driving out to the field with lunch was uncomfortable because the truck bounced and bumped over the rough ground. Because of the constant jostling, she asked Madge to take over that chore for the rest of the season. Emma also came out on weekends and helped clean house. Madge took over cooking duties, bringing something from home in the morning and staying to help Sara cook supper. They became great friends during that time.

On November 10th, after lunch, George went back to chiseling and Paul left to help Glen Babson finish his harvesting. Glen was always a little late but he had helped George and Paul make hay many times and Paul felt obligated to help him finish. Sara told Madge she was going upstairs and lie down for a while.

"Go ahead," said Madge. "I'm going to bake a cake for tomorrow."

An hour later, Sara started to feel pains in her stomach. She got up and went downstairs to take an antacid pill.

"What's wrong, Sara?" Madge asked.

"I don't know. I have a pain in my stomach. It kind of comes and goes," Sara replied.

Madge looked at her and said, "My land, girl, you're having labor pains. How far apart are they?"

"About every twenty minutes."

"You sit down," Madge ordered. "I'll run and get George. He knows where Paul is."

Madge tore out the door, and drove the old pickup out to the field, where she stopped George in the middle of a round. "Sara is having contractions," she said excitedly. "Can you find Paul?"

George shut off the tractor and hopped into the truck beside Madge. In the farmyard, he raced to his pickup and headed for Babson's. He returned with Paul in about fifteen minutes. Now Sara's contractions were ten minutes apart. Sara had contacted Dr. Julia, who would be waiting at the hospital when they arrived.

Madge warmed up the car and backed it out of the garage. Sara was waiting and ready as Paul bounded downstairs to take off his coveralls. There was no time to change his clothes. He emerged in his work jeans and flannel shirt. He helped Sara to the car. Once Sara was safely inside, Paul pointed the car down the lane.

In the house, George was dialing 9-1-1. "Jill, this is George Maas. We're having a baby, No! No! Sara and Paul are going to have a baby and they're going to need an escort. They just left the farm. Is there anyone available?"

"Yes, I can have Dick at the blacktop in about two minutes. Congratulations, Grandpa," Jill said with a laugh.

On the highway, Dick pulled alongside their car and gave them a thumbs-up. Then he turned on the lights and siren and led them to the hospital. In ten minutes, they were pulling up to the emergency room doors, where two of the hospital staff members had a wheelchair waiting. They helped Sara out of the car and into the chair.

By the time Paul had parked the car, ridden the elevator to the third floor, and donned his scrubs, Sara was already prepped and ready. The contractions were even closer together now and Dr. Julia was busy giving orders to her staff. Sara looked at Paul. Though she never screamed, she moaned with each push and squeezed Paul's hand tightly. A nurse dabbed away the sweat on Sara's face as she continued to cope with the pain as best she could.

Sounding like a football coach at a high school game, Dr. Julia said, "Just one more push, Sara. I can see the head. You're doing terrific. Come on, you can do it!" Sara screamed as she gave one last push, and Dr. Julia said, "That's it! The baby's out. My job's over, but your job has just begun. You have a beautiful baby boy." She then looked at Paul and said, "Mr. Maas, would you like to cut the umbilical cord?"

Cassie then wrapped the baby in a warm blanket and handed him to Paul to present to Sara. As Paul handed the baby to Sara, he said. "I'm so proud of you, honey. You did a great job! Thank you."

"Have you picked out a name?" Cassie asked.

"Edward Jon Maas," Paul and Sara answered together. Then Sara added, "That's J-o-n, without the H."

The nursing staff got Edward cleaned up as Sara was wheeled to a recovery room. She would stay at the hospital for two or three days. Saturday Paul took Sara and Baby Eddie home to the farm. It would be the beginning of many good times.

Since Sara was still tired from the delivery, Emma spent a few days with Sara on the farm to help her get into a routine. Getting Ed to nurse wasn't as easy as they'd first thought, but in just a few days, his nursing became stronger.

By January, Sara and Paul decided she would become a stay-at-home mom. Crops and prices were good, so her extra income wouldn't be necessary.

Farmers were optimistic as 1977 turned out to be another good year. It looked like the Russians would continue to buy U.S. grain, which was good cause for optimism.

Paul changed to thirty-inch row spacing, which meant they had to buy a new planter, two rear-mounted cultivators, and a new corn head. While dickering on the corn head, the John Deere salesman also talked them into a two-year-old 7720 combine. It meant their farm equipment would be totally green.

A week after New Year's Day, 1978, Sara announced to Paul she might be pregnant again. After a visit to Dr. Julia, she came home all a-glitter. She was due in August—Sara thought mid-August, but Dr. Julia predicted the 25th. Sara and the doctor wagered a Whitey's malt on whose prediction would be closer. Winter and spring passed with no problems during the second pregnancy.

On their anniversary, Sara again wore Mrs. B's nightgown, but this time she was eight months pregnant and the nightgown didn't cover her front side very well. As she walked into the bedroom, Paul started laughing. Sara was tired and hot and had swollen feet, so she didn't see what was so funny—until Paul made her look at herself in the full-length mirror.

"I'd like to have a picture of this for posterity," Paul said. Sara gave him a dirty look as he ran to grab the camera.

"You'd better take a side view. A full front would be pornographic," she ordered.

Early in the morning on August 15th, Sara nudged Paul and said, "I think we'd better go to the hospital."

As Sara got dressed, Paul called Madge, because she was closer than Emma and didn't have to go to work. When Madge answered sleepily, Paul said, "Mom, we've got to head for the hospital. Can you come out and stay with Eddie?"

Madge snapped awake and replied, "Sure, I'll be there in fifteen minutes."

By the time Paul had alerted the hospital and was helping Sara to the car, Madge was pulling into the driveway. When she stepped out of the car, Paul and Sara laughed to see her still in her nightgown and slippers and wearing one of George's old denim shirts.

"I'm glad there were no cops around," Madge confessed as she took little Eddie out of Paul's arms. "I didn't stop at one stop sign. I'll have to call George later and have him bring me some decent clothes. Now you get going. You don't want to have the baby on the way. I'll take good care of Eddie."

When Paul and Sara reached the hospital, they learned that Dr. Julia was out of town, so her partner, Dr. Lisa Connors, was going to do the honors.

In less than an hour, Dr. Connors announced, "Congratulations! You have another bouncing baby boy."

As Cassie wrapped the baby in his first blanket, she asked, "What are you naming this little one?"

"Timothy George Maas," Sara said proudly. Then she added with a smile, "Oh, and you can tell Dr. Julia to make my Whitey's malt a blueberry."

Chapter Fourteen
—It's a Girl!—

In 1980, Ed was due to turn five in November and Tim would enter the terrible twos in August. July 25th marked Paul and Sara's fifth anniversary, and as always, the weather was hot and sultry.

Sara and Paul planned to go out to eat in celebration of the occasion. The idea was thwarted because their regular babysitter was at church camp and both grandmas were busy that night. In the end, it didn't really matter, because they were both too tired from the heat to go out. They decided to celebrate at home with the boys.

Sara baked a chocolate cake with "Happy 5th Anniversary" on the top. She found some Neapolitan ice cream in the freezer. After supper, they all had ice cream and cake.

Eddie asked, "What's an anniversary?"

"Well, it's like a birthday, but it's the day your dad and mom got married," Sara explained.

"Oh," said Eddie, his curiosity satisfied. He was more interested in the cake and ice cream.

After they had eaten, Paul suggested they all go out and sit in the front porch swing, which could easily seat two adults and two kids. All of them were wearing their sleeping clothes—the men of the household in PJ bottoms and t-shirts and Sara in her short summer pajamas.

Paul took off his t-shirt to be cooler, and Eddie, wanting to be like his dad, took his off, too. Then Sara removed Tim's shirt.

Eddie looked at Sara with a curious eye, and before he could ask, she said, "I think I'll keep mine on for now. I'm not that warm."

As they sat, Paul began telling stories, starting with Goldilocks and the Three Bears, then moving on to Paul Bunyan and Babe, and finishing with Henny Penny. Soon Tim was almost asleep leaning against Sara and Eddie was rubbing his tired eyes.

"I think it's time for some young men to go to bed," Paul announced.

Sara picked up Tim and Paul gave Eddie a ride upstairs, where they put them to bed and turned on their fans. Soon the room would cool down and the boys would be asleep. Before they started back downstairs, Sara quickly went into their bedroom and changed into Mrs. B's nightgown. She and Paul went back down to the porch swing, where they talked about the weather, the effect of the Russian embargo on farmers, and children.

Paul asked, "Do you want any more children, hon?"

"I think a little girl would round out the family, don't you think?" Sara replied.

"Yeah, but what if we get another boy?" Paul asked.

"That would be okay, but I'd still like a little girl."

"If the fourth one's a boy, then what?"

"We'll give up."

"Let's do it this way," Paul suggested. "If the next one is a girl, we'll quit. If not, we'll try one more time. Agreed?"

"Agreed," Sara said, putting her head on Paul's lap.

She had to bring her legs up a bit, so she stuffed her nightgown between them. She ran her fingers through his chest hairs. There were definitely more than twenty-five now. He ran his fingers through her hair, while running the other hand over her upper body, caressing each curve. He undid the three buttons at the top of the nightgown and slipped his hand inside. As he tickled her nipples, Sara giggled.

"I wish we could go to the dune," said Paul.

"We can't leave the boys," Sara replied.

"I know."

"We could go out on the front lawn, though," Sara said, looking up and smiling. "We could hear them from there. Wait here. I'll get a blanket from the den."

They spread the blanket on the grass between the oak trees, where they'd have a beautiful view of the stars and the half moon. They stood looking at each other, then embraced and kissed. As Sara untied Paul's sleeping shorts, they loosened and then slowly fell to the ground. Paul slipped the nightgown off Sara's shoulders and let it slide down onto the blanket. They stood naked in the moonlight, feeling the warmth of their skin against each other's bodies.

They sank down to the blanket. Soon they were locked in a romantic embrace. They lay next to each other for a moment. Sara raised her head, listening. "Was that Timmy?" she asked.

"I didn't hear anything," said Paul.

"There, I heard him again," Sara said, she stood and walked toward the house. Paul propped himself up on his elbow and watched her cross the yard.

"It must be a mother's ears," he thought as she stepped onto the porch, turned, and motioned for him to follow.

With a sigh, Paul got to his feet, picked up the nightgown and his shorts, then he grabbed the blanket. When he reached the porch, he tossed the blanket onto the swing. It would need to be shaken before they brought it back inside.

He locked the screen door behind him, and headed upstairs, where he found Sara in Tim's room, holding him against her shoulder as she rocked slowly in the old rocking chair. He wished he had a picture of such a lovely sight—a loving mother holding her child. Tim must have wet his night diaper, since it was sitting on the changing table.

As Paul paused to imprint the picture in his mind, Sara put her finger to her lips and pointed toward Eddie's room. Paul went and checked on him, and found Eddie curled up in a ball. Apparently, he had gotten chilled by the fan as it blew directly on him. Paul covered Eddie with a sheet and turned the fan slightly away. Almost instantly, Eddie stretched out across the bed.

Paul then went to their bedroom and turned on the fan, though a gentle breeze was starting to come in through the open window. He turned back the covers and sat on the edge of the bed until Sara finally appeared and stood in the doorway.

"What's the matter?" she asked.

"Nothing, I just feel wonderful about tonight. You, me, and the boys make a great family. How did I ever find you and how did I ever convince you to marry me? It was a miracle, don't you think? And just look at you standing there. You're so lovely, like a goddess. I love to watch you move. I love you so much."

Sara smiled and said, "Let's continue this conversation in bed. I'd love to hear more about your thoughts."

At the end of September, Sara thought she should pay Dr. Julia a visit. She'd missed her period again and those funny feelings were returning to her tummy. When she saw the doctor, she first mentioned the Whitey's malt she'd won a couple of years earlier.

Dr. Julia laughed and said, "Alright, how about double or nothing on this one?"

"It's a deal," Sara replied.

This time Dr. Julia chose April 25th and Sara chose April 15th. During one of the ultrasound tests, the doctor let the secret slip when she announced, "It looks like she's doing fine." With the addition of a little girl, their family would be complete.

During the winter months, Paul and Sara asked Eddie if he would like to move to the northwest bedroom. It was bigger and he'd have more room for his farm toys. Eddie's old room would become Tim's and Tim's would be for the new baby, since it was closest to the master bedroom.

They spent several weeks painting and filling the baby's room with new little girl furniture and it was ready in early April. The 15th went by, but the baby still hadn't arrived, and on Saturday the 25th, Emma came out to help Sara since the long pregnancy was wearing the poor girl out. Sara decided to lie down on the couch while Emma watched the boys and baked a cake.

A few moments later, Sara walked into the kitchen and said, "I think it's time to call Paul." She turned on the new CB radio, which Paul had installed just for that purpose and said, "Breaker, breaker. This is Long Tall Sara, calling Big Boy. Do you read me?"

"I read you loud and clear," Paul's voice replied.

"It's time for you to come home," Sara said. "My pains are fifteen minutes apart. Mom can watch the boys. You'd better hurry."

"I'll be there as soon as I can. I'll call Dad and he can finish up here at Becker's. Hold on, Long Tall Sara, I'm on my way!"

Just then the radio began to chatter with the voices of truckers tuned in to the same channel.

"This is Rubber Duck. You'd better get there in a hurry, Big Boy. It sounds like you don't have much time. I think Long Tall Sara is about to pop. Is this your first?"

Sara laughed and returned his call, "Rubber Duck, this is Long Tall Sara. No, it's is the third. Don't get too far away. I might need that semi to haul me into town."

"Anything I can do for you?" Rubber Duck asked.

"Well, you might get me an escort."

"Sure thing! What's your twenty?"

"Have them meet us at 170th and Highway 38."

"Ten-four, Long Tall Sara. Good luck!"

A few minutes later, Paul roared into the farmyard in the old pickup, and dashed to the garage to get the car. In the house, he hurried downstairs and washed his face and hands. Emma threw down some clean clothes Sara had in the wash basket, then she and Paul helped Sara out to the car.

Gravel flew as they roared down the lane. On the blacktop, they found a patrolman waiting to escort them to the hospital.

This time it took a mere twenty minutes for Sara to deliver a seven pound, twelve ounce baby girl. Dr. Julia looked at Sara and said, "Make mine chocolate, please. No, make it two!"

When asked the baby's name, Sara replied, "Jennifer Julia Maas." Then she added, "I'm afraid the middle name is for a neighbor lady who lived across the ravine from me when I was a little girl. She was like a grandma to me. I hope it doesn't hurt your feelings."

"Heck, no!" the doctor said with a smile. "Julia's a great name, no matter what. I've had it all my life. I was named after an aunt that my mom stayed with."

Paul gave Sara a hug and said, "Okay, ladies, I'm buying. Hon, you'll want blueberry, right? And Dr. Julia, you wanted two chocolates."

"Right," said the doctor. Then she turned to Cassie and said, "Cassie, what flavor do you want? Paul's buying."

Everyone laughed, and even little Jennifer Julia Maas seemed to be smiling.

Chapter Fifteen
Sara's Chickens

The 1970s had been great years for farmers with farm commodity prices at all-time highs, but in January 1980, President Carter announced an embargo of many products going to Russia. The USSR had invaded Afghanistan and the USA had decided to punish them.

When the embargo went into effect in January 1980, corn prices fell from $2.90 per bushel to $1.60 in less than a month. Soybeans declined from $9.00 to $5.00. Farmers who had borrowed money to purchase land or make expensive improvements were caught in a trap as their anticipated income disappeared.

It was the beginning of a long economic depression in agriculture. Many good operators went into bankruptcy. The banks did everything they could to help and extended credit as far as they could, but many farmers didn't survive the crisis.

George had a difficult time sleeping after attending bank board meetings. It was difficult telling a neighbor he had to sell out or face foreclosure. It was a sad time—and the saddest part was that the embargo didn't work. America's trading partners refused to join the embargo and they continued to sell to Russia. Brazil and Canada took away U.S. markets that had taken years to build. Because of an ill-conceived government mandate, American farmers would now have to spend many years rebuilding those markets.

The Maas farm felt the pinch, but not as bad as many others. They hadn't made any large purchases, and the only capital they had to borrow was for replacement cattle and for spring seed, fertilizer, and chemicals. All new machinery acquisitions were put on hold.

There was much less money left over for living expenses than had been the case previously, and it was a crisis that would last for the entire decade of the '80s. The only time prices briefly recovered to their former levels was in 1988, when a severe drought hit the Midwest, but no one had any grain to sell.

In the fall of 1986, Sara decided she could help with the money shortfall on the Maas farm by raising chickens. They'd provide eggs and there'd be some left over to sell, and the roosters could be butchered for meat. It seemed like a good plan, so she went to the extension office and picked up some poultry bulletins.

Madge had raised chickens when she was younger, so she agreed to help. Paul wasn't excited about the venture, but the old chicken house wasn't being used, so he agreed to give it a try.

During the winter, Paul bought a small building at a neighborhood farm sale to be used as a brooder house. George helped purchase feeders and chick water fountains. He also knew some turkey growers around West Liberty and got one of them to sell him some turkey bedding to get started. Later he ordered bedding by the truckload and stored it in the old hog house.

In March, Sara ordered 100 pullets and fifty cockerels from the co-op. She also bought 100 pounds of chick feed. The first week in April, Sara went to the co-op and picked them up. The chicks came in boxes of 100, and when she opened the box, all she could see was fuzzy little yellow birds, all peeping and wanting to get out.

Madge came out to help get everything set up. She explained how each chick had to have its beak dipped in the waterers so they'd know where the water was. They scattered some chick feed on the newspaper floor. When the kids came home from school, they hurried to the brooder house, where Madge showed them how to hold the fragile chicks. Jenny loved to hold the fuzzy chicks next to her cheeks. Sara went to the house and got the camera. She took several photos of Jenny cuddling the chicks.

Everyone was excited, but baby chicks aren't cute for long, and within a few days, their wing feathers began to grow. The newspapers were removed and feeders were placed in the center of the floor. The chicks grew quickly. Although they lost a few along the way, Sara was proud that they ended up with more than ninety layers and forty-six roosters.

In late August, the kids returned to school, so Sara had some time to herself. One Wednesday, she decided to go to the church's young mother's meeting. She planned to leave an hour early so she could stop in and see Mrs. Becker.

The Beckers had been their landlords for many years. When her husband died, Mrs. Becker had stayed on the farm for a couple years and George used to check in on her every morning. One day he found her lying at the bottom of the basement stairs. She had fallen and had been lying there for several hours. George called an ambulance and got her to the hospital, but Mrs. Becker had never felt comfortable living by herself again.

Finally, her two daughters convinced her to move into an assisted living facility in Wilton. She sold the farm to George and Madge on a contract so she'd have some annual income. All the members of the Maas family continued to visit Mrs. Becker because her daughters lived some distance away. She always liked company, especially Sara, who would tell her all about the condition of the crops and how things were going on the farm. Mrs. Becker had also raised chickens in her younger days, so she often gave Sara advice.

Sara showered, dressed, and since she had plenty of time, she decided to peel the potatoes for supper. As she began to peel, she decided she didn't want to get potato starch on her dress, so she took it off and continued peeling the spuds in her bra and half slip. A few moments later, she heard a commotion in the brooder house.

"Maybe a raccoon or an opossum is in with the chickens," she thought. "I'd better run out there and check."

Since no one was around and she didn't want her dress to smell like a chicken house, Sara slipped on her tennis shoes and quickly ran toward the brooder house. When she arrived, she saw that it wasn't a raccoon or opossum—it was their old tomcat. He was so scared by all the commotion. He was cowering in the corner. Sara picked him up by the back of his neck and just as she was tossing him out the door, she saw a pickup coming up the drive. It was Larry Dawson, the feed salesman.

"I'll just have to wait here until he leaves," she thought.

She stepped behind the door and watched Larry. He wasn't a tall man and he'd eaten too many donuts at the Wilton Café, but his clients were loyal to him because he treated everyone fairly and never used any high-pressure tactics. His only fault was that he was a great talker.

Sara watched as Larry got out of his truck, went into the shop and hollered for Paul. Then he went to the back door of the house and rang the doorbell. No one answered, even though the radio was playing. He took out a business card and put it in the crack of the screen door. He walked back and got into his pickup—but he didn't leave. Instead, he parked his truck under the oak trees and sat there in the shade to go over some invoices. Sara was trapped in the brooder house in her underwear, but what could she do?

"I could just walk to the house like this. I'm sure Larry has seen women in slips before. I'll just be brave and act shocked," she thought— and immediately changed her mind.

Larry was one of the biggest storytellers in the county and he'd spread the episode far and wide. The first week he'd tell the true story, but the tale would get taller and taller with each retelling. The second week she'd only be in a bra and panties, then it would be only panties and no top, and finally she'd end up totally naked. She decided she just couldn't take the risk. He had to leave sometime.

To her chagrin, she saw more dust coming up the lane. She saw it was Paul, which could be good or bad. He might get Larry to leave or they might talk for hours. Either way, she'd have to wait them out.

She watched as Paul and Larry talked for awhile. She heard Paul say he had to get going. Larry said goodbye and started his vehicle. As soon as Larry's pickup had disappeared down the lane, Sara hurried toward the house. Paul was surprised when he saw her coming, wearing nothing but a bra and a half slip.

"Where in the world have you been?" he asked.

"In the brooder house," she replied, shaking her head.

Sara confessed the whole story, and as Paul chuckled, he said, "Boy, wait until I tell Larry about this one."

"Paul Maas, if you ever tell anyone about this, I swear that I will never speak to you again!" Sara snapped with fire in her eyes.

Paul knew by the tone of her voice she meant what she had just said, so he promised never to reveal her secret. Suddenly, Larry's truck came roaring back up the lane.

"You remember what I told you, Paul!" Sara scolded as she dashed into the house.

Larry never got out of the truck. He just rolled down the window and said, "I forgot to ask if you needed any lick tanks for the stock cows this winter. There's a special on this month." Then he added, "Is Sara around? I've got a new sweatshirt for all the wives. What size would she be?"

Paul answered solemnly, "No, she's not here, but I'd say she'd take a women's medium tall. About the lick tanks, I guess we can use eight."

"Okay," said Larry. "Gotcha down, thanks. I'll see you next month. Tell Sara I'll have to bring her sweatshirt next time. I don't have any talls with me."

Larry backed up his pickup and headed down the lane again. Sara was out the door before Paul had a chance to go inside. "I'm late for my meeting," she called over her shoulder. "I won't be able to see Mrs. Becker now. I'll run the errands afterward. Tell the kids I'll be home at four."

Sara's chicken enterprise turned out to be a success. They laid plenty of eggs and Sara found a number of people in town preferred fresh farm-raised eggs to those from the store and were even willing to pay a little more for them. The roosters provided many good winter meals.

The next spring she ordered fifty pullets and fifty cockerels. Madge showed her how to cull the older hens and save about half for next year. The culls were butchered for stewing hens, and many of them were donated to church for their annual bazaar and supper.

Sara worked out a chore schedule for Eddie and Tim, telling them if they hunted the eggs and fed the young birds in the summer, she'd split the profits with them. It was an opportunity to teach the boys work ethics and money management. Paul had agreed to include the chicken feed and bedding in the cattle expense because he wanted the project to work. It wouldn't have been quite as profitable if all costs were considered and he didn't want the boys and Sara to get discouraged. In the end, he decided, the benefits of fresh eggs and meat were difficult to price.

Chapter Sixteen
Dry as the Desert

The winter of 1988 was mild and what snow did fall melted quickly. In March the weather was warm and dry, which made for easy calving. The new calves never got chilled and the lots were easy to keep clean.

It was dry enough in late March to seed the oats and alfalfa. There were few years in which they could do field work that early. April brought a few showers, but not enough to slow down fieldwork. By mid-month, the soil temperature was above fifty-five degrees, warm enough for the corn to germinate, and Paul started planting earlier than he'd ever done before.

The lack of rain started to become a concern, but it always seemed to rain in the nick of time. However, the dry trend persisted and since moisture wasn't available in the top two inches of the soil, Paul and George decided to lower the planting depth to three inches. It was a chance they had to take. If it rained, fewer seedlings would emergence, but if it didn't rain, the seeds would need the moisture at the lower level.

Time after time, the forecast would promise rain and the radar would show a line of showers advancing across Iowa; but by the time it got to the eastern part of the state, it had either dried up or lasted for such a short time, only a small amount of rain fell. By June the corn was about twelve inches tall and the soybeans were approaching the sixteen leaf stage. The ground in the pastures had big cracks in the surface.

They started to bale alfalfa the first week in June, and because of the lack of rain, it was harvested without any rain damage and had a beautiful green color. The re-growth from the crowns started immediately, but the hot, dry days presented problems. Rain usually destroyed the leaf hopper eggs, but since there was no rain, their population exploded. The bugs crawled upon the new leaves and sucked them dry. The co-op was kept busy spraying for hoppers, but even with those control measures, the second cutting of hay was small. Hay for feed was sure to be at a premium next winter. They could only hope that the rain would return by the time the third cutting was ready.

As June dragged on, rain was spotty and infrequent. The corn plants tried to protect themselves by rolling up their leaves, nature's way of keeping the moisture from escaping. At night they unrolled their leaves and tried to grow. The temperatures in June topped 100 degrees several times, and most cornfields looked more like fields of pineapples and pastures began to dry up.

July promised some relief. On the fourth, it rained an inch and a half—the most rain since March—but there was no more for two tortuous weeks. Seven of those days saw the temperature soar to more than 100 degrees, and the nights seldom fell to less than seventy. The soybeans were still in the vegetative stage and wouldn't set pods until August, which would give farmers a chance to salvage a bean crop, but corn was at the critical pollination stage. The silks dried in the extreme heat, meaning the ears wouldn't be filled to the end of the cobs. Some stalks aborted their ears completely, and in some areas, the corn didn't pollinate at all, leaving just an empty cob on each stalk.

Prospective yields were being lowered every day it didn't rain, but somehow the Chicago Board of Trade seemed oblivious of the conditions in the Midwest and commodity prices failed to rise. They wouldn't realize the full extent of the drought until fall.

The torrid temperatures also affected the cattle in the Maas feedlot, since they couldn't move to a hill where a breeze was blowing like the stock cows could do. One afternoon, Paul noticed one of the steers breathing heavily. A few moments later, the steer collapsed and died. Knowing that the steers were overheating, Paul got the garden hose, attached it to the hydrant outside the lot, and began sprinkling as much water as he could on the animals.

Just as George arrived to help, another steer collapsed. They simply couldn't get water on them fast enough. George suggested, "Let's call the fire department. Maybe they can bring water out and spray the cattle."

"Good idea," Paul agreed. "We're going to lose even more if we don't do something soon. I'll see if they'll come out."

Within twenty minutes a tanker and a pumper truck arrived and firemen quickly began showering the cattle with thousands of gallons of water. Within ten minutes, the cattle were breathing normally again.

Paul pulled the dead animals out of the lot and called the rendering plant, but he was told they couldn't get there until the next day. Paul covered the animals with a tarp, hoping they wouldn't deteriorate too much. Something had to be done to prevent the same problem from happening again. If they could install a sprinkler system above the cattle, the fine mist would evaporate and cool the surrounding air. He headed for town to buy some plastic piping to install the system.

The misting heads were more difficult to find. Paul called several livestock equipment dealers before he located the proper size. They were located at a dealer in Vinton.

"Dad, why don't you and Mom drive to Vinton and pick up the sprinkler heads? Sara, Eddie and I can have the pipes installed by the time you get back."

In a couple hours, they had the pipes installed, thanks to Eddie's help. He stood in the skid loader bucket and nailed the pipe hangers onto the rafters while Paul maneuvered the machine. Sara handed lengths of pipe to Eddie and he slid them into the hangers. Paul coached him how to glue the pipes together. When George and Madge returned at 9:30, it was Eddie who stood in the bucket again and installed the sprinkler heads.

By eleven, they were done and George turned on the water. A fine mist fogged out of the sprinkler heads and cooled the air instantly. From that day on, the heat losses were over in the cattle lot, but the drought continued.

The pastures were soon gone, and although it was an ironic joke, Paul swore he could see a worm crawling across the ground at fifty feet. They were forced to feed the hay they'd made in June, and George started to look for more hay to buy from the neighbors. The pond continued to be the main watering hole for the stock cows, but it was evident that it would soon be dry because the fish were dying. The grass crackled like paper when they walked on it. Paul could stick his hand down past his knuckles in some of the cracks in the ground. Everyone prayed for rain before it was too late.

The cattle weren't the only animals suffering. The day after the cattle scare, Eddie came running into the kitchen from the henhouse where he'd been feeding the chickens. "Mom, the chickens are dying. There's nine or ten already dead. They're standing around with their wings out and mouths open. I found more dead ones in the brooder house."

Sara followed Eddie out to the henhouse and saw that he was right. The same thing was true in the brooder house. There were dead chickens strewn everywhere. She hurried to the house and called Mrs. Becker, the most knowledgeable chicken person she knew.

"Hello, Lila," she said when Mrs. Becker answered the phone. "How are you? Are you keeping cool?"

"I'm fine. How's your chickens?" asked Mrs. Becker. "I've been meaning to call you. I've been worried they were going to get too hot."

"That's what I'm calling about," Sara said. "We lost several today. How can I keep them cool? I can't spray them with water like cattle, can I?"

"I used to put shallow pans of water all around the building," Mrs. Becker replied. "When chickens get hot they don't move. They just stand there and die. My husband used to say they were too dumb to know where the water was. Try that and I think you'll save the rest. Call me back if you have any more questions, and take care yourself in this heat, dear. It's awful."

Sara found some low pans and even took some cake pans out to the chickens, which quickly found the water and began to drink. It would be Eddie's job to keep the pans full until it cooled off. He and Tim hauled pails to the chickens many times that week, but it worked. Sara called Lila back in two days to thank her and told her she'd take her out to lunch to repay her.

The air conditioner they had installed in the upstairs hall window ran continuously. Sara hung a blanket across the stairway to keep the cool air upstairs. At night it gave them an oasis from the sweltering heat. The main floor rooms seemed to the catch the few breezes coming from under the oak trees or could be ventilated by fans. The lawn didn't need to be mowed for weeks. Sara watered her vegetable garden, but the flowers would have to fend for themselves. Food was necessary, but not flowers.

Paul laughed at her when she undressed one night, calling her his three-tone woman. Her arms and legs were a deep tan. Her back and shoulders were a lighter color because of being covered by her blouse, but the sun still burned through the cloth. The parts covered by her bra and panties were white. She had to admit she wasn't a fashion model, and neither was Paul.

After the children were in bed the night of their July 25th anniversary, Sara put on Mrs. B's nightgown, walked into the den, and twirled around, making the nightgown swirl in the breeze. Paul looked at her and smiled, but Sara knew he was getting depressed because of the weather. She had to find a way to get him out of his funk.

"Let's go out to the dune," she said. "The children are asleep, and if we walk, we won't wake anyone."

"Sounds good to me," Paul said.

They put on their tennis shoes and started toward the dune. The moon was about three-quarters full. As soon as they reached the other side of the gravel farmyard, Sara took off her sneakers and continued walking barefoot along the dusty road. The dust was cool on her feet. There was a small gate into the field where the dune was located, put there on purpose, just for people to go through. They passed through the gate quietly. In fact, Paul had hardly said a word the whole way.

Sara looked at him and said, "I'll race you to the top."

As she took off, Paul half-heartily chased her, but he didn't feel much like racing. When they reached the top, Sara undid the three buttons on the nightgown, revealing a deep cleavage. It was open almost to her belly button. Again Paul smiled, but that was all.

The dune couldn't work its magic that night. The grass, what little there was, was burnt and brittle. It had refused to grow back after the last mowing and was short, stubbly, and sharp. The breeze was still there, but the leaves rustled like dry corn in the fall. The tinder-dry corn tassels rattled in the wind. Everything they saw and heard reminded Paul of the dire situation their farm was in.

"Maybe this wouldn't be a good thing to do," Sara said softly. "The grass is sharp and the ground is hard. I think our own bed would be nicer, don't you?"

Paul nodded. Sara took his hand as they turned and headed back toward the house, kicking up dust as they went.

Finally, Paul said, "How will we make ends meet, Hon? We've already lost about two thousand from the dead steers and the spider mites."

"Honey, we've done it before," Sara said intently, "and we can do it again. It'll rain sometime. It always does. God won't let it be dry forever."

"I don't know," Paul said softly. "I just hope He turns on the faucet soon. We're going to have to borrow just to get through this year. Thank goodness Dad says he doesn't need any rent money. He says he and Mom will catch up next year."

"I know, but next year will be different," Sara said, squeezing Paul's hand. "You just wait and see."

"You know, you're starting to sound like a farmer," said Paul, genuinely smiling for the first time that night. "You're right, hon. There's always next year."

"Well, I *am* a farmer," Sara said, pushing against Paul playfully. "At least, I'm a farmer's wife."

Paul turned and looked into Sara's eyes. "Do you think maybe that nightgown might have rain magic in it?"

"I don't know," Sara said with a smile, "but what have we got to lose?"

Sara started to dance around Paul like a ballerina on stage. She raised her hands and preformed a not-so-prefect pirouette. She quickly changed her style and sashayed back and forth, flipping her gown up and down like a follies dancer. Finally, she began to sing, "Rain, rain, rain on the corn, rain on the beans, rain on the grass, rain so I can have my honey back."

Her singing finally made Paul laugh out loud. "If I didn't know you better, I'd think you were drunk."

She danced and sang all the way back. At the hydrant in the backyard, they washed their feet with the garden hose. "Turn around so I can wash off the back of your legs," Paul said.

She turned around to let him, but Paul started spraying the middle of her back. She screamed as the cold water hit her, then quickly turned and tried to grab the hose, but he continued to spray her until the nightgown was sticking to her body, revealing her every curve.

They wrestled playfully until Sara got control of the hose and stuck it down the front of Paul's shorts. Only then did he finally reach for the hydrant handle and shut off the water. It was the first good laugh they'd shared in weeks.

In the house, they hurried downstairs to the laundry room, where Paul slipped off Sara's nightgown and stood looking lovingly at her naked body. Once they were dry, they headed for their bedroom, but Sara took a few moments to peek in on the kids before she joined Paul in bed. They held each other all night long.

Early the next morning, Sara thought she heard thunder. She looked out the window and it looked like rain, but it had looked like rain so many times that summer that she couldn't get too excited. She rolled over and put her leg over Paul's—her favorite position—and fell back to sleep.

A short time later, a loud crack of thunder woke them both. Paul got up and peered out the window. Outside, the wind was blowing dry leaves across the yard and bending the cornstalks. Within moments, rain began to beat against the window pane.

"Maybe we should put our pajamas on, in case we have to head for the basement."

They reluctantly dressed. Paul settled back in next to Sara and they snuggled together, saying nothing, listening to the rain. It continued to rain for about thirty minutes. The lightning and thunder began to dissipate, but the rain continued.

"Let's get the kids up and play in the rain!" Sara said excitedly. "This is a day they need to remember."

Before Paul could answer, she was already walking down the hall, announcing, "Wake up, kids! We're all going to run outside and play in the rain."

"Like this? In our pajamas?" Eddie asked sleepily.

"Sure! That'll make it more fun. You boys take off your tops. No sense in getting them soaked."

The boys tore off their tops and headed for the door. Paul said he was going to check on the cattle and the rain gauge at the barn, and Eddie said he'd go along. They both gasped as the rain pelted against their bare skin.

Tim wailed, "Wait for me!"

In a second, he was chasing after them. Jenny looked at her mom. "Mommy, can I take my top off, too? I want to be like Eddie and Tim. I don't want to get my Barbie pj's all dirty and wet," she whined.

Sara looked at her disappointed face. "Heck, yes, honey. They're only your brothers. Soon you won't want to go topless around them, so let's see if we can find something in the wash basket for you to wear outside. Here, put on this pair of Tim's old shorts."

Jenny pulled on Tim's shorts, and began to cry. "These are too big!"

"I'll get a safety pin and we'll cinch them up, okay?" Sara said with a smile.

Sara searched in the junk drawer, found two safety pins, and pulled the waist of Jenny's shorts tight. Then, giving them a quick tug to make sure they wouldn't fall down, she said, "They're a little big in the legs, but they'll do. Now, let's get outside and play in the rain!"

Sara and Jenny laughed and shrieked with joy as they splashed through the puddles in the lawn. "Let's go check the chickens, Mommy," Jenny suggested. "I'll beat you!"

Together they raced ran down the path to the henhouse, where they found the chickens content to watch the rain from the safety of their shelter. Then they scurried to the brooder house, where the pullets were obviously afraid of the noise of the rain on the roof. They were cowering in the corners, but they were fine.

On the way back to the house, Jenny found some shiny rocks along the path, probably residue from an earlier building project. She picked up three or four of the rocks and put them in the pockets of her shorts.

As they approached the garage, they saw Paul and the boys returning from the cattle lot. They stepped in every puddle they could while they were crossing the farmyard. "Two inches in the gauge!" Paul said happily. "You should see the steers. They're just standing in the rain, getting cool."

"Just like us!" Jenny added.

"That's right, hon, just like us," Paul said, scooping his daughter up and giving her a hug.

The boys stood under the eaves of the garage and let the water pour down on them from the corrugated steel roof. It was a joyous time for everyone.

"Let's go run in the garden!" Tim suggested.

"Okay, but stay on the path and be careful. It'll be slippery," warned Sara.

"I know, Mom. That's what makes it fun!" Tim replied.

"I don't want to go to the garden," said Jenny. "I want Daddy to swing me around and around in the front yard."

"Okay, I'll go to the garden with the boys," said Sara. "You and Daddy play in the front yard."

Paul carried Jenny out to the front yard and began swinging her around by her arms. As she squealed with delight, her too-big shorts, weighted down with the rocks, began to slide down her legs.

"Stop, Daddy!" she screamed. "My pants are coming off!"

Paul set Jenny down and helped pull her shorts back up. Then he picked her up again and tossed her high into the air, catching her by the arms as she came back down. He whirled her around as she giggled, her feet dangling off the ground.

"Do it again, Daddy. Swing me around," she begged.

"Okay, one more time. Then Daddy needs a rest."

As Jenny swung through space, one of the safety pins let go and her shorts weighted by the stones went flying off into the wet grass. Laughing, Paul retrieved the shorts, but before he could help her put them back on, she took off running. As she ran bare through the warm rain, Paul thought she looked like her mother in miniature—a beautiful smile, dark brown hair, a well-tanned body, and skinny. He finally caught her under the old oak tree, where he knelt down and re-pinned her shorts.

As he worked, Jenny put her arms around his neck, kissed him on the cheek, and said happily, "I love you. You're the bestest Daddy in the whole wide world."

Paul hugged her back and said, "Thank you, sweetie. You want a piggyback ride?"

Jenny climbed on his back and put her arms around his neck, then he grabbed her legs and around the yard they went. When they reached the front porch, he gently set her down on the steps.

"Maybe you should put those rocks in your pockets on the steps.

That way you won't lose your shorts," said Paul. "Here comes Mom and the boys. I think we better quit. You're wearing Daddy out." As Sara and the boys drew near, he shouted, "Let's play football! Eddie and me against the rest of you."

"I don't want to play," said Tim.

"Me, neither," echoed Jenny.

"Okay, you guys wait on the porch," said Sara. "Eddie, it's you and me against Dad."

The three of them hurried over to the side yard next to the garden, where Eddie and Sara huddled to decide their strategy. Sara went long for a pass, but Paul knocked it down. On the next play, Paul caught Eddie and pulled him to the ground, then tackled Sara, and as she fell, the top button on her pajamas popped open, but she didn't care.

On the final play, Sara shoved Paul aside and he fell into a huge water puddle. Then she ran long and Eddie hit her with a perfect pass. The bottom button on her pajama top came undone as she ran for a touchdown. Sara spiked the ball and did a victory dance as Eddie ran over and gave her a high-five.

Paul, still sitting in the mud puddle, cried, "Unnecessary roughness! How about a flag, ref?"

"Sorry," said Sara as she and Eddie piled on top of Paul.

In the free-for-all that followed, Sara's last button popped open. She quickly grabbed both sides of her top and pulled them together, but it didn't seem to faze either Paul or Eddie. They were too busy wrestling and laughing.

"Want a rematch?" asked Paul. "This time it's Eddie and me against Mom."

"You're on!" said Sara.

She re-buttoned the middle button on her top and play resumed. Eddie threw a pass, but the slick ball wobbled and fell short. On second down, Paul played quarterback and passed the ball to Eddie, but Sara caught him before he made it to the end zone. On the next down, Eddie threw a wobbly pass that Sara intercepted. Paul grabbed for her, but all he got was her blouse. As he tugged on it, the button pulled free, leaving Sara to run toward the opposite end of the yard with her top flying out behind.

At the sidewalk, she spiked the ball again and did another victory dance as Paul and Eddie looked on, knowing they'd just been beaten by the lady of the house. She then realized her top was undone. She again grabbed both halves and put them together, giggling like a little girl.

"One more game!" Paul yelled.

"Not right now," said Sara. "You guys play catch. I'm going to check on Tim and Jenny."

As she came around the corner, Sara saw the two little ones lying naked on the grass, each with their feet under a downspout, letting the rainwater flow up their legs and over their stomachs, laughing with joy. When Tim saw Sara watching them, he quickly retrieved his pajama shorts and said, "Jenny, Mom's watching. Put your pants back on."

Jenny just looked at Sara and said innocently, "You said it was all right, Mom. He's just my brother."

Sara smiled. "It's fine, sweetheart, but you should probably get your bottoms on before Eddie comes around or he'll tease you guys forever."

As her children pulled on their shorts, Sara re-buttoned her top for the second time, just as Eddie and Paul came around the corner.

They all made one more trip through all the big mud puddles, then Sara announced, "Okay, everybody, it's time to get some breakfast. Everyone to the hose to get legs and feet washed off. Then take showers— boys in the basement, girls in the upstairs bathroom. I'll make pancakes for breakfast. It'll take a little longer, but it'll be worth it. I promise."

The boys were done with their showers first, and Eddie started setting the table while Tim got out the syrup and butter and Paul gathered the ingredients and found the mixing bowls. Sara and Jenny came down with their heads wrapped in towels. To Sara's surprise, all the boys were wrapped in towels.

Eddie said, "There weren't any clothes in the basket, Mom. We even brought the basket up so you wouldn't think we're fibbing."

Sara put both hands to her face in mock horror. "Well, Land of Goshen," she said. "I reckon you fellas will just have to go upstairs and find some duds. I must have put them away." As the boys turned to leave, she added, "You might as well leave those wet towels here so I can wash them."

They tossed their towels in a corner and streaked through the living room. The women of the house laughed as they watched the nude Maas men disappear up the stairs. By the time they returned, the batter was mixed and the griddle was hot enough to start the pancakes.

When they were all seated around the table, Paul said, "First, let's give thanks for the rain. Heavenly Father, thank you for this wonderful rain. It replenishes the soil so the crops and the grass can grow. Forgive me for doubting the power of Your mighty hand. Thank you for blessing Sara's nightgown to bring the rain. Thank you for Sara, because she's my rock and makes me believe in You—and in myself. I can't think of anyone else I'd want to live with. You've surely blessed me. Thank you, too, for my children. They're the best gifts in the world. Help me to help them learn and grow. And finally, bless these pancakes as they feed our hungry bodies. In Jesus' name, we pray, Amen."

"And all God's children say, 'Amen!'" Sara agreed.

"Amen!" everyone repeated.

Sara couldn't keep up with the demand for pancakes. Her family ate them as fast as she could make them, but she didn't mind a bit. What was even more wonderful was that Paul seemed to be his old self again, and she was grateful.

As they finished eating, the rain was letting up outside. Paul went back out to recheck the rain gauge, and when he came back, he said there were three inches in the gauge. He went downstairs and returned a short time later, carrying Sara's wet nightgown in his hand.

"This nightgown truly is magic," he said, giving her a hug. "Don't ever lose it."

"I don't plan to," Sara replied, squeezing his waist.

"I believe God has blessed this nightgown. If we believe in its power and with God's help, are answered," Paul said softly. "I know it's too late to help the corn much, but it will definitely help the beans and the pasture."

It rained two inches in the next four days, and by mid-August, six more inches had fallen. The soybeans set pods and filled nicely, but the corn was nearly a total loss. The grass in the pasture started to green up and the creek flowed again, giving the cows plenty of fresh water, but it took the pond all winter to refill. It took nearly twice as many acres as normal to make the silage that year. The corn yields varied from sixty bushels on the good ground to less than twenty in the poorer soil.

The government stepped in and granted help for the drought-stricken farmers. Corn prices topped $3.00 a bushel, but no one had any corn, so it really didn't matter much. The soybeans yielded well. Their ability to wait until the rain came helped yields immensely.

The harvest, though short, went well, and as Sara said, "Next year will be better. It's God's promise."

Farmers are always optimistic. There's always another year. The next crop will be better. There's always hope. They began looking forward to 1989, and one day the disastrous year of 1988 would only be a memory to talk about around the kitchen table.

Chapter Seventeen
Sweet Corn Party

In rural America, many work events center around the whole family. One of those events is canning sweet corn. Seed corn companies often provide free sweet corn seed as a gift to customers for buying their hybrid seed and like most farm families, the Maas sweet corn patch was planted near the buildings so their dog could keep the raccoons out. Raccoons are one of Mother Nature's smartest animals. They seem to know exactly when the sweet corn is ready for harvest. There are many remedies to keep the raccoons from being first in the patch, but ol' Shep or Fido is the best deterrent.

When the corn is ready, there's a small window of time to pick, shuck, and can or freeze the golden kernels. This requires all hands on deck—parents, grandparents, children, sisters and brothers, and any in-laws one can gather. The more persons helping, the less work for everyone and it becomes a social event.

The first summer after Paul and Sara married, Sara's folks and Paul's sister, Sue, volunteered to help. Paul, Sara, and George picked the corn early in the morning. By the time John, Emma, Madge, Sue, and her kids arrived; the hayrack was full of unhusked ears. Sue was eight months pregnant so her participation was limited to babysitting and preparing lunch, but she was there to participate in the chatter and kidding. She also received her family's share of the corn. Two years later, it was Sara who was eight months pregnant, so she was the designated babysitter.

This year, Sue's boys, Seth and Noah, helped husk corn until they got bored. This took about fifteen minutes. Then they disappeared to the barn or the creek. As they grew older, their time working the corn pile was extended. But during their early teen years, they still only lasted until lunch, and disappeared on Uncle Paul's Go Getter or their dirt bikes.

The year after the great drought, Sue just brought Missy and little Josh with her. Her older boys each had jobs in Waterloo. Missy was Eddie's age, thirteen, and the two of them were like brother and sister. They rode bikes together, climbed in the haymow, and played in the creek, but not until the corn was husked and de-silked. Sue stayed at her parents' house, but all the kids stayed with Uncle Paul and Aunt Sara, doubling up in the beds or sleeping in the camper.

Sara's folks arrived early in the morning to help pick the corn. Paul pulled the hayrack into the corn patch and everyone tossed the ears onto the rack. They had to wear long pants and long-sleeved shirts to keep the corn leaves from cutting their skin. When about 700 ears were harvested, Paul pulled the rack under the old oak trees, where the husking and brushing of the corn silk off the ears began.

There was an occasional "Ugh!" or "Gross!" from the kids when they found an earworm hiding under a husk. That part of the ear was then cut off and discarded. The husks were tossed into the skid loader bucket, and when it was full, Paul ran it over to the feedlot and dumped the husks over the fence, where the steers enjoyed the fresh fodder.

As soon as four dozen ears had been cleaned, the women headed for the basement, which was the processing plant. Cover cloths and old sheets lined the floor to catch any stray kernels or corn milk that escaped the cutters, who used sharp knives to remove the kernels from the cob.

As the kernels piled up in the cutter's pans, the packaging and freezing crew scooped up the corn and put it into large pans. They cooled it with ice cubes and added salt and sugar to the mix. It took about twenty-four ears for each batch, and each batch filled four quart-sized freezer bags. The final step was pouring the golden kernels into plastic freezer bags and placing them into the freezer. Altogether, they generally processed about 120 quarts of corn, which was plenty for everyone until the next year.

Everyone switched jobs frequently to avoid boredom and overwork, and once the men had finished the husking, they joined the ladies in the basement. The constant chatter and kidding made the job go faster, and by 2:00, the job was done, except for cleaning the counters and utensils. The old deep freezer had to work overtime to freeze all the bags.

Finally, the floor coverings were taken outside and given a good shake. The ones with the most debris on them were hung on the clothesline and washed with the garden hose. At 3:00, everyone rested under the oak trees, the men in one circle and the women in another.

As Sara was walking onto the porch to join the others, she found Eddie and Missy sitting on the porch swing.

"What are you kids doing?" she asked.

"Nothing, just talking," Eddie replied.

He was sitting on one end of the swing and Missy lying on the seat with her head at the other end. They were content just to sit in the shade of the porch, enjoying the breeze.

"If you want some lemonade and homemade ice cream, come around to the back door in about ten minutes, okay?" Sara said.

"Homemade ice cream!" Eddie said excitedly. "We'll be there."

"Good," Sara said with a smile. "Why don't you two go out to the barn and find Jenny and Josh? I think they're in the haymow with the kittens. Tell them to come, too."

"Okay," said Missy as she and Eddie started off in the direction of the old barn.

By the time the kids returned, the ice cream was ready. Grandpa George pulled out the beater and let them spoon off the ice cream sticking to it while Grandma Madge scooped out the creamy mixture. Sara had the toppings ready, and Sue emerged from the kitchen with lemonade. It was a perfect ending to a hard day's work.

As the afternoon waned, Emma and John announce it was time to go home. They got their portion of sweet corn from the freezer, and George and Madge soon followed, but Sue stayed until after supper.

It was 10:00 before Sara got everyone bedded down. Missy slept with Jenny instead of with Eddie, which let Aunt Sara know Missy was now a young lady and sleeping with boy cousins was no longer appropriate. Josh bunked with Tim. Eddie had his own bed. Sara knew the days of big sweet corn canning fests would soon be over. The children were growing up, right before her eyes and large caches of sweet corn would no longer be required.

As she reminisced about previous years, she recalled the year Tom and his family got in on the action. The Maas household was really filled with kids that year. When it came to sleeping, Josh bunked with Jenny, Wendy and Robin got Tim's room, Missy slept with Eddie in his room, and Tim and Jake moved into the camper for the weekend. Tom and Kristy spent the night in town with Sara's parents. Sue and Jeff retired to Wilton with George and Madge. That also meant that Aunt Sara had to prepare a huge breakfast for all the nieces and nephews, but she didn't mind at all.

During the husking, Tom announced he had accepted a job with Vermeer Manufacturing, a maker of unique construction equipment and haying equipment in Pella, which meant they would be moving closer to Muscatine. Kristy had decided to become a stay-at home mom until the children were out of school, and she laughed as she wondered how a McWilliams family would be accepted in a Dutch community.

Jake helped pick and husk that year, but was thoroughly bored until Paul let him drive the Go Getter. He drove around the farmyard and up and down the lane all afternoon. Wendy had just turned fourteen, too young for her to stay at home but too old to play with Robin, Missy, and Eddie. She read a book and entertained Jenny and Josh. Robin, Missy, and Eddie were all ten that year and the three of them hung around together all weekend.

Missy was a freckled, peppy girl with sun-bleached hair who wasn't afraid of anything. She'd pick up frogs, toads, and bull snakes and she'd stick her hand under an old brooding hen to get to the eggs. Chicken poop between her toes didn't phase her one bit. Robin, on the other hand, was a beautiful, shy girl with long dark hair. Today she was as cute as a bug, because Aunt Sara braided her long hair into two long pigtails. They hung down her back like two dark ropes. She was afraid of many of nature's creatures. Eddie proudly showed the girls around the farm. They climbed in the haymow, played with the kittens, and rode their bikes around the farmyard.

After lunch, Missy begged her mom and Aunt Sara to let them go to the creek. The moms finally relented and gave their permission to go for two hours. Sara packed an old lunch box with water and cookies and an alarm clock set for 3:30 so they would know when to come back.

About 4:00, the three vagabonds returned to the house, giggling, and singing. Their arms and legs were covered with mud. Sara took one look at them and said, "Okay, everyone to the showers. Girls upstairs, Eddie to the basement. Kristy, will you help the girls find towels?"

The kids left for their respective bathrooms. Sara got Eddie his swimming trunks, and when Kristy came down to the basement laundry with the girls' clothes, she started a load of wash.

"Hey, Kristy, look at this," Sara said, holding up two pieces of Eddie's clothes.

"What do you see?"

"There's mud on Eddie's undershorts, but none on his outer ones. And look at this. There's mud on the girls' panties, too. You know what? I'm thinking we have some skinny-dippers in the family."

Just then, Sue entered the washroom and added with a smile, "And I'll bet Missy was the one who talked them into it. That girl will be the death of me yet—but I'm surprised she got Robin to go skinny-dipping. She's always been so quiet."

"It's always the quiet ones that surprise people most," Kristy said. "This is good for her, and I think it's all right at this age. They grow up so fast. If it wasn't for Tom and Judy Collins, I'd be an old maid. My mom never told me anything about sex or love. I suppose she was afraid to."

"Judy Collins? That's a name I haven't heard in a while. Whatever happened to her?" Sara asked.

"She went with my brother for a long time," Kristy replied. "Then they just drifted apart. At our last class reunion, she told me she was married to a career Navy man and had five kids. She was always a favorite date with the boys. She was good-looking, had big boobs, and was kind of wild. Young guys go for that, I guess."

"You were best friends with her," Sara said. "I remember her coming over with you to see Tom. How did you and Tom meet anyway?"

"It was kind of a surprise," Kristy responded. "Judy and I were in the backyard sunbathing in early June. We were lying on our stomachs and had unsnapped our tops. We had our radio blasting away and didn't hear my brother Bill and Tom sneak up on us with cups of ice water. They tossed the water on our backs and we both screamed and sat up—leaving our tops behind! Luckily for me, I had grabbed my top and was only exposed for a second, but not Judy. She was mad as a wet hen. She stood up and started chasing my brother, screaming, cussing and topless. She slapped and hit him until he finally grabbed her in a bear hug. Only then did she realize she was topless. She ran screaming back to the blanket and rolled herself inside. Then she got up, glared at Bill, and marched inside. Bill laughed so hard he could barely stand up."

"What about you two guys?" Sara asked.

"Tom, bless his heart, walked over, knelt down, and apologized," Kristy replied. "Then he bent over and gave me a peck on the cheek. He walked me back to the house and asked if he could take me to a drive-in movie the next night. I said yes, and the rest is history."

"That's a funny story." said Sue, joining in the laughter. "I don't know Tom all that well. We only see each other at family gatherings, but if he's anything like his sister, he has to be great." Sue looked at Sara and added, "You're like the kid sister I never had. The way you take care of this farm and Paul is amazing."

"She's like a sister to me, too. I grew up with three brothers. I never had anyone to talk to until I met Tom's sister," Kristy chimed in.

"Well, thank you, sister-in-laws," Sara said. "I kind of like you, too."

"Hey, do any of you beautiful women want to go swimming with us?" Paul called down the basement stairs. "We men and the kids are ready to go."

"I didn't bring a bathing suit," Kristy called up. "I guess I'll stay here."

"I bet I can find one that will fit you," said Sara. "All I have are two-piece suits, though. I can't find anything else to fit my tall body. You're about the same size on top, and I've got a couple older ones with smaller bottoms, since my bottom sort of expanded after three kids. Let's go see what we can find."

The three women went up to the kitchen and announced that they were going along. Sue would stop in Wilton to get her suit. Madge and George volunteered to go to Happy Joe's for pizza while everyone was swimming.

It was late before everyone finally made it to bed, and the next morning, Paul returned to the house to find coffee and rolls waiting after chores. His dad had raided the local bakery before he came out. Right after lunch, Sue and Jeff gathered their crew and share of the corn and headed home to Waterloo. Tom and Kristy stayed until afternoon, vowing to visit more often since they had moved closer.

Sunday night's supper consisted of leftover pizza. After the long weekend, Sara was too tired to cook. They all went to bed early. The sweet corn was done for another year.

Chapter Eighteen
Paul's Close Call

On their anniversary, Paul, Sara, and the kids went to Happy Joe's to celebrate. When it was time for bed, Sara took Mrs. B's nightgown out of its box and put it on as the kids headed off to bed.

As Paul and Sara watched the news in the den, Paul said, "I must have eaten too much. I've got a stomachache. I'll take some Pepto-Bismol and go to bed. Maybe we'll have to postpone our usual anniversary celebration, hon."

"That's okay," Sara said, giving him a hug, "It's only a day, and every day is special with you."

The next morning Paul was still feeling ill. He finished chores and stayed on the sofa most of the day.

"Maybe you should go to see the doctor," Sara volunteered.

"If I don't feel better tomorrow, I'll go," Paul agreed.

The next day he felt somewhat better and seemed to improve a little each day until a week after Labor Day, when he started cutting silage. He worked long days, but the pain in his abdomen persisted and although it came and went, Paul felt weaker following each episode.

The day he finished the silage, the pain grew intense, sending Paul to bed early with a promise he'd visit Dr. Barnes the next morning. At 10:30, he went into the bathroom and vomited. It was full of blood. Shortly thereafter, he had diarrhea, which was also bloody.

"Sara, I need some help," Paul called from the bathroom. His voice was barely above a whisper.

Sara ran to the bathroom and saw blood on the stool and lavatory. It was also running down Paul's legs. "My god, Paul, what's happening?"

"I don't know," he said weakly, "but I can barely stand up."

Sara helped Paul to the shower, got him undressed, and started to clean him off. She was afraid that he was hemorrhaging internally. She screamed down the hallway, "Eddie! Wake up! Call 9-1-1! Dad's sick. Get an ambulance!"

Eddie peeked into the bathroom and saw the blood running down his dad's legs. Instantly he turned and ran to the bedroom and dialed 9-1-1. When the emergency operator answered, he said urgently, "This is Ed Maas. My dad is bleeding and needs an ambulance. Please hurry. We live at 3370 170th Street."

"We'll be there as soon as we can. Keep your dad lying down. Is he bleeding because of a cut or injury?"

"No! He's bleeding out of his butt and he's vomiting blood."

"Okay, Ed, an ambulance is on the way. Now don't hang up. Just lay the phone down so I can hear what's going on."

Eddie laid the phone on the nightstand and ran back to the bathroom. He helped his mom get his dad back to the bedroom, where they sat him on a towel at the edge of the bed. Paul moaned and lay back on the bed, conscious, but very weak.

"An ambulance is on the way," Eddie said. "I think I can hear the siren now."

The operator on the phone started talking. "Mrs. Maas, this is Jill Borden. Is there anything I can do?"

Sara picked up the phone and reported to Jill, "We can hear the ambulance now. They can't be far away. Thanks, Jill."

As Sara grabbed her bathrobe and wrapped it around her bloody pajamas, she said, "Eddie, get in the chest of drawers and get your dad some boxer shorts and a t-shirt—quick!"

They'd barely gotten Paul dressed before the fire truck and ambulance were pulling up outside. Soon Fire Chief Joe Hagan was knocking on the door. Eddie led firemen and EMTs upstairs to the bedroom, where they quickly put Paul on a backboard. It took four of them to maneuver Paul down the stairs, where they transferred him to a gurney and rushed him out to the ambulance.

"Do you want to ride with us, Mrs. Maas?" Chief Hagan, who was also one of the EMTs, asked.

Realizing what she was wearing, Sara exclaimed, "I can't go in my pajamas. I've got to put on some different clothes."

Joe said, "I'll tell you what. We'll send the ambulance on ahead and you can ride with Deputy Berry when you're ready. You know Mrs. Maas, this is the hardest part of this job—taking someone you know personally to the hospital. I'll tell the deputy to wait for you."

"Thanks, Joe," Sara said. As the ambulance sped away, she turned to Eddie and said, "Call Grandma Madge and tell her they've taken your dad to the hospital. Then ask if she can come out and help get everyone off to school."

"Okay, Mom," Eddie replied as they turned to go back into the house. "Dad's going to be alright, isn't he?"

"I'm sure he'll be fine," said Sara, putting her arm around her son. "I've got to change clothes in a hurry. I'll call you in the morning before you go to school."

At the hospital, Sara found Paul lying in a bed, his body full of tubes and patches. Nurses were making him as comfortable as possible. Dr. Barnes had been called and would be there early the next morning. It would be a long night, but Paul seemed to be resting quietly as Sara tried to get some sleep on the room's little couch.

Madge arrived at the farm about 11:15. Eddie told her what had happened. Madge cleaned up the bathroom. She had never seen such a mess. Thoughts raged through her mind. What was happening to Paul? It was after midnight before anyone went to sleep, including Tim and Jenny, who had been awakened by the sirens and commotion.

The next morning, Madge let the children sleep as long as possible. She decided to drive them to school so they wouldn't have to take the long bus ride. Madge had to wait until George arrived with some wearable clothes. She had literally thrown some clothes on over her nightgown when Eddie called. George came early and delivered some clothes to Madge so she could take the children to school. He started chores before she returned. When he had finished, they headed for the hospital.

Dr. Barnes arrived at 5:00 that morning. Tests showed Paul had lost nearly two pints of blood and she wanted to take x-rays before ordering a transfusion. When the x-rays showed very little, she ordered a colonoscopy and an endoscopy to follow the transfusions. Paul needed to rebuild his losses before any more stress was applied to his body. Sara called home with little news. Dr. Barnes had checked in to tell her she had ordered several tests with the hope of finding out the cause of Paul's problem.

By 6:00 that afternoon, Dr. Barnes told Paul, "I think you should go to University Hospital. They have newer equipment and more doctors. I'll have you see Dr. Leon Howe. He's an internal medicine specialist. They'll get to the bottom of your problem. Is that okay?"

"Certainly," Sara replied.

On Wednesday morning, Sara followed the ambulance to the University Hospital, where Dr. Howe ordered a CAT scan on Paul's abdomen. When the results were in, he said, "Mr. Maas, we've found a large mass in the area of your small intestine. We can't be certain what it is, so I'd like to schedule an exploratory surgery on Thursday and see if we can solve this puzzle. I wish I had better news, but there's no other way to be certain of what we are dealing with. Do you want me to go ahead with the surgery? Drs. Ragan and Chou will be assisting me. They both specialize in gastro-intestinal medicine."

"Of course, Dr. Howe," said Paul. "I haven't been feeling well for about a month."

Sara nodded her head in agreement.

"Good," said Dr. Howe. "I'll have the nurse give you a time and explain the procedure. I'll see you both in the morning."

The doctor seemed so precise and self-assured that neither Paul nor Sara doubted his ability. When he had left the room, Sara said, "I'll call your mother, then mine. They'll have to get the kids off to school and I'm sure your dad will help with the chores."

When Sara called Madge, Madge asked if it would be alright with her if she called Sue to wait with Sara during Paul's surgery. Fifteen minutes later, Sue called to say she'd be on her way over to stay the night with Sara as soon as Missy got home from school. Sara then called Emma, who in turn called Tom. Less than a half hour later, Kristy called to tell Sara she'd meet them at the hospital at 7:00.

Sara and Sue got a motel room not far from the hospital. The surgery was scheduled for 7:00, but when Sara and Sue walked into Paul's room at six, nurses and aides were already getting him ready. An aide showed the women where they could wait.

At seven, Kristy arrived. "I can't believe this is happening," she said. "Paul's always been in such good health."

A few minutes later, Pastor Tom walked into the waiting room and they all prayed together. Three hours went by, then four. The more time passed, the more worried Sara became. She couldn't sit still, so she paced the room and hallway as Sue, Kristy, and Pastor Tom chatted quietly.

Just before noon, Dr. Howe finally came into the waiting room. "The surgery went fine. We found a large tumor called a carcinoid in Paul's small intestine. We removed it and about twelve inches of his small intestine, and the good news is that it wasn't malignant. We also got to it in time. There was a possibility the tumor could have ruptured on the outside of the organ and he would have bled to death internally. He's very fortunate to have received such good care immediately after the tumor burst. You can tell your son that his help probably saved his father's life. Paul should make a full recovery, since he's in great physical condition. He'll be in some pain because we had to cut a lot of muscle, but we'll continue his pain medicine as long as he needs it. The recovery period could be fairly long. He won't be able to lift more than five pounds for at least two weeks. Then he can gradually increase his activity as he feels fit. I'd say he will be back to normal about Christmas."

"Oh, thank you, doctor," said Sara, giving Dr. Howe a hug.

"Being a farmer, you need to keep him from driving tractors, climbing ladders, or any heavy lifting for at least eight weeks," Dr. Howe added with a smile. "I know it won't be easy, but I know you can do it. I'll want to see him again in two weeks. Any questions?"

"Can the kids see him?" Sara asked.

"How old are they?" Dr. Howe asked.

"Thirteen, twelve, and nine."

"That should be fine. He'll probably be here for five or six days. I won't be releasing him until he's eating again," said the doctor.

"Thanks again for taking care of my husband," Sara said, wiping tears from her eyes.

"No problem, Mrs. Maas. I'll either call or see you every day until Paul's released."

When Dr. Howe left, Sara hugged Pastor Tom and asked him to thank God for His help and everyone who helped today. As he began to pray, Sara finally broke down, no longer able to control her emotions now that it was finally over. Sue and Kristi sat on either side of her, holding her hands and wiping away their own tears.

Pastor Tom had to leave, but told Sara he'd be back in the morning. Shortly after he had left, a nurse came into the waiting room to let them know Paul had been returned to his room.

Sara entered the room first and found Paul awake, but groggy. Sara walked over and gently kissed him on the forehead.

"It's over, honey," she said softly. "I'm right here to take care of you."

Paul smiled weakly, then closed his eyes and drifted back to sleep.

Several times over the next few hours, Paul had spasms of pain that caused him to grab the bed rails and shake them. It happened once when the nurse was checking in.

"My, my," she commented, "he sure is strong. I hope the bed holds together. I was in the OR with Dr. Howe and he mentioned that there wasn't an ounce of fat on Paul's body. He has muscles like a college athlete."

Sue called her folks and Kristy called Sara's parents to tell them the surgery went well. Then they each called their husbands and let them know they'd be staying another night. By nightfall, Paul could have a little water and ice.

Sara told Sue and Kristy, "I'm going to stay here. Why don't you two go and get a bite to eat."

They agreed and told Sara they'd bring her back something. She was holding Paul's hand as they left.

About an hour later, Sue and Kristy returned with a ham sandwich and a soda for Sara. She didn't realize how hungry she was until she took a bite. Even though the sandwich was soggy, it tasted very good. The women decided to take shifts through the night. Sue would take the first shift, then Sara, then Kristy.

At ten o'clock, Sara and Kristi left for the motel. Sara was exhausted and fell asleep before Kristy, so she changed Sara's alarm to 5:00 instead of one. Then she set hers for 1:00 to give Sara some much-needed sleep. At 1:00, Kristi returned to the hospital and relieved Sue, explaining what she had done.

"I'll try to make her put some clothes on before she leaves," Sue said with a smile. "When she finds out it is 5:00, she's going to be hard to stop."

As Sue slipped into the other bed at the motel, Sara didn't even move, even when Sue stubbed her toe on a chair and began hopping around, trying to stifle a few choice words.

At five, Sara's alarm sounded and Sue heard Sara exclaim, "My gosh, I'm late! How could I have set the alarm so wrong?"

"Calm down, Sara," Sue assured her. "Kristy took your shift. She reset your alarm so you could get some sleep. You just be sure to put some clothes on before you tear out of here."

Sara was thankful for Kristy's consideration. Knowing that Kristy was taking care of Paul, she showered and put on a little makeup before she left for the hospital. When she arrived in Paul's room, she found him sleeping, with Kristy sleeping in a chair beside the bed, her head resting on the mattress.

Sara gently tapped Kristy's shoulder and whispered, "Kristy, wake up. I'll take over now."

Kristi lifted her head, looked at Sara, and said, "I guess I fell asleep. Paul's been comfortable. He woke up an hour ago and asked for you, but I told him you were sleeping. Then he said, 'Good! She looked so tired.'"

Sara smiled as her eyes welled with tears. As she fumbled in her purse for a hankie, she said, "Kristy, I love him so much. It's hard for me to see him hurting."

"I know," said Kristy, patting Sara's hand. "You and Paul have a special partnership. I love Tom, but it's being together all day that binds you two so closely. I wish more of us could experience that same feeling."

"You'd better get back to the motel or you'll look like me tomorrow," Sara joked.

"Right, and I don't want to miss breakfast with Sue. She's a hoot, isn't she?" Kristy said.

"Yes, I've got some great sister-in-laws, and one is sort of crazy," Sara agreed.

Although they hadn't known he was awake, they heard Paul say, "You're talking about my sister, aren't you?"

His comment made all of them laugh, but Paul grimaced because laughing made his incision hurt.

"I had better be going. See you both in a couple hours," Kristy said as she put on her jacket.

As Kristy walked out, Sara asked Paul, "How are you feeling?"

"Sore—and hungry," he replied.

"I can let you have a drink of water, but you can't have any solid food for a couple days," Sara said. "You do know that the doctors removed twelve inches of your small intestine, right? It wasn't malignant, so you won't have to go through chemo or radiation, but you won't be able to lift anything for at least eight weeks. We'll have to get some help for the harvest, but don't worry. We've been in tight spots before. There's always a way."

"I know, hon," Paul said drowsily. "Now I think I need to get some more sleep."

When Sue and Kristy returned at eight, they found Paul watching TV and Sara asleep in the chair.

"Who's watching who?" Sue teased. With that, Sara woke up, so Sue added, "Why don't you get some breakfast? I'll watch my little brother. Kristy, you go with her and make sure she eats something. We'll plan our day when you get back."

At noon, Kristi said she thought she'd head for home since Paul was out of danger. Sue said she'd stay until her parents arrived in the afternoon.

When George and Madge arrived at 2:00, it was obvious Madge was quite shaken about her son's condition, but George immediately began planning how to bring in the harvest without Paul.

"I'll just hire someone," he said. "Maybe Sam Goodman can help. He does a lot of custom work."

"Oh, hush up, George," Madge snapped. "Paul's in no shape to talk the harvest."

About a half hour later, they said their goodbyes so they could get back to the farm for chores. Sue was going to leave with them.

"Don't chase any of the nurses, little brother," Sue said as she left the room, "and you'd better keep an eye on Sara. There are some pretty cute doctors around here."

Emma took care of the kids that night. She and John would bring the kids to visit Paul on Saturday.

When the weekend came, Emma, John, and the kids tiptoed into Paul's room at 10:00. Paul was feeling better, but he was asleep. Jenny and Tim were very quiet, and the moment that Jenny touched her dad's hand to see if he was alive, he woke up.

"Hi, Sweetie Pie. How are you?" Paul said.
"Are you going to be alright, Daddy?" Jenny asked softly.

"I'm going to be just fine," he answered.

Tim didn't say a word. He was busy looking at all the gadgets and monitors surrounding his father. Eddie was more emotional. He'd seen all the blood that night and had helped get his dad to the ambulance. Just as Eddie was reaching for Paul's hand, Paul coughed and grimaced from the pain. Eddie couldn't stand it anymore.

He laid his head on Paul's chest and sobbed, "Oh, Dad, don't die. We need you!"

Paul gently stroked his son's dark hair and said, "Don't worry, son. I'm not going to die, and Dr. Howe told me that you were a big help to your mom that night. I want to thank you for being so brave, but I'm going to need you to keep helping around the farm until I can get on my feet again, okay?"

Eddie raised his head and nodded. Sara stepped forward and gently pulled Eddie away from the bed, wiping tears from her own eyes. Emma and John were also sniffling and blowing their noses. It was a beautiful thing to see a father and son so closely connected.

Paul stayed in the hospital for another five days before the Dr. Howe released him with strict orders: No lifting! No climbing ladders! No tractor driving! For at least eight weeks! It would be a challenge, but the consequences of breaking the rules were great.

Chapter Nineteen
Good Neighbors

It was George's turn to worry. How were he and Sara going to get the harvest done? She was a good tractor driver, but she wasn't familiar with the drying system. He could drive the combine, but Paul hadn't even begun to get it ready for harvest. He must have looked worried at the Wilton Coffee Shop when he went for his morning doughnut and coffee with the boys.

Sam Goodman asked, "How's Paul doing, George?"

George explained the situation in detail and added that he was worried about how Sara and he were going to get everything done. The kids were still too young to help very much.

"George, my friend," said Sam, "by now you ought to know you'll get your corn and beans in. With all the times you and Paul helped the rest of us in our time of need, I think it's time we repaid the favor. What you do say, boys? Think we need to have a combine party? When the crop's ready, George, we'll all come over and cut the beans. Then we'll come back and get the corn. Don't worry, and tell Paul and Sara not to worry, either."

A resounding "You bet!" came from everyone at the table and those overhearing the conversation at the nearby booths.

When Paul came home from the hospital, he didn't feel strong enough to venture outside. He even had to be helped up and down the stairs. The bandage covering his incision had to be changed two or three times a day because of seepage from the wound. It took Sara twenty minutes to change the cloth, and all Paul could do was lie still while she worked.

His breakfast consisted of oatmeal or pudding, since he was limited to soft foods until the wound stopped draining. It would be two weeks before he could have a hamburger, and that would have to be with no ketchup or mustard. Spicy foods were also a no-no. He could have soft serve ice cream because of its low butterfat content. Sara could tell he was feeling better when on one of their ice cream runs, Paul noticed neighbors combining soybeans. He hoped their neighbors would be able to keep their word.

Early October, Paul was sitting on the front porch. George and Sara had just finished chores. George was sitting on the porch rail talking to Paul when Sam Goodman's pickup pulled up the lane. He stopped under the oak trees, walked up the front steps, pulled up a chair beside Paul, and asked, "How many acres of soybeans and corn are we talking about, Paul?"

"About 300 acres of soybeans and 400 of corn," Paul replied.

"Well, we'll need at least six combines for the beans," said Sam. "Are you going to store any?"

"We'd like to," George said. "We usually store about 4,000 bushels in the old bin at Becker's, but this year anything goes."

"Tell you what I think," Sam said. "Why don't you store 7,000 or so in the bins here at the home place? You won't have time to move corn around much this year. I'd store the beans because they don't need to be dried. You've got two drying bins that hold about 25,000 bushels of corn. That will feed your calves, right? I could rent the two bins at Becker's for my soybeans. I'd fill them first, then bring my ten-inch auger over here to fill yours when we come to do your beans."

"You don't have to rent the bins. You can use them for free," said Paul. "Your help with the harvest is worth it."

"That's not necessary," said Sam. "Boldt's and Conner's will furnish the semis to deliver to Central Corn. Three hundred acres should be about 15,000 bushels. I'd put seven here at home and ship the rest. How do you feel about that?"

"Sounds like a good plan, Sam. I knew you'd figure something out," George said.

"Now we have the beans taken care of, Paul. How are you, anyway?" Sam asked.

"I'm getting better. Just haven't got any strength. I'm as weak as a kitten and I've still got three weeks with this belly wrap. I really can't thank you enough for helping us."

"Think nothing of it, Paul. You'd be the first one there if it was me. Now the corn will be a little more difficult. Four hundred acres equals about 60,000 bushels or more. That's a big figure for one day. Do you think George and Sara can fill the drying bins?"

"Sure, she's the best tractor driver for miles around," George chimed in.

"I thought so. I think the Petersen brothers and I can sneak in here between our dryer fills and open up the fields. You and Sara can fill the two dryer bins here. The rest can go to Central Corn. Dan talked to them and they're going to close the elevator for half a day when we do your corn. They'll only take corn from here. Any trucker looking for something to haul can come here and get a load."

"Super! That's a great worry off our backs," Paul said. "I know Sara will be concerned about feeding everyone. How many do you think we'll have?"

"The bean day she'll only need some kind of afternoon lunch for the boys. There will be about twelve to fifteen men. We won't get started much before noon. They can eat lunch before they come," said Sam.

"She and Madge and Emma can handle that. The corn crowd will be different, though. They can start in the morning."

George said, "We could clean up the shop and eat in there. It's warm. We can get some tables and chairs from church, but we'll need some kind of number for how many to feed."

"No problem. I think my wife and Madge can round up enough

neighbor ladies to help serve lunch. I'd say there would be close to thirty hungry guys to feed. It will be a blast. Well, I'd better be going. See you soon if it's not raining. I'll be around to set up the auger, George. Take it easy, Paul. We'll get everything done. Don't you worry," Sam said as he left the porch.

"It's sure great to have good neighbors," Paul sighed. "They never let you down."

October 10th dawned bright and sunny. By 10:00 the first combine pulled up the drive. Sam's farm assistant set the big auger in the bean bin. By noon each operator was greasing his machine and mounting the head to his combine. The chase wagons were lining up along the lane. Three big 600-bushel wagons and tractors sat by the bins. Boldt's had two semis idling on the road. The co-op was there to furnish everyone with fuel.

The first machine to start was the Petersen's new John Deere, its thirty-foot header gobbled up the standing soybeans. Dust and chaff flew out of the rear of the combine. Don Dietz followed with his Case IH. Two of the smaller combines headed to the field across the creek. It was cut into small rolling pieces and their twenty-foot headers were more adaptable to the terrain.

At noon a surprise combine arrived. Joe Ewing, from near Bennett, pulled in. He knew George through the County Board of Supervisors Association and had heard about the party. He enlarged the color scheme with his big yellow New Holland machine. Sam sent him and one of the Strongs to the Becker place along with the semis. Sam enjoyed masterminding the whole operation and keeping tabs on everyone by cell phone or radio. His calculations showed that they were harvesting close to sixty acres an hour and would be done by five.

He told Sara to have a small lunch planned about 3:00. Most of the wives of the combiners had sent desserts with their men for lunch, so it was a virtual smorgasbord of the finest baked goods in the county. Each woman had her specialty and had sent it in abundance. Sara and Madge and Emma packed all the cookies and brownies and cakes into the pickup.

Madge dashed off to Muscatine to pick the children up early from school. Sara wanted them in on the excitement. John and Emma drove the truck to the field and Sara loaded Paul into the van. He also wanted to be a part of the day.

Sam Goodman made sure all the men arrived for lunch at about the same time. He had also contacted the *Muscatine Journal,* which sent out a reporter and photographer. The reporter interviewed several men and Paul and Sara. The local TV station was also on the scene with a camera and reporter, telling everyone the story would be on The Good News segment of the 6:00 and 10:00 news.

Lunch lasted half an hour, and featured lots of good-natured kidding between the men, each trying to outdo the others with their stories. They kidded George about having to pay a lot of income tax because of the good yield. He said he'd be glad to pay, if he really was going to get as much as they said. Paul leaned against the van during most of the lunch period, but he finally had to sit in a lawn chair Sara had brought along, showing the others that he wasn't just faking his illness. Most of the guys stopped and talked with him, and by the time the lunch break was ending, Paul was having trouble holding back his tears.

Sam broke up the lunch break by announcing, "Boys, we'd better get back to work if we want to get done before dark."

Joe Ewing told Sam he'd quit around 4:30. He wanted to be able to drive home before dusk, but he'd be back in the morning for his header. Sam agreed, saying he wanted everyone home before dark, since big machines and narrow roads were a bad combination in the fall.

As Eddie admired Dan Petersen's new combine, Dan said, "Want to ride in it, Eddie? I got an extra seat in the cab."

"I sure would!" Eddie said, looking at his mom.

When Sara nodded, Eddie quickly climbed into the cab, smiling from ear to ear.

As the women gathered up the leftovers, Sara helped Paul back into the van. As he was waiting for her to finish, Glen Babson walked over to Paul and said, "You've helped me so many times and always refused any pay, so I'm glad I finally get a chance to repay you. If Sara or your dad needs any help weaning calves, please call me. I'll be more than glad to come over. You're my best neighbor."

"Thank you," Paul replied, his voice cracking.

As Sara and Paul drove slowly from the field toward the house, they passed Dave Petersen, who was repairing a broken section on his grain head. A gust of wind blew bean dust off the back of the combine. It swirled around and soon Dan was dusting himself off.

"Remember when you helped me fix that old 1460?" Paul said with a smile.

"Do I? I'll never forget it. I can still feel that dust," Sara replied, shrugging her shoulders as if they still itched.

"For years after that episode, I'd get sleepy in the cab and remember looking at you with no shirt on, and that would wake me right up," Paul said. "You had on white underpants with pink roses and a pink elastic waistband. "

"Wow!" said Sara with a smile. "I remember no shirt, no jacket, no bra, and as I recall, I took off my jeans because they were full of dust, too. I had nothing on but my underpants. I guess I was just crazy in love, but it was kind of fun."

"I don't know about you, but I'm still crazy in love with you," said Paul.

"That talk will get you in trouble in bed, though we'd have to be careful with your incision."

"I'll take that chance. I'll rest up the whole afternoon if I have to."

Back at the house, Paul collapsed on the sofa, exhausted. He could hear neighbors pulling out and saying their goodbyes and promising to return in a couple weeks to do the corn. That night the event did make the airwaves. In fact, it was on the national news because one of the major networks picked it up for their own good neighbor segment.

The first week in November, Sam Goodman and Don Petersen took turns opening up the cornfields and helping Sara and George with the drying bins. Paul was feeling stronger and helped with the management. This time there were eight combines, seven chase wagons, and ten semis.

The sheriff sent two deputies to direct traffic. Sara let Ed, Tim, and Jenny stay home from school so they wouldn't miss the show.

The neighborhood wives helped prepare and serve the noon meal in the cleaned-out shop. There were roasters of ground beef and chicken, all kinds of salads, mashed potatoes, baked beans, and corn. For the dessert there were ten different kinds of homemade pies and cakes. If the men went back to the field hungry, it was their own fault. Many wrapped up some cookies and cake for later in the afternoon.

"If you see my combine sitting still, don't worry. I'm just taking a nap," Dan joked. "All this food is going to make me sleepy."

"I've got a whole bunch of firecrackers to wake you up," Sam responded with a chuckle.

By nightfall the corn was finished. Some stayed and visited with Paul, but most said they'd be back in the morning for their combines. The elevator closed at 4:00, so several truckers were forced to dump their loads the next day, but none seemed to mind. Paul and George thanked everyone for their help and returned to the house.

"You know, you work all your life to help others. You never figure they'll have to help you," George mused. "It's great to have such wonderful neighbors and friends. My dad used to say that you can't farm without your neighbors, and I guess that's still true."

The next week, Paul mailed thank you notes to all those who had helped. Just before Thanksgiving Day, he also placed a thank you ad in the local paper. It read: "To all our friends and neighbors who helped harvest our crops: The American farmer is always in friendly competition with his neighbor and desires to do his best with his own farm. He constantly looks over the fence to see what his fellow farmer is doing, but the best of his character shows when one of his neighbors, because of health or some other reason, can't harvest his crops. Then he drops what he's doing and hurries to help his friend do whatever is necessary. This year our friends and neighbors came to our aid, and we want to say thank you, and God bless each and every one of you. We know we'll never be able repay the amount of help you've given us. Madge and George Maas, Sara and Paul Maas, and family."

Chapter Twenty
Triumph and Tragedy

When Ed (as he now liked to be called) began his senior year in high school, he also began what would probably be his last active year in 4-H. He had shown beef animals, both steers and heifers, since the age of ten. His dad and Grandpa George had helped in the early years, but for the past several years, he had pretty much been on his own. He'd had some success, but never a champion in any class. That year one of his entries bloomed at fair time.

He placed first in the crossbred steer class, then showed for Grand Champion and received the Reserve Champion honor. It was the best he'd ever done. He decided to try his luck at the state fair, and the entire family was on hand to see him take first in his class again. When competing for Grand Champion, he again came in second, but Reserve Champion at the Iowa State Fair was a goal far greater than he'd ever dreamed.

To top off his 4-H experience, a cattleman from Texas offered to pay a premium for his steer. He wanted Ed's animal for his own show herd at the Texas State Fair. It didn't take Ed long to make up his mind. The extra money would go toward college.

In September, Ed started as a middle linebacker on the football team. He liked contact sports, whereas his brother, Tim, preferred singing in the school choir. Ed worked hard and was fairly good, making the All-Conference team and receiving several local honors, but basketball was really Ed's sport. He was 6'4" like his dad and packed strong shoulders and legs. He also had a deadly three-point shot from the corner.

Ed was a gifted athlete, but he had to give some credit for his success to Tim. Tim stood 6'9" and was a talented basketball player, but also was a gifted vocalist, so he had to make a choice between chorus and basketball. To make the decision easier on Tim, the choir director and the basketball coach worked out a schedule that would allow Tim to do both. It meant the Muscatine High basketball team had two Maas brothers as starters—Tim as center and Ed as a power forward. They were the cornerstones of the team.

The true powerhouse of the league was North Scott High Lancers of Eldridge, who amassed a 26-0 record that year, led by Kevin Staub, a prolific scorer. Muscatine tied with two other teams for second place in league play, but they managed to make the state tournament play-offs. The Muskies had taken the Lancers into overtime at their game in Muscatine, North Scott's only close game during regular season play.

North Scott rolled through their sub-tournament opponents with ease, but Muscatine was in the other bracket and won their early games, which set up another meeting with the Lancers on a neutral court in Davenport. Sara's parents had always had season tickets and followed the Muskies through good times and bad. They weren't about to miss a game in which two of their grandsons were starting. They came early to the farm and rode to Davenport with Sara, Paul, and Jenny in the van. They also picked up George and Madge in Wilton.

All seven walked into the gym together. Jenny soon found some of her school friends and disappeared, but the adults had six seats in a row. The men sat at one end of the row and the women at the other. Unexpectedly, Mrs. Staub, the grandmother of the North Scott's star player, sat down beside them. Madge recognized her from the State Cattlemen's Association and knew that she always looked down on the Muscatine crowd.

They exchanged greetings, but it soon became evident that Mrs. Staub would be controlling the conversation, going on and on about how great her grandson was and how he was being recruited by a number of Division I colleges. She went so far as to say her family had already bought their tickets for the state tournament. They'd made reservations at a Des Moines motel for all three nights because she was sure North Scott would win the state championship. Finally, as the game was about to start, she asked Madge about her grandsons.

Madge looked Mrs. Staub in the eye and said, "I have two grandsons playing tonight and they both start. We haven't bought tickets for Des Moines, but maybe we'll get some after tonight."

Mrs. Staub looked surprised, and turned her attention to the team introductions. The Muskies had been designated the visiting team, so they were introduced first.

"Starting at forward, 6'4" senior, Ed Maas," the announcer said, "and at center, his little brother, a junior at 6'9", Tim Maas." The crowd laughed as the announcer continued, "At the other forward, 6'3" senior, Jeremy Cousins; at guard, 5'11" senior, Josh Logan; and at the other guard position, 6'1" junior, Thad Jefferies."

The Muskie five waited at midcourt as the North Scott starters were introduced. The last player introduced was Kevin Staub, and the Lancer fans went wild.

The referee tossed the ball at center court and Tim easily controlled the tip. Jeremy Cousins found Ed standing all alone in the corner and threw him the ball. Ed caught it and swished a three-pointer. Now it was the Muskie fans' turn to go crazy. Staub took a pass and drove for the basket, but he found Tim in his way, his arms up straight, and bowled him over. He made a face as the ref called him for charging, but said nothing. The quarter ended with Muscatine up 12–10.

The second quarter started with Cousins stealing the ball from Staub. He passed it to Ed, who hit another three-pointer. Staub tried to penetrate the MHS defense, but Tim blocked his shot. Ed recovered the ball and threw an alley-oop pass to Tim who had quickly hustled down the floor. Tim grabbed the ball in stride and stuffed it with a thunderous dunk. To make matters worse for the Lancers, Staub picked up his second foul on the play as he tried to block Tim's dunk.

Staub immediately lost his cool and shoved Tim as he tried to get up after the foul had sent him sprawling. He picked up an intentional foul, which gave the Lancer coach no choice but to send him to the bench for the rest of the half. Although he was hurting from the hard foul, Tim calmly sank two free throws before he, too, went to the bench. The half ended with the Muskies leading, 24–18.

Mrs. Staub had nothing much to say during halftime, but she did managed to tell Madge that North Scott was a second half team and would soon get back on track. When the second half began, it appeared Mrs. Staub might be right. North Scott scored six straight points to tie the game. Mrs. Staub started to smile.

Then the Maas brothers began to take charge of the game. Ed stole the ball twice, each time hitting a three-pointer. Tim blocked two more shots. Staub hooked Tim with an illegal elbow, picking up his fourth foul.

"They're just picking on him because he's the star," Mrs. Staub lamented. "The refs are out to get him."

Muscatine led 48–36 as the fourth quarter began. Staub drove the ball the length of the court, but ran into Ed under the basket, picking up his fifth foul. He went ballistic, screaming at Ed and the referee. He finally had to be physically removed from the court by several players and coaches.

After that, the fight seemed to go out of the Lancers and Muscatine won the game, 62–48. Mighty North Scott had been defeated and wouldn't be going to Des Moines. Before the game was over, Mrs. Staub stood and left, not even looking at Madge. Madge glanced at Sara and Emma and flashed them an impish smile.

In Des Moines, the Muskies won their opening round game, but lost in the semifinals to Ankeny. Ed didn't continue his sports career that summer. He needed money for college, so he worked for a local seed corn company all summer. He drove the de-tasseling rig and met a cute auburn-haired girl named Carol Wilson who rode the outside basket on his rig. While most of the girls wore as little as possible to get a good tan, Carol wore a blouse and shorts. She seemed above the others in maturity and Ed enjoyed her company at lunchtime. He asked for a date, and soon she was his only date. Ed graduated from high school in early June. He had the traditional afterschool party, a big barbeque. This was surely Ed's year.

Later in June, the corn needed to be delivered to the river terminal. Paul was busy making hay and chopping haylage. They decided to have Boldt's haul the corn. They could come with two trucks, but only one driver. George and Jerry Boldt worked out a system. George would fill the trucks and Jerry would deliver. The two started on the second bin of grain.

The first load came out easily. Then Jerry parked the second truck and headed for the river with the first. George began to fill the second. About halfway through the loading process, the corn stopped flowing from the bin, so George climbed the ladder to check on the problem.

A few moments later, Paul pulled into the yard with the round baler and noticed that the auger was running and corn was overflowing the sides of the trailer. He turned off the auger, but George was nowhere around. Just as Jerry was arriving with another truck, Paul looked up and saw the open bin entry door.

"No, Dad!" he shouted as he clambered up the ladder and peered into the bin.

He saw George's cowboy hat on top of the grain and a glove lying on the cross auger of the stirring system. Paul rushed down the ladder and headed for the shop as Jerry stepped out of the truck.

"Dad's in the bin!" yelled Paul. "Call the fire department! I'll get a cutting torch. Hurry!"

Sara heard the commotion and came running. She opened the walk-in door as Jerry helped Paul start to burn through the steel panels in the doorway with the cutting torch. The smell of burnt corn permeated the air and white smoke from the hot galvanized steel rose from the torch.

Finally the first panel gave way and corn began pouring from the opening. Paul immediately started cutting another hole as the firefighters arrived and began slicing more holes in the side of the bin with metal cutting saws and pulling metal away from the bin. An auger was thrust into the opening to unload the corn onto the ground.

Finally, one of the firefighters at the top of the bin hollered, "I see his head! I'm going in. Someone hold my safety rope!"

As the first firefighter crawled into the bin, the others widened the hole so another man could go in. Within seconds, they had uncovered George's head, but his body was lifeless. They pulled George's body out of the corn and slid him over the grain to the door. Paul helped lift his dad from the bin and then sat on the ground, cradling his lifeless body in his arms.

"Dad, you old fool," Paul sobbed, "Why did you go in there? Why? Why?"

Sara put her arms around Paul as the firemen gently pulled George's body from his grasp. They loaded George into an ambulance, but it was only a formality.

"We'll take the body to the hospital," the fire chief told them, "because it's the law. Do you want me to go over to Madge's or will you?"

"We'll tell Mom," Paul choked. "I don't want her to find out from someone else."

Sara and Paul returned to the house, changed clothes, and headed for Wilton. When they arrived, Madge met them at the door. The look on their faces told her something was wrong.

"It's George, isn't it?" she asked.

"Yes," Paul said, his voice quivering. "He smothered in the grain bin. I can't understand why he went in, Mom. We tried everything we could, but we couldn't revive him. I tried, Mom."

"I'm sure you did, son," said Madge, tears streaming down her face. "Sometimes only God knows why." Then Madge began to wobble and only managed to say, "Paul, I think I'm going to faint" before she collapsed in his arms.

Sara helped Paul get Madge into the house and onto the sofa. When she came around, Madge asked softly, "What do we do now?"

"First, we'll have to call Sis. I'll phone her right away," Paul answered.

"Would you like to stay with us tonight?" Sara asked.

"Maybe I should. Sue won't be able to come until tomorrow."

When they got home, the phone was ringing. It was Sue. She insisted on coming down right away. It would take three hours, but she'd be there as soon as she could. Ed and Tim were called at the seed corn plant. The supervisor told Paul he'd send them home as soon as they came in from the field. Sara called the Wilton pool to get a hold of Jenny. Everyone was waiting in the living room when Sue arrived. Though she was generally calm and stable, Sue was obviously upset when she arrived. Paul hugged his sister and explained all the events leading up to finding their dad. The next day, they all went to the funeral home to make arrangements. Afterwards, they met with Pastor Tom. Jeff and the kids showed up a little after noon.

After a death in the Midwest, visits with the family are expected. Usually the day before the actual service, people arrive at the funeral home to offer their condolences. George Maas was well known and well liked and had helped several families get started. As a county supervisor, he was also sympathetic to the needs of city dwellers. Realizing there would be a large number of people coming, they set visitation hours from 1:00 to 8:00.

Pastor Tom suggested they move visitation to the church, where friends could sit in the pews while they waited. The first couple hours went well, but all the standing and visiting was very tiring and Madge needed a chair after three hours. By seven everyone had been seated for short periods. The last person finally left at 9:00 that night. More than 800 mourners had passed through the church that day.

The funeral was held the next morning and the church was filled to overflowing. Pastor Tom told the mourners that George had followed Jesus' teaching by helping to take care of the sick, feeding the hungry, and clothing the naked. He didn't know one person who had ill feelings toward George, and certainly God would have a fine place for him in heaven. During the service, Missy sang "Amazing Grace" and "The Old Rugged Cross," two of George's favorite hymns.

Many cars followed the family caravan to the cemetery. After the graveside service, the church women served lunch, and by 4:00, it was all over. Just before they left for Pella, Kristy and Tom visited with Madge and Paul. Although they'd only known George from family events, he had become a part of their lives and they would miss his laughter and jokes.

Paul was especially shaken by his dad's death. Only four days earlier he and George had been planning their future, but now his world would be changed forever.

As the days went by, Madge came to the farm less often. The Maas children returned to their summer jobs and Sara had to do her best to replace George when it came to helping Paul. Some chores in the house would have to wait because Paul needed her now more than ever.

In August, Sara began processing tomatoes into sauce and the delicious smell filled the air. She was expecting her dad, who had been coming to the farm more frequently. Fixing things around the farm had always been George's job, but John had stepped into that role after his death.

The kitchen phone rang, and when Sara heard the tone of her mother's voice, she knew something was wrong. "What's the matter, Mom?" she asked.

"Sara, your dad just had a heart attack. The ambulance is here now, but I know he's gone. He was mowing the lawn. When I heard the sound keep coming from the same spot outside, I went out to investigate and found him lying beside the mower. I called 9-1-1, but it was too late. Can you come in right away? Mrs. Hyman is here now. She came over just as soon as she saw the ambulance. Oh, Sara, what am I going to do?"

"Of course, Mom," Sara said, already removing her apron. "I'll be right there."

Sara turned off the appliances and called Paul on the cell phone with the sad news. "Mom just called. Dad had a heart attack. She needs me. I'm going down immediately."

"I'll be right in and I'll go with you," he said. "The hay can wait."

When Sara and Paul arrived, Emma was as distraught as Madge had been at the loss of her husband. Several neighbors were also at the house. As she was trying to console her mom, Madge walked in the front door. She had been in town and was stopping by to invite Emma to a luncheon at her church. She was shocked to hear the news and instantly threw her arms around Emma. If anyone in the world knew what Emma was going through at that moment, it was Madge.

As she finally regained her composure somewhat, Emma said, "We have to call Tom and Bob. We shouldn't make any decision without them."

Sara called Tom first, and Tom told her that he and Kristy would be there in two or three hours. Bob was on a business trip to New York, but his company chartered a private plane to fly him and his family home to be with Emma by the next morning.

Sara decided to stay with her mom that night. They contacted Emma's pastor, who arrived within an hour. Paul took Madge home and went back to the farm to do chores and to tell the children that they had lost their Grandpa John. The next day the family would have to plan another funeral.

John McWilliams was known mostly where he worked and at church, so his visitation lasted only four hours, but more than 200 people came to pay their respects. At the funeral, the minister praised John's work in the church. John's granddaughters Robin McWilliams played a piece on the violin and Penny McWilliams sang "In the Garden." Paul's sister's family couldn't attend, but they sent a lovely floral arrangement and condolences. Sue called Sara the day after the funeral. They talked for over an hour.

Bob and Tom stayed with their families for two days after the funeral. The three siblings and Emma had to meet with the attorney. The second afternoon was spent writing thank-you notes. Bob's company jet arrived on Thursday morning to fly him and his family back to Kansas City. Tom and Kristy left about three in the afternoon. Sara collapsed on the sofa in the den and finally had time to reflect.

"What a year!" she thought. "We never know what the Good Lord will do. He gives us good feelings and sad feelings, but He never forgets us. Even during the sad times our devotion to Him should never waver. Praise be to God and His Son, Jesus."

Chapter Twenty-One
Moving On

The first fall after George's death proved how much he had actually done for Paul. Sara tried to step in and fill the gap left by George, and although she was no stranger to the harvest, she'd never done it on an everyday basis. Several times Paul would have to come in from the field to repair a simple breakdown. Since the wagon tongues were heavy, hitching them up was a difficult skill to master. Just being out of line a few inches caused her much frustration.

At the end of the day, Sara's muscles ached, and by the end of the season, her back was in constant pain. She went to therapy in Muscatine twice a week to get relief. During the winter, they attended some machinery shows and found a quick hitch system that would save Sara from getting in and out of the tractor cab to hook and unhook the wagons. She could do it by just backing up into the hitch. They also purchased a new grain auger with a swing away hopper. Now Sara could unload with less effort. Paul invented a hydraulic system to help open the slides on the wagons.

The goal was simply to survive until Ed finished college at Iowa State in three years. When he graduated, he returned home to start working with his dad. He continued dating Carol Wilson, who had one year left at Drake University. They were wed as soon as she graduated in June.

During the next six years, Sara and Paul became grandparents several times over. Aaron, Isabelle, and Isaac were born to Ed and Carol. Sara and Paul gave Ed and Carol two acres at the end of the road to build a new home just a half mile away.

Tim graduated from Iowa State with a degree in mechanical

engineering. He married a young lady named Angie, and was hired by John Deere. He and Angie added three girls to the growing list of grandchildren—Karen, Kourtney, and Kylie.

In early August, Ed and Carol met Tim and Angie at Adventureland in Des Moines for the weekend, leaving Paul and Sara home alone to do the chores. Saturday was a typical warm summer morning. After they'd finished eating breakfast, Paul said, "Let's go right out and check the cows."

"In our pajamas?" Sara asked.

"Sure, why not? It's warm, and everybody's gone, so no one will see us."

"Okay, I'll get my sandals," Sara said, wondering what Paul had in mind.

"I'll get the Go Getter and meet you out back," said Paul with a smile.

They got into the UTV and headed down the pasture lane. Sara opened the gate. As she stood and waited for Paul, the morning sun felt warm on her back. After Paul had whizzed through, she closed the gate and climbed back into the vehicle. She unbuttoned the bottom two buttons on her top. Now more of the breeze could reach her skin.

Her top floated in the wind as Paul drove up and down the hills like a teenager. When they came to the top of a ridge, they saw the cows in the slough below, grazing contently. Paul gave Sara, his funny sexy smirk, then reached over and unbuttoned her last button, letting the top fall open. Now she knew he had something on his mind! As they rode down toward the creek, she re-buttoned her top unconsciously. Paul watched, but didn't say a word.

When they pulled to a stop in the middle of the creek, Sara asked, "Now what?"

"Oh, nothing," Paul replied. "Want to ride down the middle?"

"Are you crazy?" Sara shrieked as Paul gunned the UTV, throwing water and mud high and wide. A few moments later, he stopped for a moment and stripped off his t-shirt.

He looked at Sara and said, "Why don't you take your top off, too?"

"Are you possessed?" she said with a laugh. "You haven't acted this way since we were young."

"Yeah, I know," he said. "I'm feeling a little young this morning, and we're alone. There's no one around to see you half naked but me and the cows."

"Well, I really don't want to take it off completely," Sara confessed, "and I don't think you're feeling young. You're just horny, Big Boy. How about I just leave it unbuttoned?"

"Fine with me," said Paul, "but we haven't been able to play like this for a long time. Ready for some more? Let's go check the pond tank."

Paul gunned the Go Getter again and they raced toward the pond. He stopped at the top of the dam's crest. Both of them exited the all-terrain vehicle and Sara leaned on the front while Paul walked down the bank toward the tank. She watched him, clad only in sandals and pajama bottoms, as he picked his way to the tank.

"Only on a farm, could you check the cows in your pajamas," she thought.

Sara turned her attention toward the pond. The pond was quite large by farm pond standards, covering nearly two acres. The water stayed fairly clear because the pond was fed by a spring and three tile lines. There was a small boat dock jutting out far enough from the berm to clear the edge moss and duckweed. Two inner tubes always hung on one of the posts, although no one had been swimming that year.

At the back of the pond was a small beach. When the pond was first constructed, George hauled many loads of sand from the dune to create a small sandy area in the water and added washed sand from the Muscatine Island sand pits to give it a clean covering.

Paul and Sara had spent many hours on that beach with family picnics and swim parties for the children. Jenny and her friends had used the beach for sunbathing when she was in high school. Now the beach was overgrown with joint grass and weeds, but the surface of the pond was beautiful as it rippled in the morning sun, reflecting the blue sky and the willow trees along the edge. Above the surface, swarms of gnats did their frantic dance, and here and there little columns of vapor spiraled up into the warm air.

Sara walked over to the dock and sat on the small bench between two of the posts as Paul approached the badlands, as he called it, in front of the tank. The water tank sat on a large slab of concrete at the base of the dam. It was supplied by a pipe running through the dam from an intake deep in the pond. The water was always cool, and the cattle preferred pond water over creek water, but getting to the slab sometimes was a challenge. It was always wet at the base of the dam due to seepage, and the cows made deep pocks in the mud with their hooves, sometimes ten inches deep.

The dried tops of those pocks were sometimes sturdy enough to walk on, but there was always a chance of miscues and that was why Paul called it the badlands. Paul was wishing he'd worn his work boots instead of just his sandals. He gingerly picked out his mud pinnacles as he neared the tank, and finally stepped onto the concrete slab, breathing a sigh of relief.

He checked the tank and scooped out some leaves and one drowned bird. Birds often landed on the leaves and leftover grass and, forgetting they weren't ducks, sank and drowned. When Paul finished, he looked back at the UTV, but Sara was nowhere in sight.

"Where is that woman?" he grumbled. "I don't understand her sometimes. There are days she accepts my advances, but other days she won't. We're the only people here, so what's wrong with taking her blouse off? She runs around in the house with nothing on all the time. Only yesterday I came in for supper and she was setting the table stark naked. When I asked her why, she said she'd just taken a shower and hadn't taken time to go upstairs to get dressed."

As he thought about that incident, he smiled at how beautiful Sara was. They'd been married thirty years and he was still filled with desire for her at the sight of her nude body. They had all day to relax and enjoy each other. Who knew what might develop?

Paul worked his way back across the mud domes and hurried up the slope, where he saw Sara sitting on the dock. She'd brought the old comforter and had spread it out on the boards. He hurried over and sat beside her. She seemed to be in a trance.

"A penny for your thoughts," he said softly.

"I was just thinking," she said dreamily. "Remember all the times we picnicked on the beach? Remember the day Tim dove off the dock and swam over to us? He was so proud. Then there was the time Jenny found that box turtle and wanted to take it home. We finally convinced her to leave it here because this was his home. I came back the next day with her to bring him some food. Do you think we should clean up the beach? Maybe Ed and Carol will enjoy the pond like we did."

"I don't know," Paul replied, "but we could ask. Times have changed since we had little kids."

"Remember when we came out here a week before we were married?" Sara asked.

"Do I?" said Paul with a smile. "How could I ever forget?"

"We were sort of naughty that day, weren't we?" Sara said with a giggle. "I mean, we went skinny-dipping and we weren't married yet."

"Well, you started it," Paul teased. "First, you decided we could go swimming in our underwear. Then you climbed up on the dock and took your sexy blue panties with the lace panels on each side and your blue bra off right in front of me."

"Boy, you don't forget much, do you?" Sara exclaimed. "I remember you sort of egging me on."

"Yeah, I probably did, but you were hotter than a firecracker. I still can remember seeing you standing there with nothing on. We were sort of crazy, weren't we?"

Sara touched Paul's hand. "Do you want to go skinny-dipping again? You wanted me to take off my top earlier and I wouldn't do it, but I'm thinking now would be a good time."

"Yeah, I was thinking along those lines," he returned, "but you don't have to. We can just sit here."

Sara stood, unbuttoned her top, slid it off her shoulders, and let it drop to the blanket. Then she stepped out of her pajama bottoms, struck a sexy pose, and dove into the pond.

"Come on, Big Boy," she called as she surfaced. "Let's see if you remember what I taught you."

Paul took off his shorts, but before he jumped in, he tossed the two inner tubes into the water. Once in the water, they each climbed into a tube and paddled around.

"You look as good as you did thirty years ago," Paul said.

"Yeah, right," Sara replied. "I'm twenty-five pounds heavier and my boobs sag way down. You do know, flattery will get you nowhere, except maybe a good night in bed. Oh, by the way, did you notice? Boobs float! I didn't do a bad dive, though. I know I can't swim as far anymore."

As the warm sun washed over them, they floated lazily and reminisced.

"Did you know I was on the pill when we were out here that night?" Sara asked.

"No, I didn't!" Paul said in surprise. "I didn't even know contraceptives existed back then."

"Had you ever seen a girl naked before me?"

"Besides my sister, only one, and she was Katy O'Malley," Paul said. "I'd almost forgotten about her."

"Katy O'Malley! Who's she? I've never heard of her. I thought you told me about all your old girlfriends."

"I did, but she was more of a playmate than a girlfriend. She came from a big family with lots of older brother and sisters. Her dad always called her 'Oops.' They lived on the old Noll place. Her dad worked in town and her mom worked at the hospital.

"In the summer, Mom babysat her. She was the same age as me, so we played together all the time. When we got old enough to go to the pasture, we played in the creek and the woods. She could think up stories and work them into our play. We played house, doctor and nurse, pioneers, and many other things.

"Sometimes we played with the kittens in the haymow, and one day it was really hot up there, so I took my shirt off. She looked at me and took her top off, and we just went on playing. We did that several times. She was too young to have any breasts, so we never gave it any thought.

"One day we went to the creek. Katy had been reading *Little House on the Prairie* and *Little House in the Big Woods*, so she decided we should play pioneer. We waded in the creek to take our pioneer baths."

"This could be getting good," Sara teased.

"We found a deep water hole next to the bank. She pulled up her shorts as high as she could as she slowly crept into the deep water. She could tell the water was still deeper near the cut bank. I stood back and watched. Katy turned and said, "Let's take all our clothes off. Then we can go to the deepest part."

"No way!" I answered.

"'Oh, come on, chicken. I won't tell if you don't,' she teased me.

"With a couple splashes, she made for the opposite bank. I followed. She stripped off her clothes and went splashing back into the deep waterhole. The water came to her waist. She definitely wasn't shy. She sat down in the water, now it came to her neck. She started to pretend she was taking a bath. I shyly turned my back and slowly took my shirt, shorts, and underpants off. I tried to back into the water so she couldn't see me and didn't see the rock under the surface. I stepped on it and fell down right in front of her. I landed in her lap. I remember looking up at her from my prone position. Katy laughed as she helped me up, saying I was very slippery. I remember looking at each other once, but we soon forgot all about our nakedness. It was fun splashing in the water. We were only ten years old at the time, but we actually played naked in the creek several times that summer. Katy could dream up the most novel reason for us to take our clothes off. We never got caught. It was all innocent fun."

"You naughty little boy!" Sara said, playfully splashing water at Paul.

"Katy moved to Des Moines the next year. I never saw her again. I never went skinny-dipping with any other girls, although there was one right before our wedding," Paul said, giving Sara a wink.

"You know, it's about eight," Sara said with a laugh. "I suppose we'd better go back to the house. You go up on the deck and I'll throw the tubes up."

As Paul climbed the ladder and stood waiting for the tubes, Sara said, "Now there's what I like to see—I like my man naked."

"That's what you told me thirty years ago."

"Well, I haven't changed my mind."

Paul caught both tubes and hung them on the post, then turned and saw Sara floating on her back, her eyes closed. What a sight! She hadn't changed in thirty years, except that her hair had grayed a little. He was a lucky man.

When Sara joined him on the dock, Paul pulled her close as they sat on the blanket to let the sun dry them off. Paul's body had developed a small paunch and his chest and back were covered with a mixture of gray and brown hair—and there were way more than the twenty-five chest hairs she had counted so many years earlier. She had also developed a larger waistline, had stretch marks from having three children, and the muscle tone in her upper arms was gone.

"I think we've aged pretty gracefully," Sara finally said with a warm sigh.

Paul said, "Sara, I want to ask you something."

"This must be serious," she said. "You never call me Sara unless it's something important."

Paul gave her a playful nudge. "Last week, Darwin Petersen asked if I'd run for county supervisor. Nate Howell, who replaced Dad on the board, is retiring, and his party doesn't want to lose the seat. I've been thinking about it, but I want to know what you think."

"I think it would be great," Sara said happily. "You'd do a good job. Your dad would be mighty proud and your mom would be pleased."

"It would mean more time away from the farm," Paul added, "but maybe it's time we turn the operation over to Ed and Carol. He's been working here six years, and he knows how I think, so he wouldn't do anything foolish. I trust him."

"Boy, you're full of surprises today," said Sara. "I think Ed would do a fine job. How soon is this all going to happen?"

"Well, the election's in November, so I'd have to sign the nomination papers by August 30th. We could hand over the books and management to Ed in January."

"I think that sounds like a plan," said Sara. "Let's put our pajamas back on and head back. We can have lunch at Shorty's Restaurant."

"Let's live dangerously," Paul said with a devilish smile. "Let's forget the pajamas. I've never ridden with a naked lady in an UTV."

"You're on," Sara said. "Let's go."

As they folded the blanket, Paul commented, "Do you realize next July I'm going to walk my little girl down the aisle? I've been waiting for that day for a long time. It seems like only yesterday she was asking me to give her a piggyback ride."

"Well, come on, old man," Sara teased. "Do you need me to help you to the UTV?"

"I don't think so!" Paul said, racing her back to the Go Getter.

They took the long way back. Paul said it was to check out the cows again, but it was really because he loved having his naked wife beside him. He liked the way certain parts of her body swayed and bounced as they rumbled along.

Sara was a little nervous as she opened the gate with no clothes on. She quickly returned to her seat after shutting and latching the gate. Paul approached the corner of the barn cautiously to make sure no one was sitting in the drive waiting for them. Instead of stopping by the house gate, he put the machine away in the machine shed, then he made her walk carrying her pajamas to the house—it worked until Sara saw the dust from a car coming down the road. They dashed into the house and ran upstairs where they could shower together. Paul gave her a good back scrub and massage.

"Let's go back to bed," Sara said with a sly smile. "We can always catch Shorty's later."

* * *

The next week, Ed, Carol, and the kids returned and Paul asked Ed if they had an evening so he and Sara could present him with a proposal.

Ed looked at his dad questioningly and said, "I think Thursday night would work. What's on your mind?"

"Well, I don't want to give it all away, but I'll give you a clue," Paul replied. "I'm thinking about running for county supervisor and I'm wondering what you and Carol would think about that." Unable to wait, he then smiled and said, "And your mom and I have decided it's time you took over management of the farm. If I win the election, I'll be away from the farm more. What do you think? I have to register by August 31st."

"Gee, Dad, you're just full of surprises, aren't you?" Ed said, shaking his head.

"That's exactly what your mom said when I asked her."

"I think you'll make an excellent supervisor. We'd have to make some adjustments on the farm, but Carol should be agreeable. Maybe she could quit her job and help me like Mom helped you. Let's plan on Thursday night unless Carol says we've got something else going on."

"Thursday will be fine," Paul agreed.

Ed called Carol at work and she said Thursday would work. She also suggested a barbecue on the patio with hamburgers and hot dogs. She'd talk to Sara when she got home from work. When Ed told Paul the plan, he agreed to everything—except that he'd bring steaks for anyone who wanted one, since it was going to be a special occasion.

The weather was warm and beautiful that Thursday evening. The kids had just finished their first day of school and were full of news for Grandma and Grandpa. Ed grilled the steaks to perfection and plenty of hot dogs for Aaron, Isaac, and Isabelle. Paul gave the blessing and then everyone said, "Amen!"

After supper the children played outside until the light faded, then Carol hustled them off to bed. When she returned, Paul began to lay out his proposal.

"If I get elected, I'll have to spend one day a week in Muscatine at the weekly meeting, and I'll have to do whatever else supervisors do. It'll average two days a week and some evenings. Those are the minuses, but the big plus is that I'll be on the county health plan, which means Carol will be able get health insurance from the farm. Sara and I think it's time to turn the operation over to you two. I could find some other part-time job if I don't get elected, but we'll cross that bridge when we get to it."

Carol said, "I've been thinking since Ed hinted to me what might happen tonight. Because I'm a CPA, I could do the books here and do taxes for other people from a home office. I'm committed to Burt for this year, but then I can go out on my own. I'd only take on enough clients to be finished by the first of April. The rest of the year I could help on the farm."

"Sounds good," said Ed as Paul and Sara nodded their approval.

"Also, since Ed has two siblings who don't farm, we may want to form an LLC to have some job protection. You know I love Jenny and Tim and I don't believe either of them would do anything rash, but things can change. I've seen businesses destroyed because of sons and daughters squabbling over who gets what."

"That makes good sense, too," Paul said.

"The problem would be if something should happen to you and Sara at the same time," Carol continued. "We might be forced to buy out the other two, and we couldn't afford an expense like that. One of my clients had to sell their family farm and work somewhere else after his mother died. It was sad."

Paul smiled at his daughter-in-law and said, "You've been thinking about this for quite a while, Carol, haven't you? And I think you're right. Let's look into forming an LLC or a corporation. Sara and I would never want this farm to be a burden for you. Do you think we could have something in place by early next year?"

"I sure do," Carol replied. Then she paused before adding, "You know I support the other party, Paul, but if you run, I promise to vote for you. You'll make a great supervisor. In fact, I'll be your campaign manager if you want."

Paul filed for the supervisor position the next day, and by the middle of September he was campaigning all over the county, promising nothing but honesty and integrity. Sara did her part by attending all the meetings. She loved to tell people what Paul stood for and what he wanted to do for the county. Carol also did a good job managing Paul's campaign. She made sure he was at all the right events and had access to any questions that might be asked ahead of time.

John Worthington, Paul's opponent, was also a farmer. He ran a large farm with his two sons. They operated several thousand acres and had a large hog finishing enterprise. Both men were well known in the county.

When the first Tuesday in November arrived, Paul and Sara went to party headquarters at Eagle Ridge Restaurant to watch the returns. Carol, Ed, Jenny, and Jason came to the restaurant late, and Tim surprised them by arriving from Dubuque. At 10:00, the first returns started to come in, and Paul's election was never in doubt. He led from the first report. At midnight, John Worthington called to congratulate him and wished him well. Paul would be the new member on the board of supervisors of Muscatine County.

December was even busier than usual. Paul attended several supervisor meetings so he could be up to speed when he took office. They had Christmas at Ed and Carol's. Tim and Angie and their family came Christmas Eve and stayed for Christmas, since Angie's family had held their celebration the previous week. Jason and Jenny came to the festivities late because of an early Christmas calf delivery. Jenny laughed, saying it wouldn't be the last time they would be late.

Sara and Paul gave Ed a desk nameplate that read: "Ed Maas, Farm Manager." Then they gave Carol one that read: "Carol Maas, The Real Boss."

"I think next year will be one we'll all remember," said Paul happily.

When a Governor's Ball invitation came in the mail, they accepted. The dance would be held in the Fort Des Moines Hotel ballroom. Jenny and Carol spent several Saturdays helping Sara find the perfect long black evening gown covered with silver sequins. It also had a short jacket to cover her shoulders, and she looked elegant because of her height.

Paul rented a tuxedo but bought his own shoes. In January, they headed for Des Moines, where Sara was the talk of the crowd, since there were few women there who were both tall and beautiful. Her brown hair, streaked with strands of gray, accented her shimmering gown as she glided around the floor with Paul as if they'd been doing it all their lives. Paul beamed with pride while dancing with her.

Several people noted that Paul might be starting on long political career. The new governor stopped by their table to greet them and to tell Paul he hoped they might find time to sit down for a talk about the needs of his county. It was an enchanting evening.

Chapter Twenty-Two
—Goodbye at the Dune—
The Nightgown Moves On

Carol finished her income tax clients early and then resigned from her job and took over management of the farm's records. She had retained an attorney, Jim Taylor, in January. He was experienced in agricultural law and had accomplished several farm reorganizations. The farm became Maas Farms, Inc. on March 1st. Ed was president; Paul, vice president; Sara secretary; and Carol, treasurer. Tim, Angie, and Jenny were directors, with Jason to be added after Jen's wedding.

Ed became the main checker of the cows, installing a small camera inside the calving area so he could check on the animals from his home. This meant Carol would never have to pull calves at 11:00 at night as Sara had done, although Carol did her share of getting the calves started.

Carol loved being a stay-at-home mom. Working with Ed appealed to her and she could be home for the children when they returned from school each day. She was also anxious to drive the tractors as her mother-in-law had done for so many years.

Sara found she had time on her hands, so she volunteered at the elementary school, helping young readers with disabilities. She also accepted various positions in the church women's organization. She enjoyed being with other women and spent many evenings with Paul attending meetings associated with the county board.

Paul found the new job more time consuming than he'd planned. He had to review many issues that had been left on the table before he took office. There were also more night meetings than George had attended, since the board had been given more responsibilities due to state and federal mandates and cutbacks. He enjoyed the challenge, despite the long hours.

Spring planting went as scheduled. There were some rain delays, but with the help of Carol and Sara, Ed got the field work done.

In the last week in May, Paul was due to be at a morning committee meeting. Sara could hear Paul showering upstairs as she fried eggs and bacon for breakfast.

As he stepped off the stairs, Paul said, "Sara, I feel funny. My right arm is numb."

Before Sara could say anything, she heard him fall. She ran to his side, screaming, "Paul, what's happening?"

"I don't know," he said weakly, his speech was slurred.

As Sara tried to help Paul sit up, she looked into his eyes and saw that they barely focus.

"Paul," she said, "I think you're having a stroke. Stay right there. I'll call the ambulance."

She quickly dialed 9-1-1 and when a woman on the other end answered, she said, "This is Sara Maas. I believe my husband has had a stroke. I need an ambulance immediately."

"We'll be there as fast as we can, Mrs. Maas," assured the operator.

Sara hung up the phone and ran back to where Paul was slumped against the wall. She pulled out her cell phone and called Ed.

Ed answered, "What's up, Mom?"

"It's your dad! I think he's had a stroke. He fell down the steps and he can't speak. I've called the ambulance, but please hurry!"

"I'm on my way. I'm just coming through the pasture gate. I'll call Carol."

Sara heard the UTV roar around the buildings and slide to a halt. Ed was by her side in seconds. He cradled his dad's body in his arms, but he didn't respond. He just stared and moved his mouth as if he was trying to say something but couldn't.

Sara was hysterical. She ran from window to window, watching for the ambulance. Carol arrived before the EMTs, but she said she had heard the sirens, so they'd be there soon. Carol went out to the kitchen and turned off the burners Sara had forgotten in her panic. The frying pan was red hot. The smoke alarm was sounding, because of the burning bacon. Carol scrambled to get it turned off.

The ambulance arrived and the EMTs took Paul's vital signs before wheeling him out to the vehicle. They asked Sara if she wanted to ride with them, but she was so upset she didn't know what to do.

"You'd better go with them, Mom." said Ed. "Carol and I will be there as soon as we get things settled around here."

Sara held Paul's hand as they left the farm, but on the way, it seemed as if he was having another seizure. He lost consciousness and didn't respond to any stimulus. At the hospital, he was whisked into ICU.

Dr. Barnes looked concerned as she approached Sara after examining Paul. "Paul's had a severe stroke," she said. "He has some bleeding in his brain, but we won't know how much damage has been done for a few hours. There are drugs to alleviate the damage, but I don't know if we got them administered in time. I'm sorry, Sara. It's difficult to have to give you this news. I've contacted the university. Dr. Dave Kindler is a neurologist and he's making a special trip here to see if he can help. Right now, Paul's condition is too fragile to be transported."

"Thank you, Dr. Barnes," Sara said shakily. "Can I see him?"

"Absolutely. Stroke victims can hear but can't respond, so you can talk to him."

Sara entered the ICU, where Paul had wires and tubes coming out of his body. She grasped his hand and squeezed it. She bent over, found a spot on his forehead not covered by patches, and kissed him softly.

"Oh, Paul, my love, don't leave me," she whispered. "I don't know how I can live without you. We have so many years ahead of us to do the things we couldn't do when we were farming. Please, God, don't let him die! I love him so much."

When Carol and Ed arrived, Ed didn't know what to say. He'd seen his dad like that one other time when he was twelve. Carol gave Sara a silent hug. Her father-in-law was as important to her as her own dad. He'd always treated her as his daughter. She broke down and sobbed on Ed's shoulder, then excused herself and left the room.

She met Tim and Angie in the hallway and told them to go right in. Tim went in and talked to his mother, but Angie stayed behind to help Carol collect herself.

Jenny was on a field trip with her agriculture class and was delayed getting there, but when she arrived, like Ed, she found herself speechless. Her dad was lying in a hospital bed, unable to communicate. Her dad, who was supposed to be giving her away in two months. Her dad, who had swung her around that rainy morning until her pants fell off; her dad, who had taught her how to lead a 4-H calf, ride a bike, drive a tractor, and love the outdoors.

Jen hugged her mother and said, "What are we going to do, Mom? I'll help any way I can. He *has* to be at my wedding."

"I know, honey," Sara said softly, "but I'm afraid we've got a long road of recovery ahead of us. Your dad will do the best he can. You know he will."

Dr. Kindler examined Paul, studying test results and meeting with the staff for at least an hour before talking to Sara and the rest of the family. "Mrs. Maas, your husband had several small strokes right after the first one and his condition is critical. I'm not going to paint you a pretty picture. If he recovers, he'll probably never return to his normal activities. He may get some functions back, but there's no way to know how much. We'll monitor his progress for several days and he should stabilize in a week or two. Then we'll reevaluate his condition. I wish I had better news, but I don't. I'm going to confer with the staff at the university to see if they have any other suggestions."

The vigil of taking care of Paul then began. Tim and Angie stayed overnight. They had made arrangements with friends to take care of the kids. Sue told Ed she'd be there in the morning. It was hard to convince Sara to leave Paul's bedside.

They worked out a schedule. Jenny would start as soon as school let out and stay until ten o'clock. Ed would relieve her and stay until three in the morning. Sara would go from three until Carol arrived at nine or ten. She'd then sit until three, when Sara would return and wait for Jenny. Madge would fill in if needed. The first weekend, Sue arrived from Waterloo and relieved Carol.

Paul's condition never seemed to change, though some days the doctor got a little response. Sara started to get the house ready for Paul's return. She ordered a hospital bed and lifts and enlisted visiting nurse care for help bathing Paul. The dining room was converted to a recovery room, and she would make other changes as the need arose. She and Paul would still live a life together, even if it wouldn't be the way she had planned.

Paul was to be released from the hospital on a Friday. Sue and Jenny would be available to help the first few days. Jenny was almost done with school for the year and would move out to the farm for a month or two. Sara insisted that her wedding not be delayed. Paul wouldn't have wanted that to happen.

The night before his release, a cold front pushed through the Midwest and there was a potential for tornadoes. Sara and Jenny were at the hospital and went into the hospital lounge for a break as rain pounded against the window panes and chunks of hail pelted the roof.

Suddenly the lights went out, and only flashes of lightning lit the room. Although it seemed like a long time, it was less than thirty seconds before the hospital generators kicked in and the lights came back on. In Paul's room, monitors were screaming when Sara and Jenny went back in. Nurses were attacking Paul's body with shockers and medications, but the line on the screen was flat.

Sara knew what had happened. She watched for a while and slowly approached the bed, even though the staff tried to keep her away.

"Please, please let him go," Sara said softly. "God has called him home, and he'll be waiting for me when I get there. He's never broken a promise. Please, let me be alone with my husband for a moment."

The staff departed, taking as much of the equipment with them as they could. Jenny put her arm around her mother's shoulders and cried.

"We had a wonderful life together," Sara said, her voice barely above a whisper. "It seems short to us, but in God's eyes it was long enough. Your dad was my rock. Now I'll have to go it alone, just like your grandmothers have had to do. Everything was going to be so great. His supervisor's job, turning the farm over to Ed and Carol, and looking forward to retirement—it was all coming together. We never know what God has planned for us, but we have to believe He's doing the right thing. We'd better call Ed and Tim and tell them their dad has gone to heaven."

Sara touched Paul's cold hand and kissed his lifeless cheek. Life as she had known it was over. All that was left was the body of the man she had loved for so long. Sara turned and she and Jenny left the ICU. They walked slowly to the waiting room and waited for a nurse to bring the release papers.

As they walked across the wet parking lot, the sun suddenly emerged from the clouds and a multi-colored rainbow appeared in the eastern sky—God's promise that He would never forget His people.

Sara looked up and smiled. "That's Paul," she said, "saying goodbye and telling us to carry on."

The next day the families planned Paul's funeral. In typical Midwestern fashion, visitation was planned for the day before the service at the Wilton church Sara and Paul had attended all their married lives. Pastor Tom came out of retirement to officiate. Visitation started at 2:00 and continued until nine. It was supposed to have ended at seven, but the line was so long that they stayed until everyone had been given a chance to offer their condolences. The family was exhausted when it was over.

The morning of the funeral began with an incredibly beautiful sunrise. Jenny got up to help her mother, but Sara was nowhere to be found. Jenny found a note on the kitchen table that read: "I wanted to greet the sunrise from the dune. I think Dad might be there, too."

Jenny slipped on her tennis shoes and ran to the dune in her pajamas. She found her mother sitting on the old park bench and looking at the long rows of new corn.

"Mom, are you alright?" Jenny said. "Do you want me to sit here with you?"

"Sure, Jen. Sit down."

"It's pretty here, isn't it?"

"Yes, your dad and I spent many hours here. Sometimes we just sat and talked and sometimes we'd end up making out. We lay right here on a blanket the whole night of our wedding and watched the sun come up over the cornfield. We stood here, naked, starting our new life together. We were in charge of a little piece of God's beautiful earth. A man and a woman, part of God's creation."

"Just as God clothed the land with grass and trees, He clothed us and made us fruitful. It was the greatest feeling I'd ever known. We were at the beginning then, and now I'm sitting here at the end, alone, wishing I could hold Paul one more time. But that's not going to happen, is it? Paul would want me to get on with my life, but he didn't tell me how difficult it would be without him."

"Jen, a farmer loves his land. If you fall in love with a farmer, you learn to love the land, too. They both will love you in return and will always be a part of your very soul," said Sara. Then she looked at her daughter and added, "What I'm going to do next is going to seem crazy, but this is how we started, and this is how I want to finish."

She stood up and kicked off her shoes. Then she sighed heavily, unbuttoned her pajamas, took them off, and stood naked in the morning sun. Her skin was no longer soft, she had a small tummy, and her breasts sagged. Although time had been good to her, she was an older woman. Tears streamed down her cheeks as she let Paul go.

"Good bye, Big Boy. See you later. Wait for me." She whispered.

A breeze started at the dune and crossed the field. The corn leaves rustled and waved. Sara knew it was her Paul leaving. She gave the breeze a slight wave.

After a few moments, Jenny stood and handed Sara her clothes. "That was beautiful, Mom," she said softly. "I think Dad knows we're all here for you and we always will be. This land will always be the Maas farm, and you and Dad have always taken care of the land God entrusted to you."

Sara turned to her daughter and sobbed, "Oh, Jen, how can I live without him? Why did God take him so soon? I wasn't ready for this."

"I know, Mom," Jenny said, putting her arms around her mother. "No one is ever ready."

Jenny helped Sara get dressed and then they slowly walked back to the house. As they reached the barnyard, Ed appeared.

"Where have you two been? I was getting worried. How come you're just wearing your pajamas?"

Jenny said, "Mom just wanted to see the dune one more time with Dad so they could say their final goodbyes."

Ed could tell by the tears in his mother's eyes and the streaks on her cheeks he should ask nothing more. As Sara and Jenny made their way toward the house, he turned and went to finish the chores.

The day turned out to be one of those rare days in late spring with blue skies and a few puffy clouds. The grass was green and the peonies were in full bloom. Sara's brothers, Bob and Tom, and their families arrived early. Jeff and all the children had arrived the night before. The church was overflowing and the county offices closed for the day so employees could attend.

After the graveside service, the church ladies served lunch. By 3:00 it was over and the family drove out to the farm. Jenny stayed overnight. Tim and Angie also stayed, with the kids sleeping at Carol's.

The next day began with reading sympathy cards and letters, and the afternoon was filled with writing thank you notes. They received more than $3,000 in memorial funds, which they decided should be given to the church for a future project in Paul's name. That night, Tim and Angie went back home to Dubuque and Sue's family left for Waterloo. Madge and Emma came by and the three of them reminisced and told stories about their husbands. Emma stayed the next three nights.

June passed slowly. The Muscatine County board named a country road in Paul's honor: Paul Maas Avenue. Ed's children kept Grandma Sara busy attending ballgames and swim meets. Sara spent many evenings at the cemetery, praying at Paul's grave. Time may cure all wounds, but Sara's would take a long time to heal.

July was hot and sticky. Jason had a busy month and Jenny barely saw him. Two weeks before the wedding, they went to Red Rock Lake with Jason's parents to spend some time together before the wedding and to get everything finalized.

The first week of August, the wedding was three days away. Sara called Jenny and asked if she had a few minutes to spare.

"Sure, Mom, what's up?" Jenny asked.

"You'll find out when you get here. There's something special I want to give you."

"I can be there about three. Is that okay?"

"That will be perfect!"

At 2:30, Sara went upstairs to her bedroom, opened the top drawer of her dresser, and pulled out the box containing Mrs. B's magic nightgown. She wouldn't need it anymore, and it was time to pass it on to her own precious daughter. She held it up and smiled. Life was going to go on, exactly as it should.

About the Author

Bob Bancks retired after farming for forty-eight years in eastern Iowa. His writing is based on his own experiences and those he has heard about from his neighbors over the years. As Bob says, "Farming is a great way of life and although it does have its ups and downs, the rewards are great." He and his wife, Jane, worked together to raise their children in a manner not unlike the one portrayed in *The Nightgown*.

CPSIA information can be obtained at www.ICGtesting.com
Printed in the USA
BVOW03s1858061113

335516BV00001B/2/P